CODE *of* HONOR

HORNET: BOOK 4

CODE *of* HONOR

HORNET: BOOK 4

TONYA BURROWS

Entangled Publishing, LLC
2614 South Timberline Road
Suite 109
Fort Collins, CO 80525
Visit our website at www.entangledpublishing.com.

Amara is an imprint of Entangled Publishing, LLC.

Edited by Heather Howland
Cover design by Kelly Martin
Cover art from Shutterstock and Bigstock

Manufactured in the United States of America

First Edition October 2017

Chapter One

In a moment of blinding clarity, Dr. Tiffany Peters knew she was dying.

It didn't scare her. The macabre had fascinated her throughout her life, and her death was no different. The clinical part of her brain reeled off the symptoms of death, and her body was checking every box. She wished she could document what was happening. Doctors and scientists had spent centuries trying to understand death. She wished she could tell someone how it felt, but when she opened her mouth, no sound escaped.

The hotel room around her swam in and out of focus, and each breath was a chore, like an elephant sat on her chest. Her belly felt full. She bet if she cut herself open, she'd find a whole lot of blood in there.

She was so damn cold.

A bullet to the stomach wasn't how she'd expected her life to end. Tiffany wasn't a particularly adventurous person. She liked routine, and was okay with sticking to her little corner of the globe and viewing the rest of it through the viruses she saw under her microscope. In a few months, she was supposed to get married—though now she knew that would've been a mistake. She'd planned to have a couple of kids. Maybe win some recognition for her work in virology. She always figured she'd live long enough to see her grandchildren grow up, then die old and frail like most people.

Never in her wildest dreams had she expected to be hemorrhaging internally on a hotel bed in a five-star Caribbean resort during a hostage situation.

Funny how only one week could change so much.

A flash of movement at the foot of her bed caught her attention, and she blinked to clear her vision. Someone was pacing there. A young man with a mean, hard-edged face and cold eyes. She remembered him, the kid with the orange sneakers. He was part of the group of people trying to keep her alive, but he was different from the rest of them. He was trouble.

"This whole thing is fucked," he said, and it took her a long moment to realize he wasn't speaking to her, but into a cell phone. "I warned Briggs this was a bad idea, but he's lost his goddamn mind and taken the whole fucking hotel hostage. Dr. Peters is dying. Dr. Oliver is MIA. And HORNET is everywhere."

Hornet? Like the bug? What did that have to do with anything? But one thing he said did make sense to her.

Dr. Oliver is MIA.

Claire Oliver, her best friend and research partner, had somehow escaped this hotel of horrors. Claire was safe. She was okay. Tiffany grasped the thought, held it tight, and something loosened inside her. Another tether holding her to life snapped free.

The kid in the orange sneakers stopped pacing at the foot of her bed and stared at her. His features showed no concern, no empathy, nothing but mild annoyance. He noticed she was awake and met her gaze. She thought his eyes cold, but they weren't even that. They were dead, with no flicker of humanity on the other side. She thought she'd seen evil before—the man who had shot her less than six hours ago had certainly seemed evil at the time. But she was wrong. That man had been a human making bad decisions. This kid was a psychopath.

"Sir," he said evenly into the phone, all the while holding her gaze. "If I mop up this mess, it's over. My cover will be blown."

Mop up.

He meant kill her. Would he find Claire and kill her, too? Oh God, and there was no way to warn her.

Tiffany tried to sit up, but she barely had the strength to lift her head. She opened her mouth, tried to call out, to warn someone, but all that came from between her dry lips was an inhuman moan. Even though she was dying and could feel her body shutting down one process at a time, she still had to try. For Claire's sake.

"Yes, sir," the kid said and then pocketed the phone. He shook his head and produced a gun.

This was it, she realized. He'd pull the trigger, and she'd be gone before she even registered the pain. She turned her head slightly, looking for the door, praying nobody walked in and got caught in the crossfire. There was no help for her, but if she could save someone else…

Except she and the kid weren't alone in the room. On the queen bed next to hers lay an unconscious blond man in a bloodstained New Orleans Saints T-shirt. She remembered him. Jean-Luc? She'd heard someone call him that during one of her bouts of consciousness. He'd rescued her from the floor of the hotel's lobby, had brought her here, to safety in this room. And now he'd die, too. All for helping her.

She looked at the kid again and choked out, "Please, don't."

"Sorry," he said, not sounding the least bit sorry. "You've outlived your usefulness, Dr. Peters."

Yeah, that's what he thought.

Tiffany sucked in a lungful of air and screamed with everything she had left in her. The sound that tore from her throat was raw, ragged, primal.

It was the last thing she ever did and, in the split-second before the bullet struck, she hoped it was enough to save the blond man.

Chapter Two

ONE WEEK EARLIER
FRIDAY, JULY 17
ALTA, WY

Where the hell was his son?

Jesse Warrick took off his Stetson and shielded his eyes against the afternoon glare of the hot Wyoming sun as he scanned the land around the barn. He knew Connor was awake. He'd hoisted the kid out of bed himself—and, Jesus, Mary, and Joseph, why was the boy in bed at three in the afternoon anyway?—but now Connor was nowhere to be seen.

Again.

Ever since Jesse's ex-wife had shipped their fifteen-year-old son to the ranch, Connor had been nothing but a pain in the ass. Lacy had all but given up on their son as a lost cause after his most recent run-in with Las Vegas law enforcement. She'd made it clear that she didn't particularly care if he came back because he was "corrupting" her younger children. As if those kids' well-being was somehow more important than her oldest child.

Classic Lacy behavior. As soon as the road got a little bit bumpy, she bailed and went in search of greener pastures. That was exactly what had happened to their marriage. Jesse had really meant his vow of "till death do us part." Lacy had meant something more along the lines of "till I find a better alternative." And she had. Her current husband owned a casino and a couple hotels.

But shipping her son away? It was a new low for her.

And he still hadn't figured out how to break it to Connor.

Not that Connor was even talking to him at the moment. And even if he were suddenly in a chatty mood, Jesse wouldn't be able to have a rational conversation. The kid had been tap-dancing on his last nerve for weeks. Sulking, mouthy, defiant, stubborn, and too damn proud for his britches. Connor had all of Jesse's and his ex-wife's worst qualities.

God help them.

Jesse drew a long, slow breath to combat the temper heating the back of his neck and resettled his hat on his head. Well, there was work to be done whether or not Connor showed up for his chores. He walked into the barn, grabbed a pitchfork, and got to work mucking out the horse stalls. He lost himself in the task until his muscles burned and sweat dripped down the side of his face. The ranch—and the physical labor that came hand in hand with it—was his happy place, and he was in desperate need of some happy these days. Especially since he was still coming to grips with the fact he would never have an MD after his name. No med school wanted a former Army medic with a less-than-honorable discharge under his belt. He'd received another rejection just this morning.

"Warrick."

At the sound of his name, Jesse straightened with another scoop of dirty hay on his fork and found Gabe Bristow standing in front of the open stall. "Hey, boss." He dumped the load in a wheelbarrow, then propped the pitchfork against the wall and stepped out of the stall. "I thought you were meetin' us in Martinique."

Gabe inclined his head. "That was the original plan, but I wanted to check things out around here. Quinn's kept me up to date on the training facility. It's not the same as seeing for myself."

The facility, planted on a stretch of land bordering Jesse's ranch, was a new project for HORNET and, save for a few small-time missions, had been the team's main focus. "You know Quinn. He has that place runnin' like a well-oiled machine."

"Yeah, I'm sure he does." Gabe hesitated a beat, then added, "How has he been? Any issues with the mandatory medical checks?"

"Nope. He still don't like 'em, but he doesn't complain." Quinn, the team's XO, had a traumatic brain injury that he'd done his damnedest to hide until their last mission had forced him to reveal it. Since then, he'd had surgery to correct the blackouts he'd been dealing with and was under orders to undergo a monthly physical.

Gabe cracked a smile. "Mara's doing?"

"My guess." Jesse still wasn't 100 percent comfortable with his baby cousin and Quinn together, but there wasn't much he could do about the relationship at this point. Quinn and Mara were planning a fall wedding, had a ten-month-old daughter together, and now Mara was heavily pregnant with their son. Not that he wanted to break them up. Mara was good for Quinn, and they were goofily in love. Just wasn't a comfortable thing to think too much about.

Jesse swiped off his hat and mopped the sweat from his forehead with his arm, taking those few seconds to study Gabe with his practiced medic's eye. Gabe had been wounded during a mission a year and a half ago. They'd nearly lost him, and then he'd been wheelchair bound for close to a year. Now he was walking again with his usual cane, which he'd always had due to a previous injury. He wasn't nearly as muscular as he'd been, but he'd regain that in time with training. Other than the weight loss, he looked the picture of health. Still...

"What about you? How are you feelin'?"

Jesse'd never say it to Gabe's face, mainly because Gabe wouldn't have wanted to hear it, but he'd been worried about the man. Especially during the months Gabe had been stuck in a wheelchair. Former SEALs like him made the worst patients, and for a while, when doctors were telling him he may not walk again, he'd withered to a husk of his former self. Almost as if he wanted to give up, which was completely unlike Gabe "Stonewall" Bristow. Depression had been a mighty weight around the big guy's shoulders until one day he'd suddenly thrown himself into his rehabilitation with the same single-minded determination that had seen him through SEAL training. Jesse didn't know what had prompted the sudden change, but suspected Gabe's wife Audrey had lit a fire under his ass.

Audrey should be sainted for that because the man standing in the barn now was a complete one-eighty from what he'd been at this same time last year.

Thank Christ.

"I'm, uh, good." Gabe changed the subject fast, as he always did when someone brought up his brush with death. "There's something Quinn and I would like to talk about if you have some time to swing by the facility this evening."

"I was plannin' on it. Mara invited me for supper."

"Good. See you then."

Jesse replaced his hat on his head and watched Gabe leave. What was that all about? Despite the usual hitch in his giddy up, he appeared to be moving painlessly again, carrying himself like a man once again comfortable in his own skin.

Huh. Gabe had never been the type to beat around the bush, so the fact he didn't come right out with whatever was on his mind was puzzling. Guess he'd find out soon enough.

Jesse grabbed the pitchfork and returned to mucking out the stall. He had five more to do before supper since his son had disappeared on him. He didn't mind the labor. It cleared his head like nothing else could, but the fact Connor had shirked his chores once again rankled. The kid was going to learn some goddamn responsibility if it killed him.

Frustrated with it all, Jesse stabbed at the hay a little too hard and the pitchfork stuck in the wood floor, jarring him all the way up to his teeth.

"Whoa, cowboy. The floor's already dead. If you want to kill something—"

Figured. How was it the one person he'd done his damnedest to avoid always seemed to find him? He didn't bother glancing over at Elena Delcambre, his cousin Mara's best friend, who had somehow managed to become the only female member of HORNET. And had been a massive thorn in his side ever since. He scooped up more hay. "Are you offerin' up yourself?"

Lanie snorted and leaned a shoulder against the stall door. "You'd like to stab me, wouldn't ya?"

He would, but not in the way she meant. Ever since she'd talked her way onto the team, he'd wanted nothing more than to fuck her—an urge he viciously fought. He'd first met Lanie when she was his son's age. She'd visited the ranch for a summer with Mara, and she'd been all long, gangly limbs, with frizzy hair and braces. He wanted to keep that image of an awkward teenage girl front and center in his head, because if he saw her as the woman she was now, he'd end up doing things he'd most definitely regret.

The darkness that had consumed him after Delta Force

kicked him out was always hovering right there, a ghost at the edge of his consciousness, waiting to devour him. And now, after three failed marriages, he'd learned nothing ever stuck, not even the people who were supposed to love you. Every loss took a little piece of him with it. And he had so very little of himself left to give. He was done. No more women. No matter how appealing this particular one was.

"Hey," Lanie said and straightened. There was a note of concern in her voice. "What's up with you? You're not taking jabs at me like usual."

Sighing, he forked up another mound of fresh hay from a nearby pile and shook it out across the floor of the stall. "Gabe was here."

"Yeah?" She took hold of the wheelbarrow full of dirty hay and pushed it down to the next stall in line, then grabbed another pitchfork. She never shied away from dirty work, whether in the barn or behind enemy lines, and it was something he'd always admired about her. "I thought he was meeting us in Martinique next weekend. What did he want?"

"He said he and Quinn want to talk to me about somethin'."

"That's...cryptic. Weird."

It was. "Probably about the trainin' exercise."

She paused from scooping out the stall and grinned over at him. "That's going to be fun."

"You're just lookin' forward to a weekend at Tuc Quentin's resort when it's over."

"Well, duh. Who doesn't look forward to island time? I'm gonna break out my little red bikini and catch some rays while sipping on a coconut drink."

He scoffed. "You can be such a girl sometimes."

"I *am* a girl. No, wait—" She straightened and peeked down the front of her tank top. "No, yeah, they're still there. Definitely female. Whew."

The move drew Jesse's gaze to her chest and his throat dried up like he'd swallowed a mouthful of sawdust. Yes, definitely female. The woman had curves in all the right places…a fact he worked hard to forget. Easier to do when he saw her as just another one of the guys.

"But it's not only the resort time I'm looking forward to." She leaned on her pitchfork and grinned. "I can't wait to scare the bejesus out of our trainees."

He cleared his throat and went back to shoveling like humanity depended on him to clean this stall. "Hmm. Yeah. Trial by fire."

"Is there any other way?" She went back to work on her own stall. "Besides, these kids have it easy. Nothing we can throw at them will be as bad as my first mission with y'all. But I intend to do my best. Like I said, it's gonna be fun."

Jesse had been anticipating the weeklong training mission, too. It was guaranteed to be a good time. The whole team back together again, playing war games out in the jungles of Suriname, scaring some of the FNGs—fucking new guys—followed by a weekend debriefing-slash-retreat at Tucker Quentin's 5-star resort on Martinique. But now that Connor was here…was it right for Jesse to leave the ranch? His parents would most certainly watch Connor for the week, but there was no telling what kind of trouble the boy would get into. Already in the short time since he'd arrived, he'd been in several fights, had been caught drinking and smoking, and had stolen money out of Jesse's wallet. Which Jesse hadn't called him on yet.

"Earth to Jesse," Lanie said and clanged her pitchfork on the side of the wheelbarrow a couple times. "Hey, space cadet. What's with you?"

He looked at her. Sweat glistened on her brown skin from the effort of mucking out the stall and a sprig of hay clung to the dark ringlets of her ponytail. Dressed in jeans and boots, her bra strap slipping down her shoulder from under her tan tank top, she'd never looked more beautiful. Every thought in his head disappeared except one: he wanted this woman. Had for a very long time. Lanie wasn't so much the one who got away as the one who might have been, had their circumstances been different when they met as teenagers.

Goddammit. Figured she'd come barreling back into his life after he'd sworn off women.

He opened his mouth to give her some BS excuse, but an alarmed shout from the front of the barn had them both whipping around, ready to spring into action. They looked at each other, dropped their pitchforks, and ran for the door.

Outside, two guys rolled around on the ground, sending up plumes of dirt as they pounded the hell out of each other. One was Connor, his tawny hair matted down with sweat and dust and blood from a cut above his eyebrow. The other looked to be one of the younger recruits from over at the training center.

Jesus, he'd told Quinn that Christian Schumacher was too much of a wildcard—and between Ian Reinhardt, the team's explosives expert, and Jace Garcia, their duplicitous pilot, the last thing they needed was any more wildcards. Problem was, even though Quinn was a hard-ass, he had a soft spot for lost causes. He was reluctant to write anyone off.

Jesse, not so much. In his book, you broke the rules, you faced the consequences.

Schumacher had Connor pinned now, and pulled back a fist for a lights-out blow.

Enough of this bullshit.

Jesse waded into the fight and yanked Schumacher off, tossing the guy as easily as a bail of hay. Connor scrambled to his feet and would have launched another attack if Lanie hadn't caught him around his skinny waist.

"Get him out of here," Jesse said over his shoulder. Then

he stood, arms crossed, and stared Schumacher down. "What the fuck do you think you're doin'?"

Schumacher growled and shoved himself to his feet. "Kid kept running his punk-ass mouth."

"Yeah, exactly. He's a kid. Fifteen-years-old. And you're, what…twenty-two, three? You're the adult here, so goddamn act like one."

Schumacher wanted to take a swing. Jesse saw it in his eyes, and silently goaded him to do it. Jesse would take a punch if it meant that mean-spirited fucker got kicked out of the program.

But the kid backed down and stalked away.

Jesse closed his eyes and breathed out slowly.

Okay, one down. Now to deal with Connor.

Somehow, he didn't think that would be as easy.

Chapter Three

Lanie hauled the boy away from the fight, dodging fists as she dragged him into the barn. With a frustrated grunt, Connor shrugged her off and paced between the stalls, swiping at his bleeding face with the back of one hand.

God, he looked like his father.

Not so much the hard-edged, bottled-up man Jesse was now, but Connor very much reminded her of the boy he'd been back when she first met Jesse. All long limbs, tall and skinny, with the same blue eyes and shaggy hair. Except Connor's hair was lighter, tawny instead of the dark umber of Jesse's. And there hadn't been quite so much anger in Jesse's eyes at this age. No, for him, the anger had come later in life. Looked like Connor was getting an earlier start down that road, and her heart ached for him. She'd been forced to watch from a distance as his father wrangled demons strong enough to make a full-grown man self-destruct. It wasn't fair that a boy should face those same demons.

"Connor—"

He smacked her hand away. "Don't. You're not my mom."

She stepped back. "No. I'm not, and I don't want to be. But you look like you could use a friend."

"I don't need you."

"Or anyone, huh?" When he looked up sharply, she offered a smile. "I remember feeling the same way at fifteen. My parents weren't around much, either, so I had to be tough. I thought I could take on the world by myself, and didn't need anything from anyone. I wasn't entirely wrong, but I wasn't entirely right either." She reached into the tack room on her right and grabbed a bandana someone had left behind on the bench. She held it out to him. "At least stop the bleeding."

He snatched it away, but stared down at it for a second like he had no idea what to do with it. And in that second, his tough guy act faded away and she glimpsed the lost little boy underneath. Then he folded the bandana and pressed it to his forehead with a wince.

Sighing, she leaned against the door of a stall. "Why weren't you in here helping your dad? He was counting on you, ya know."

"For slave labor." Connor's lip curled as he glanced around. "I don't like barns. I don't like horses. I don't know why I'm even here."

"Jesse wants you here."

"No, he doesn't. He's always been too busy to care about me."

"That's not true."

"Is so." He started pacing again, just like his father did when he was agitated. The similarities were uncanny. "You said your parents weren't around?"

She managed to hold back the wince. That was a can of worms she hadn't meant to crack open. "Dad was a Texas Ranger. He was killed on the job, and after that Mom had to work a lot to keep the lights on."

"But they cared about you?"

A vice clamped around Lanie's heart and she had to draw a breath to ease the tightness. Peter Delcambre had been married to the job and was gone from their family long before his death, and Sharon had never recovered from the trauma of it all. She'd checked-out, mothered on autopilot until Lanie left for college, then up and disappeared. But Lanie had to think they'd loved her as best as they were able. "I think all parents love their children. Some just don't know how to show it."

"I don't think so." Connor shook his head, scuffed his bright red Vans in the scatter of hay on the concrete floor. "My whole life, I've been an inconvenience."

"*No*." Lanie infused the word with conviction. There was a lot she didn't understand about Jesse Warrick, and even more that drove her crazy, but she knew for certain he'd never view his son as an inconvenience. "Connor, no. Jesse doesn't think that about you."

"Yeah, sure." He rolled his eyes in the snarky way only teenagers could master. "Neither of them wanted me, you know? Now Mom's happy with her new family and her perfect children. She doesn't want me around anymore. And Dad's always off fighting another war. He never cared about me." He jerked his chin in the general direction of the training center. "But he cares about those guys. They're like him, and I'm not."

Ah-ha. So that was what this was all about. "Is that why the…" She made a vague motion toward her own face, indicating the bandana he held to his head.

He tossed the bandana aside. "Schumacher's an ass. He wouldn't shut up about his new sneakers. I said they were ugly, and he threw a punch. He started it, but I would've finished it."

She decided now was not the time to remind him that he'd have been knocked sideways if his father hadn't stepped in and saved his skin.

The barn door creaked open and Jesse stalked inside, his features set. Anyone who didn't know him would think he was calm, but she saw through the facade. Inside, he was boiling. Holding it back, though, as usual. For once, she'd like to see him let it go, lose control. It'd do him good to release some of the tension perpetually knotting his shoulders.

"Connor," he said in a painfully level tone.

The kid's spine snapped straight, readying for another fight. In that respect, he wasn't like his dad. He didn't hide what he was feeling. His expression was a whole damn novel of anger and resentment that anyone could read.

Oh no. This wasn't going to go well.

• • •

Jesse was so focused on his son, he forgot Lanie was there, too, until she stepped between them and held out her hands. "Whoa, hold up, guys. You're both angry, so let's take a minute."

He glared at her. Unflinching, she glared right back. And, goddammit, she was right. He needed to take a breather because he was seconds away from an explosion. Connor could push his buttons like nobody else—except for Lanie. It was hard to say which of them took more delight in needling him.

He drew a breath, then another, and rolled his shoulders. "Connor." He kept his voice calm and even. "Help me understand why you feel the need to keep causin' trouble."

"I'm not!"

"So gettin' into fistfights when you're supposed to be helpin' me here in the barn isn't causin' trouble?"

"Whatever." Connor stalked past him. "I'm outta here."

How the hell was he supposed to get through to the kid

when Connor ran off every time they tried to talk? "Where you goin'?"

Connor scowled over his shoulder. "Home. My real home."

"You're not goin' back to Vegas by yourself."

"Why not? You obviously don't want me here."

"Of course I want you here."

"Which is why you're taking off and leaving me on this stupid, dusty ranch?"

"I have to work—"

"You *always* have work." Connor turned away. "What else is new?"

As his son trudged toward the exit, Lanie widened her eyes at him like she expected him to say something. When he only stared at her uncomprehendingly, she jerked her chin in Connor's direction.

He still didn't have the first clue what she wanted him to say. She sighed and shook her head. "Why don't you have Connor come with us for the training?"

Connor stopped and swung back. Jesse about swallowed his tongue.

"What?" they said at the same time.

"No," Jesse added.

"Why not?" she asked. "We won't have live ammunition during the exercises and at night we're just going to sit around and BS. Maybe he'll learn something. Maybe you two will even bond. It'll be good for you both."

Jesse stared at his son. Connor stared back with eyes that were far too familiar. He'd seen those angry eyes before. They'd gazed out from the mirror at him for years. He didn't want his boy mixed up in this part of his life, but at the same time, Lanie had a point. Again. He really wished she'd stop being so goddamn reasonable.

"Would you want to go?" The question went against

every fatherly instinct he possessed, but Connor's expression changed to something other than snide indifference. He couldn't put a name to the fleeting emotion. It almost looked like...hope.

"Well?" Jesse prompted after a beat of silence.

"Okay." Somehow, Connor still managed to make his acquiescence sound sulky.

Jesse's belly knotted so tightly he had to swallow down a surge of sickness. "Whoa. I didn't say you could."

"Why the fuck not?"

"Watch your language."

"Whatever. I didn't really want to go anyway." Connor rolled his eyes and stomped away.

"Well," Lanie said as the barn door banged shut. "You handled that like a champ. Good job."

He speared her with a stare sharp enough to kill. "Don't you have somethin' to be doin' elsewhere, Elena?"

She crossed her arms over her chest, which plumped up her breasts, and made the tops of those beautiful globes peek out over her tank top. With his blood already running hot, he barely contained the urge to back her into one of the clean stalls and vent his frustration...all over her.

His cock twitched behind his fly at the mental image of her naked in the hay, sweat-slicked and writhing with pleasure as he came onto her belly.

Dayam.

Not the road he wanted to start down with her. Now or ever.

He spun away, his heart beating too hard and too high in his throat, his cock rubbing painfully against his jeans with each step he took. "Go away. I have work to do."

Behind him, she said something under her breath. Something along the lines of, "Like father, like son."

He stepped out into the hot afternoon sun in time to see

the screen door bang shut on the house. His partially deaf and mostly blind basset hound, Dozer, jumped up from a nap on the front porch and squinted at the driveway, letting out a confused *woof.* Jesse walked over and ran a soothing hand over the old dog's head.

When had his life gone sideways? Granted, his personal life had always been a mess, and maybe he'd used his career to escape the crazy. Patching up soldiers in battle gave him purpose, something solid and meaningful that he'd clung to like a life raft. But now the two worlds were colliding.

Let Connor join the training?

Jesus.

At a loss, he sat down on the porch steps. Dozer, all slobber and wrinkles, scooted closer and flopped over for a belly rub. It made him smile. This dopey-looking dog was about the only thing that could nowadays.

He gazed over his shoulder at the screen door, which hadn't shut all the way and now groaned softly in the hot breeze blowing through the valley. He hoped Lanie wasn't right about the whole "like father, like son" thing. The very idea that she might have hit the nail squarely on the head scared the ever-loving hell out of him.

Chapter Four

Dr. Tiffany Peters straightened away from the microscope and the muscles in the center of her back spasmed painfully. She'd been stooped over the lab table for too long. She'd need several hard sessions of yoga to release all the chinks in her spine, but the pain was worth it.

They'd done it. Dear God. They'd actually done it.

They'd cured viruses. Not one, not a few—but, potentially, all.

Of course she and Claire had known it worked in animal cells, and they were fairly confident it would perform the same in humans. That was why Claire was on her way to beg money for clinical trials of the drug. However, being confident something would work and actually *seeing* the results on a slide under a microscope were two entirely separate things.

Naturally skeptical, Tiffany had checked and rechecked,

and every infected and treated slide looked as healthy as the uninfected. It didn't matter the virus. Rotavirus, H1N1 influenza, rhinovirus, dengue flavivirus. She'd have to test it on some of the hotter viruses in level four containment, but she had little doubt she'd see the same results with Lassa, Marburg, and Ebola.

Their antiviral drug, Akeso, named for the ancient Greek goddess of the healing process, worked in human cells.

Tiffany jumped up and did a happy little booty shake. The idea for Akeso had started during a late-night, junk food and caffeine-fueled cram session in med school. The more she and Claire talked about it, the more they realized it might actually be feasible to introduce a drug to make virus-infected cells commit suicide, while leaving healthy cells intact.

And it worked.

It. Fucking. Worked!

Claire. She had to call Claire.

She grabbed her phone from the pocket of her lab coat, but hesitated when she saw the time. It was 2:41 a.m. Although her best friend was a night owl like her, Claire had been traveling nonstop for nearly a week, tracking a new epidemic in South America. Even if she was somewhere reachable, she was probably sound asleep. As exciting as the discovery was, it could wait until they saw each other later this week.

But she was too excited. She had to tell someone, so she grabbed her phone and tapped out a quick text to her fiancé, Paul.

Pulling all-nighter. Major breakthrough! It works in human cells! Tell you about it over dinner tomorrow night. Have a good day at work. Love you!

She waited a moment to see if she got a response. Nope. Wasn't even showing it had been read yet, and something like disappointment crept up the back of her throat. Then she laughed at herself and pocketed the phone. At one time, not all that long ago, nobody ever expected an immediate response when contacting someone. The Digital Age had created a generation of impatience, and she was right smack dab in the middle of it. Paul would see her text and respond in the morning, and that was plenty soon enough. He had a twelve-hour shift at the hospital starting at seven, and he was probably sleeping.

Okay. Back to work. Time to put together a report that might help Claire secure the funding they so desperately needed. Big Pharma never liked a cure-all, and it made investors jumpy. If they weren't successful at the Global Infectious Diseases Summit and Expo next weekend, the monumental success sitting under her microscope right now wouldn't matter one bit. Their entire project, all of their research, would come to a grinding halt without cash flow.

Tiffany rolled her stool over to her computer and fired up her techno playlist. Claire hated her taste in work music, preferring sweeping classical compositions, but that was so boring. For an overnight, Tiffany needed upbeat, bouncy, something she could get up and jump around to when she started falling asleep.

Oh, and caffeine. She needed to pour some into her system pronto or she was going to crash once the buzz of exhilaration faded. Unfortunately, a glance over at her desk showed her Diet Mountain Dew stash depleted.

Not a problem. There was a 24/7 convenience store down the street and she could use a quick walk. Be good to get out, stretch her legs.

She cleaned up her workstation and secured the lab, leaving the lights and music on since she'd be back shortly. It was a warm night, thick with the promise of a summer storm, and she breathed deeply of the damp air as she stepped out onto the empty street.

"Dr. Tiffany Peters?"

Automatically, she started to turn toward the male voice, but a niggling sense that something was off in his tone made her stop short. That niggle became a full-blown danger alarm when he crowded into her space. Oh God, was he going to mug her? And she'd left her pepper spray in the lab. She grabbed her retractable badge, intending to swipe it and duck back into the safety of the building. "I'm sorry, I'm busy."

"You'll make time for me. You have something I want." The man wore a balaclava and held a gun.

Her heart kicked and her hands began to shake as he jabbed the barrel into her spine. She fumbled the badge. He grabbed it from her and swiped it. The lock disengaged with a *ca-chuck*, and her badge retracted to the clip on her lab coat.

He nudged her with his gun. "Get inside."

"I-I don't have anything to give you."

"You have Akeso. The wonder drug."

All of the blood rushed from her head, leaving her dizzy. Akeso had the potential to save millions of lives in the right hands. In the wrong hands, it'd just become another cure the poor couldn't afford. No. That couldn't happen. She resisted his urging long enough to inconspicuously unclip her badge from her lab coat and subtly kicked it into the bushes outside before the door shut. She couldn't let them into the lab. "Akeso is just...research."

"No," he said calmly and held out Paul's phone. Her text shown on the screen. "It's more that that, and you're going to give it to me."

How did he have that phone? Terror gripped her by the throat. "Where's Paul? What did you do to him?"

"Doesn't matter," the masked man said. He nudged her down the hallway toward the lab's door with the tip of his weapon. "Open the door, Tiffany."

A chill scraped down her spine, but she held her ground. Inside the lab, her techno music continued to thump. "Akeso isn't here. I used the last of it for testing. I don't have all of the research, either."

The man spun her around and shoved the gun under her chin. "Then where is it?"

She pressed her lips together, shook her head.

The man swore. "It's with your partner, Dr. Claire Oliver. Where is she?"

"N-not here."

"Where. Is. She?" The barrel of the gun pressed harder into her flesh with each word, but she clamped her jaw shut and shook her head again. He would kill her—she was fairly certain of that—but she wasn't going to say more.

Suddenly the gun left her chin. She risked a look up at him, and saw his smile spread under the mask. He had a mustache. The red-blond bristles of it poked through the fabric. Blue eyes. Red-blond hair. Stocky. She was good with details and had to remember every one.

She flinched as he reached out, but he only ripped a flyer off the corkboard beside the lab doors. The flyer advertised the infectious diseases summit in Martinique next weekend.

He shoved it toward her face. "Claire will be there with Akeso, won't she?"

Shit. Tiffany squeezed her eyes shut. "No. She's not going. She's on a research trip in Brazil."

"Bullshit. She'll be there." He stuffed the flyer into a pocket. "And so will you."

Then, almost in slow motion, he brought the butt of the gun down against her temple. She felt the crack of it, but strangely there was no pain as the world tilted sideways. The floor was cold under her cheek. Her eyes unfocused, refocused, unfocused again, like when the eye doctor tested her for new contacts.

The man leaned down and scooped her into his arms just as unconsciousness dragged her under.

Chapter Five

Friday, July 17
6:00 p.m.
Alta, WY

Quinn and Mara's new house was a mile as the crow flies from Jesse's. Usually he walked across the fields, or sometimes he saddled a horse and rode over. But one look at the dark clouds spreading out over the mountaintops in the distance told him to take the truck. They were in for one of Wyoming's infamous storms. The air already snapped with electricity.

He glanced back at his house as he pulled open the driver's side door. His parents had come over from their place on the other side of the ranch to stay with Connor, but he felt better knowing the storm would keep the kid inside and out of trouble while he was gone.

Hopefully.

He hopped up into the cab. The truck was old and rattled with each bump as he turned it around in the dirt patch in front of the barn and pointed it toward the road. By car, the trip was more like six miles since the road skirted along the edge of Warrick land, and he took the time to let his mind wander to his impending meeting with Gabe and Quinn.

Lanie was probably right and they only wanted to go over plans for the upcoming training exercise. It was the first time the recruits would be away from the facility and no doubt they wanted to make sure everyone had his medical stamp of approval. And the recruits all did. At this point in their training, they were all a bit dinged up, but the only real medical issue had happened weeks ago when one recruit broke his leg after falling off the ropes course. He'd been treated and sent home with an invitation to come back once he healed. Other than that, the rest of them were in the best shape of their lives.

But if this little meet-and-greet was just to discuss the recruits' medical histories, why the hell wouldn't Gabe just come out and say it right there in the barn?

Lightning flashed over the mountains, momentarily lighting up his rearview mirror. He spotted a lone figure jogging along the road behind him and slowed, intending to offer the runner a lift.

Dammit. It wasn't one of the recruits. It was Lanie.

Why'd he have to glance back just then? Now he couldn't not stop. He guided the truck over to the shoulder and waited.

She slowed as she approached, her feet crunching on the hard-packed dirt, ponytail swinging behind her. Sweat glistened on her brown skin and her chest heaved with each indrawn breath.

He tried to keep his eyes on her face, and his mind on anything other than the way her tank top stretched tight across her breasts. "Not goin' to outrun the storm."

She arched an eyebrow. She did it often, and sometimes he wondered if she was even aware of the quirk.

"Was that your way of offering a lift?" she asked. "Or

are you challenging me, cowboy? Because I can't back down from a challenge."

He ground his teeth. Never took much for her to get under his skin and that, he knew, she did on purpose. "Get in the truck, Lanie."

She winced. "With the mood you're in, I think I'd rather take my chances with the lightning. I'll probably walk away less singed."

"Fine." He put the truck in gear. Lightning gashed open the sky behind them and a gentle rain splattered his windshield. It wouldn't be gentle for long. Not with the way that cloud was rumbling. He wanted to drive away, leave her to try to race the storm back to the training center, but he couldn't bring himself to take his foot off the brake.

"Lanie," he said through his teeth. "Get in the truck." He had to unlock his jaw to add, "Please."

She wiped at the sweat and rain dripping into her eyes. "Oh. Well, since you asked so nicely." Sarcasm was heavy in her tone, but she circled around the hood to the passenger side.

He closed his eyes for a moment, breathed out a soft sigh of relief, and forced himself to loosen his grip on the steering wheel. Like a burr under the saddle, she was a nagging annoyance, pricking at him with her mere presence. Why couldn't she have stayed in El Paso working for the Texas Rangers? Why did she have to go and throw in with HORNET? It had been so much easier to ignore her when he'd only seen her every ten years or so. Now that she was practically his next-door neighbor, he was lucky to get through a day without catching at least a glimpse of her.

The door's hinges squawked as it opened and the old leather bench seat creaked under her weight as she settled in. He silently thanked God the drive was only a few minutes long. As it was, it was going to feel like forever. He turned up the radio. Hopefully some classic country would curtail any attempts at conversation.

"How's Connor?" Lanie asked over Garth Brooks singing about his friends in low places.

So much for hoping for silence. "I don't know."

She turned the radio down and stared over at him. "You didn't talk to him?"

"I tried. He locked himself in his room."

She scowled. "Did you try to talk...or lecture?"

"I was only tryin' to tell him his behavior was unacceptable and—"

"Oh, Jesse." She sighed. "Do you even remember what it was like being a teenager?"

Not really. In truth, he hadn't gotten to be one for long. He'd spent most of his teenage years helping out his increasingly disabled dad on the ranch, and had joined the Army before the ink was dry on his high school diploma. Then, while in basic training, he'd gotten a letter from his girlfriend with a sonogram attached. Before he was even nineteen, he'd been a husband and a father. He'd had to grow up damn fast.

He shook his head. "It doesn't matter. The fact is, he picked a fight with Schumacher—"

"Connor said Schumacher started it."

He glanced at her. "I don't give a rat's ass who started it. Connor needs to learn to control himself. He needs to learn when to hold his temper and walk away or else—"

He'll become me.

He stopped short of saying it. Didn't dare re-open those healed over wounds.

"Or else what?" Lanie asked, a soft, all-too-knowing look in her eyes. Another reason she was dangerous. She was longtime friends with his family, knew all the ugly details of his life. She knew his temper, always boiling right under the surface, threatening to break free if he didn't keep a tight lid on it. Knew about the spiral of depression and drink that ended his Delta Force career and helped seal the fate of his failing marriage to Connor's mom. Knew about the two other failed marriages in his past.

And, goddamn her, she never condemned him for any of it.

He tightened his grip on the steering wheel and focused on the road in the increasing darkness. "Kid just needs to learn. Nothin' more to say about it."

He turned onto the lane that led to Quinn's house, where a handful of cottages huddled around the T-intersection. Back when this land used to be part of the Warrick family ranch, the cottages had been lodging for ranch hands that had families since they were close to the main road and kids could catch the school bus. Now they served as guesthouses when the guys were at the training facility—except for the first house in the row with the bright yellow shutters. Lanie had bought that one off Quinn and Mara when she decided to join HORNET. She'd since repainted it in ridiculously cheery colors and added on a room. Jesse didn't have a clue what that extra room was for since he'd never asked and he sure as fuck had never been inside, but she'd managed to turn the ramshackle place into a cozy, welcoming home.

He stopped the truck at the side of the road by her mailbox, but she didn't seem inclined to leave anytime soon. The air in the cab grew thick, started getting uncomfortably warm. He was aware of her scent, sweat and rain and something sweet like berries. It wrapped around him, more seductive than any bank-busting bottle of perfume. He didn't want to want her, but she was such an appealing combination of hard and soft, tough but gentle. She could take care of herself in a fight and wanted to be considered just another one of the guys, but he couldn't see her like that. Lanie Delcambre was distinctly woman, and his body was very aware of that fact whenever she was around.

"I have a meeting to get to," he said finally.

She nodded and climbed out. But before shutting the door, she met his gaze. "Connor is not you. Talk to him, cowboy."

Was he that transparent? "How about you stop meddlin' in things you have no business meddlin' in?"

She grinned. "*Meddlin'*"—she stressed the word, mimicking his accent— "is what I do best. Ask Mara."

Jesse sat there for several long seconds and watched her dash through the rain to the house.

Dayam. That smile.

As always, he felt a little like she'd socked him in the gut with it. All she had to do was flash some teeth and crinkle her dark eyes and all the oxygen rushed out of his lungs. Every-freakin'-time. It pissed him right the hell off.

He slammed the truck into drive and powered up the dirt road to Quinn's as lightning chased behind him. The weather tonight suited his mood. Dark and stormy with the potential for massive destruction.

Lanie was dangerous. She challenged the control he'd spent years perfecting, and he was so damn terrified one of these times she'd snap it like a twig. And if she did, they'd have a good time together, sure, but he couldn't guarantee he wouldn't go back to the man he'd been when he left the Army. All that anger. All that darkness. He didn't want to be that again. Couldn't go back. Wouldn't.

So, control. He'd just have to choke up on the reins and make sure he didn't lose it.

He parked behind Quinn's SUV and stared through the windshield at the house. He couldn't go in there as wound up as he was. He had to calm his sorry ass down.

He'd taken a few yoga classes when he'd left the Army—

though he'd deny it with his last breath if anyone asked him about it. He'd been hoping to find peace. He'd felt like a pussy the whole time—but he had learned a few breathing techniques that did help him chill out when his temper sneaked up on him. He channeled his inner yogi now and breathed in through his nose, out through his mouth. Concentrated on the simple act of sucking in oxygen and releasing it, and studied the house in front of him like he was going to be quizzed on it later.

Quinn and Mara's house was two stories, arts-and-crafts style, with a wraparound porch. Rustic, welcoming, and new enough that the elements hadn't worn the shine off it. As they were building it, he'd privately thought it was too big, but now that his cousin was pregnant again, he got why they'd opted for so much space. The rate they were going, they'd have their own army in a matter of years.

And good for them. They'd both had less-than-stellar upbringings. If they found peace by filling their home with children, more power to them. And God help them when their kids became teenagers.

Then again, he couldn't see Quinn and Mara's daughter acting out like his son was now. Bianca was a doll, and as pretty as one. The thought of seeing the little girl brightened his mood some and finally his blood pressure began to ease down.

Soft yellow lights glowed invitingly behind the windows, fighting off the encroaching darkness. Mara had chosen Santa-sleigh-red Adirondack chairs and strings of tiny white lights for the porch. Quinn—the man who bled desert beige and olive drab—hated the color and the fairy lights, but he'd indulged her like he always did.

As Jesse hopped out of the truck and dashed through the rain, he noticed two large figures in those chairs, watching the storm roll in.

Gabe's cane was propped next to his chair and his legs stretched out in front of him. Quinn was as relaxed as Jesse had ever seen him, feet resting on the bottom rail of the porch fencing. Of course he still wore his combat boots. You could take the SEALs away from the man, but you'd never beat it out of him. He lifted his beer in a hello salute before taking a swig. He wasn't supposed to be drinking. Alcohol didn't mix well with his migraine meds, but Jesse decided to let it pass without comment this time. He didn't have to watch the guy like a hawk anymore since Quinn now took his medical issues seriously, but the habit turned out to be a hard one to break.

Gabe wasn't drinking, but his medical problems were far newer than Quinn's. Jesse didn't know the specifics since he'd only treated Gabe in the first few hours after he was shot, but there had been a helluva lot of damage. The bullet had pinged around inside him like a pinball. He was damn lucky to be alive, but he was likely subsisting on a cocktail of pain meds and would be for years to come.

"Quinn. Gabe." He nodded to them, then motioned to the storm with a jerk of his chin. "Bet ya don't see storms like this in Costa Rica."

"We had a few," Gabe said, and if Jesse wasn't mistaken there was a note of something—was that wistfulness?—in his tone.

Well, of course he'd be wistful. He and his wife Audrey hadn't spent any time at their Costa Rican home during his recovery and they both probably missed the place. It was just strange hearing something other than command in the big guy's voice.

Jesse looked toward the screen door as a burst of female laughter drifted out of it. "Audrey's here?"

"Yup," Gabe said and picked up his bottle of water from the table between them. "We're looking to build a house."

Jesse swung around. "Here?"

The two men shared a look, then Gabe grabbed his cane and pushed to his feet. He was moving a little slower than he had been earlier in the day. Not bad, though. He'd come a long way.

"Let's take this into Quinn's office," Gabe suggested.

Whatever *this* was.

Jesse waited for them both to go inside before following. Toys scattered the living room, and they had to navigate around the dolls and stuffed animals to get to the office door. Mara and Audrey were at the kitchen island, conversing over…were those tubs of Ben and Jerry's? Probably. That had been Mara's main craving during her last pregnancy.

And the sight of the ice cream reminded him he hadn't eaten since breakfast. He detoured to the kitchen, drawn by the scent of something cooking. Bianca was in her high chair beside her mother, smashing what looked to be peas between her chubby fingers.

"Ladies." He bent to kiss the baby's head—yep, she definitely smelled like peas and had some stuck in her dark hair—then smiled at the two women. "You'll ruin your appetites."

"Doubt it." Mara snorted and rubbed her belly. "This boy has his daddy's appetite." She looked round and sweet and rosy with happiness. He was so glad for her in that instant, he couldn't help but give her a hug. He covered for it—the guys would never let him live it down if they knew he was such a sap—by pretending it was a diversion to steal the spoon out of her hand. He dug into the ice cream for himself.

"Hey!" She socked him in the stomach hard enough that the bite went down his throat like a rock. He coughed, eyes watering, and handed her the spoon back.

Behind him, Quinn laughed. "You should know better than to come between her and ice cream. Especially when she's pregnant."

He returned his attention to Mara. "You feelin' all right?"

She stared after her fiancé, who had continued with Gabe into the office off the living room. "I feel great," she said, but there was an undercurrent of tension in her words.

"You sure?"

"Mm-hm."

Didn't sound that way. "Everything still okay between you and Quinn?"

"Oh God, yes. I love Travis and I know he loves me. It's not that. It's…" She sucked in a breath and glanced at Audrey.

"We're worried," Audrey blurted. She nodded toward the office. "About them. We know it's just a training mission, but Gabe wasn't supposed to go and now he's being stubborn and insisting and…" Her eyes shimmered with tears and she blinked them back, shook her head. "I almost lost him last time. In more ways than you know. I-I can't… I don't know if I'm strong enough to go through it again."

Jesse's stomach twisted into a hard, painful knot. He'd suspected Gabe had struggled mentally as well as physically during his recovery, but to hear it confirmed…

Damn, it hurt.

Mara reached for his hand. "You'll take care of our guys while you're out there, won't you, Jesse?"

His gut response was to assure the women that the team wasn't walking into a real-life situation this week. But one look into Mara's dark eyes told him she needed more assurance. He squeezed her hand. "Always. I'll make sure they all stay in one piece."

"Thank you," Audrey said softly.

"I knew we could count on you," Mara added.

Yeah. They could count on him, all right.

Problem was, he didn't know if he could count on himself anymore. His ability to deal with serious medical issues in intense situations had always been the one thing he could truly rely on no matter what his mess of a love life looked like or the newest drama brewing in his oversized family back home. Medicine had been his calling for as long as he could remember...but now he just kept replaying all the things that went wrong when Gabe was shot, all the things that could have gone wrong, and all the ways Gabe could have—honestly, should have—died. Blood loss. Shock. Infection. To name a few. And Jesse hadn't been able to do any-damn-thing but sit back and watch. What was the sense in having all this medical knowledge if he couldn't do anything to help when his teammates needed him?

He realized he was standing there staring blankly at the two women and forced a smile. "I'd better go," he said around the vice gripping his throat and tilted his head toward the office.

It was the last place he wanted to go at the moment. He didn't want to talk strategy. What he wanted—no, needed—was a trip to the lake. It was the one place on earth he could clear his head and think straight. If he could get a few hours alone there, maybe he'd be able to figure out what to do about Connor and work through his sudden medical performance anxiety.

In the office, Gabe sat in the big executive chair while Quinn perched on the edge of the desk, arms crossed over his chest.

"The girls are worried about us," Quinn said without preamble.

Jesse tilted his head in acknowledgment as he shut the door. "Can you blame them?"

"No," Gabe said after a beat of silence. "And that's why we asked you here."

"Okay. You wanted to talk, so spit it out."

Gabe picked up a pen and twisted it through his fingers a

couple times. "After this week, I won't be going on anymore missions. Training or otherwise."

Jesse had started forward, but stopped like a glass wall had slammed down in front of him. "Wait." He glanced between the two of them. "What?"

Gabe sighed, set the pen down, and pushed himself out of the chair. He left his cane where it was propped against the wall and limped around the desk. "I'm not at full strength and might never be again, no matter how hard I work. It took me a while..." He trailed off, cleared his throat, and started again. "I can no longer be the kind of commander that rides to the front lines with his men. I have to think of my wife and the family we want to start. I can't give her that if I'm constantly running off to play war. And I won't"—he stressed the word with so much conviction it was more of an oath than a simple statement—"put her through the last year and a half again."

Jesse got it. He'd drawn that same line in the sand in a last ditch effort to save his marriage to Connor's mother. And look how that had turned out. But he hoped for Audrey's sake, Gabe was better at being a civilian than he'd been. "So you're leaving HORNET?"

"Not leaving. I'm still CO and Quinn is still my executive officer, but neither of us can be in the field anymore. Our roles from here on out have to be behind the scenes, which means we need a field commander who can follow orders, but who also has the ability to make split-second decisions under pressure."

He saw where this was going, and a sense of dread settled over him. "You don't want—"

"Yeah, we do," Quinn said. "If anyone can keep the team in line, it's you."

Holy hell.

Didn't they realize he was barely holding his shit together?

His son hated him, the only woman he wanted was the one he wasn't going to touch with a ten-foot pole, and he didn't even know if he was still capable of serving as the team's medic. With his recent case of the yips, he doubted he'd be able to bandage a paper cut without breaking out into a cold sweat.

And they wanted him to *take command*?

Shit.

"Guys..." His voice wobbled. Not with sentiment, though he was touched that they trusted him enough to offer the position. Nope, that wobble was all about the firestorm of panic raging inside him. He cleared his throat, tried again. "I'm okay with my current position. Ask someone else to—"

"There is no one else," Gabe said definitively.

"Think about it," Quinn added. "What are our other options? Jean-Luc? Ian? Garcia?"

Jean-Luc Cavalier, the team's linguist, drank way too much, didn't much care for rules, and was doing a damn fine job of fucking his way through the female population. He was arguably the most reckless man on the team, which put a big red X on him for any position of command. Ian Reinhardt, explosives expert, was as volatile as the bombs he defused and had a penchant for using "enhanced interrogation" techniques. And Jace Garcia? That pilot was shady as fuck. He could fly any aircraft in any situation, but you never quite knew whose side he was on.

None of them were fit for command. They were barely fit for the roles they filled now.

The look on his face must have given away his thoughts because Quinn nodded. "You see our problem here. Harvard's too young, too inexperienced—though he's been putting himself through training with the recruits and he's coming along. He'll make a good leader someday. And while Seth's managing his PTSD, we don't want to put any extra pressure on him."

"What about Marcus? He's a joker, but he knows where to draw the line, when to get serious."

"He's a possibility if you really don't want the position," Gabe conceded. "But he was never military and doesn't have the same combat experience as you do."

Were the walls closing in on him? Because it sure as hell felt the room was getting smaller.

"Listen," Quinn added after a beat. "You take the reins during this training op. After, if you still don't think you're the right guy for the job, we'll tap someone else."

One training mission. He could get through that and then politely decline their offer. He could do this. Wasn't like they'd be facing any real-world baddies this time out.

He inhaled sharply, let the breath out slowly, and gave a nod. "You can count on me."

"We know it." Quinn stepped forward and clapped him on the shoulder. "Men don't come any steadier than you, Sawbones."

Uh-huh. Steady as a rocking boat. Which explained why he was on the verge of a panic attack. His chest constricted and needed to get gone before the panic really took hold.

"Yeah, uh…" He cleared his throat to ease the tightness. "So. I have some thinkin' to do now. I'll need to take a rain check on dinner. Will you let Mara know?"

Quinn nodded. "I'm sure she'd put together a plate if you—"

"No, that's fine. I'll scrape up somethin' at home." He backed to the door, but stopped with his hand halfway to the knob as he remembered the fight from earlier. "Schumacher's a problem. He picked a fight with Connor today."

"Jesus." Quinn heaved out a sigh and pinched the bridge of his nose like he was starting to get a headache. "I'm aware. He knows he's on shaky ground. If he fucks up or mouths off just once during the training exercise, he's done."

Okay, that settled one worry. He hesitated, unsure how to approach his next question. "How would you feel if...Connor joined us?"

Gabe's brows climbed toward his hairline. "Thought you didn't want him involved in this part of your life."

Exhausted, Jesse scrubbed his face with both hands, dragged his fingers through his hair, and locked them behind his head. "I don't, but..." He dropped his arms to his sides. Shrugged. "I can't leave him here. He'll try to go back to Vegas if I do and his mom won't take him. She's washed her hands of him. Christ knows where he'd end up."

Gabe and Quinn shared a look that lasted for several seconds. The two had been friends for a long time—brothers, really, in every sense of the word but blood—and sometimes it seemed they could read each other's minds.

Finally, Quinn turned back to Jesse. "It's your decision whether you want to bring him or not. This is your show, buddy."

Annnd the panic threatened to strangle him again.

His show.

Right.

Chapter Six

Tiffany's mouth was bone dry. She couldn't remember the last time she'd had a drink, and every time she drifted off in her small, dark cell, she dreamed of jumping into a crystal clear lake and sucking it dry. She always woke up thirstier than before she fell asleep.

It had been days since the man with the blue eyes and red-blond mustache jumped her outside the lab. At first she'd been kept in a basement room with a toilet in one corner. Food and water would appear twice a day in the slot on the prison-like door.

So at least they didn't want her dead. Yet.

Then two days ago, she'd been blindfolded and hustled onto a plane. She could be anywhere in the world at this point—though if she had to guess, she'd say they'd flown her to Martinique. For all she knew, she could even be in the conference hotel. She couldn't hear any noise, though.

At least, nothing like the typical sounds of a hotel—elevator doors, muted conversations and TVs, the rattle of a housekeeper's cart. When she strained her ears, she thought she heard the sound of the ocean through the stone walls of her cell, but she couldn't be sure.

Really, at this point, she wasn't even sure of anything anymore.

She still wore the same clothes she'd had on the night her captor had abducted her, now stained and torn. She hadn't been allowed to shower or change since arriving here, and it had been over twenty-four hours since anyone had fed her.

As another cramp of hunger twisted her stomach, she let herself fantasize about going to the bridal shop and putting on her gown. All that satin and lace and pretty beadwork. She'd felt like a princess. Her mother and grandmother had cried and she'd known it was the right dress.

She'd never wear that dress again. With each passing day, she was more certain she wasn't going to live to see her wedding.

She wondered about Paul. He had to be worried sick about her, searching for her. She hoped he was at least taking care of himself. He had a tendency to neglect himself when she wasn't around to remind him.

If he was alive. She couldn't ignore the fact her assailant had had his phone.

And Claire? God. She probably didn't even realize anything was wrong. Had no idea she was walking into a trap. Once these men had them both, once they had Akeso, there was no telling what would happen.

The door smacked open suddenly, flooding her little cell with a wash of orange evening sunlight. She blinked against the assault on her retinas and gasped when a body landed with a dull thud in front of her.

Paul. It was Paul.

He scrambled to sit up and glanced around with an expression of shock and confusion on his pale face. When his gaze found her, his eyes widened. He launched across the few feet separating them and gathered her up in his arms. "Tiffany! Oh, honey, I thought you were dead."

She snuggled against his chest, torn between happiness and terror. She was too dehydrated to cry. Her eyes felt grainy, like they're been washed in sand. "What are you doing here?"

"I don't know. I was walking to my car after work, and the next thing I knew I woke up on a plane with a gag in my mouth and my hands tied together."

"No! No, no. You can't be here. You can't…" Hysteria threatened to overwhelm her. She thought seeing him again would be the happiest moment of her life. She was wrong.

"Honey." He gripped her by the shoulders and pushed her back. "Listen to me. These men are going to ask you to do something, and you're not going to want to. But you have to or they'll kill us. Do you understand? They will *kill us*."

She drew away. Something about his tone wasn't right. She'd been hysterical and terrified during her first few days of captivity, but he was strangely calm about the whole thing. He was clean, too. If he'd been taken shortly after her, wouldn't he be just as filthy?

An old niggling fear wormed its way back into her heart. There had been times when she thought Paul wasn't being truthful with her. Times when what he said and what he did didn't match up. She'd shaken them off as her own demons trying to ruin a good thing—she'd always had a tendency toward jealousy in her relationships, and hadn't wanted to scare him off by being too demanding or asking too many questions. But now…

The door opened again. Paul scrambled out of the way of the two men who entered. They blew right past him, like he wasn't even crouching there.

When the men yanked her upright, neither her legs nor her eyes wanted to cooperate. She stumbled along in the sand, and couldn't focus on her surroundings. She only caught glimpses—she'd been in some kind of storage shed, and they were dragging her toward a small concrete house. She did hear the ocean, though she couldn't see that either. The setting sun was too bright.

Once inside the house, one of the men pushed her into a bathroom. "Clean up."

She staggered and caught herself on a glossy pedestal sink. Her reflection in the mirror was startling—if she didn't know she was looking at herself, she'd never have guessed who the woman staring back was. Deep shadows colored the skin under her eyes, lines that weren't there before creased her forehead and dug grooves around her mouth. Her hooked nose had always been slightly beak-like, but now it was downright hawkish. Her eyes were too big and spooked. She looked as if she had aged ten years.

She slowly lifted her gaze to the man still standing guard in the open door behind her. She didn't recognize him.

Just how many of them were there?

He lifted an eyebrow. There was something mean and weaselly about him, and a chill scraped across her skin as he watched her expectantly. She glanced at the shower and dreamed of stepping under the hot spray, but there was no door and the weasel didn't seem inclined to give her privacy.

She wrapped her arms around herself. "Will you at least turn around?"

He didn't move, other than to pull a pack of gum from his back pocket. He folded a stick into his mouth, leaned a shoulder on the doorframe, and made a rolling motion with one hand for her to get on with it.

Nope. He wasn't leaving.

Okay. She turned her back to him and slowly stripped

off her dirty clothes. She used her stained and torn lab coat as a cover, holding it around her as she stepped over the tiled lip of the shower. The showerhead and knobs gleamed under the inset lights overhead. The walls sparkled with pretty green glass tiles. It all looked new and shiny, like it had never been used. She turned the lever and hot water streamed on, quickly filling the small room with steam. She checked over her shoulder, saw the weasel still leering at her, but decided she wanted the shower too much to care. She dropped the lab coat and stepped under the spray, letting it stream over her hair. Dirt sloughed off her body and circled the drain in gross brown water.

As she lathered her hair with the hotel-sized shampoo, she started to feel human. By the time her fingers started to prune, she almost felt like herself again.

She didn't want the shower to end. It was warm. It felt safe wrapped in a blanket of steam. But all too soon, weasel strode forward and reached in to shut the water off. He gave her body one long assessing look—he didn't appear impressed—before tossing a towel at her and finally stepping out of the bathroom. She caught the towel and immediately hid her nakedness behind the thick terry cloth, pathetically grateful for the cover.

Now what?

Tiffany glanced at the filthy clothing on the floor. They couldn't possibly mean for her to put those back on after she'd just washed off all the dirt…could they? She stepped out of the shower and over the pile, picking her way toward the door.

Weasel reappeared there with a stack of clean clothing. He shoved them at her. "Put these on."

She clutched the clothes to her chest. "Why?" Not that she was complaining, but what was the point of all this? If they were going to kill her, why let her shower and give her a change of clothes?

"Just do it." He pulled the door shut.

She was alone for the first time since weasel pulled her from her prison. Trembling, she dropped the clothes and spun in a circle, looking for…anything. A window. A skylight. Any means of escape.

There was none. For as pretty as the bathroom was, it was just as enclosed as her prison had been.

Deflated, she bent to grab the clothes again—and froze.

They were hers. The denim capri pants, one of her favorite pairs. They had been in the wash the night she'd been taken—she distinctly remembered putting them in the machine before leaving for the lab. The Wonder Woman T-shirt was the same one she'd picked up at San Diego Comicon last year. She knew it was the same because she'd spilled coffee on it and had never been able to scrub the faint stain out of the fabric. The comfy sports bra, the underwear, the slide-on sneakers—all hers.

Her clothes.

Exactly the kind of outfit she'd wear while traveling.

How was that possible?

Her hands started to shake and she drew a long, slow breath. In and out. The only person who had access to these clothes was Paul. The only person who knew what she'd wear while traveling was Paul.

It all circled back to…Paul. She'd texted him the night she'd been abducted. She'd told him Akeso worked on human cells, and then her attacker showed up with his phone.

Oh my God.

She didn't have a chance to dwell on the betrayal. A *thunk* sounded on the other side of the door and she scrambled to dress before Weasel returned. Except when the door opened, it wasn't Weasel. It was another man, fifty-ish, blond hair, angular jaw, and reddish beard. He was the man who had kidnapped her. She was sure of it, and the fact he didn't see the need to cover his face now had bile surging into her throat.

He had a hard look to him, like he'd lived through things she could only imagine.

She swallowed hard, choking down the fear. "What do you want with me?"

He smiled and rolled a suitcase—*her* suitcase—out to stand in the space between them. "You're going to meet Dr. Oliver as planned, and you're going to convince her to take you to her room, from where you'll call us."

Claire. God, she had no idea the danger she was in.

Tiffany shoved the suitcase away with her foot. "No."

"Need I remind you, we have your fiancé. Make one wrong move, alert Dr. Oliver in any way, and he'll die."

Horror zinged through her, but it was only a quick gut-reaction that she squashed. Yes, they had Paul all right. He'd probably been in their pocket all along. If "Paul" was even his real name. She was really starting to doubt that. She'd known him for two years—he'd come into her life just as she and Claire were trying to get initial funding for Akeso. Now she had to wonder if she'd ever really known him at all.

No wonder he kept pushing the wedding date back.

She'd been such an idiot. A blind, lovesick idiot.

Tears filled her eyes and she let them come. Anything to help her look more convincing because she was about to put on the act of her life. "Please, don't hurt him." She grabbed the suitcase's handle. "I'll do whatever you want."

Red Beard nodded. "That's a good girl. Follow me."

Tiffany steeled herself before leaving the bathroom. She had to make this convincing. Because while she was positive she wasn't getting out of this alive, she was going to make damn sure Claire would.

Chapter Seven

The training exercise in the jungles of Suriname had been the most exciting four days of Connor Warrick's life. He was tired, achy, hungry, in desperate need of a shower, and covered in a couple zillion mosquito bites...but also weirdly happy about the entire thing. For a little while, he had been able to throw himself into a real-life *Call of Duty* game and forget that his mother no longer wanted him and his father didn't have the first clue how to be a father.

He'd...well, he'd liked he whole experience. Really liked it. More than he'd liked anything in a long time.

The way Dad had taken charge and made things happen had been kinda awesome. The men respected him. They listened to him like he was someone important and not just some cowboy redneck from Wyoming. It was completely kick-ass. Not that he'd admit that out loud to anyone, least of all his father.

And now he got to spend the weekend here, in a crazy fancy hotel on a pristine Caribbean island. Yeah. Best week ever. Maybe there was something to this soldiering thing after all.

Across the hotel foyer, he saw Lanie drag her bags through the front door. He wasn't sure what to think about her. He liked her, he supposed, but he didn't know how to feel about her with his dad. They were totally fucking. Or if not yet, they wanted to—even though they'd spent the last week pretending the other didn't exist.

Lanie got her room key and left by the revolving door in the wall of windows that fronted the lobby. She cast only the briefest of glances in Dad's direction. He definitely saw her, but continued talking with the rest of the team, acting as if she hadn't just stripped him with her eyes.

What was this, middle school? Geez.

Another woman entered as Lanie left and several men in the lobby took notice. He studied her, too. She had shoulder-length blond hair and eyes as blue as the ocean outside the panoramic windows. She walked like a woman on a mission and she was dressed in a businesswoman sort of way, all neat and proper. Not a stunner, so why all the attention?

Curious, he glanced around at the men who'd taken notice. A couple of the older trainees, and Schumacher, the asshole. Which was just plain wrong since the woman looked to be at least ten years older than him.

Jean-Luc Cavalier also noticed her and broke away from the group. He sidled up to her and turned on a megawatt smile that Connor was sure would work.

The blonde gave him a critical up-down with her blue eyes and then scoffed. "I don't think so."

As she walked away, Jean-Luc's jaw dropped open. Closed

again. Opened. Closed. He spun to face the group, a look of genuine puzzlement on his face. "What just happened?"

"You, my man, were shot down." Danny Giancarelli, the FBI agent who had spent the week training with HORNET, mimicked a gun with his hand. "Point. Blank."

"*Non*." Jean-Luc scowled after the woman. "No way. I don't get shot down, *mon ami*."

"There's a first time for everything." Marcus Deangelo clapped him on the shoulder. "Welcome to the world of us mere mortal men. Stings, doesn't it?"

"It's the *cunja*," Jean-Luc muttered. "*Merde*. I didn't get rid of it."

"Dude. Not this again." If Marcus rolled his eyes any harder, he'd sprain them. "You're not cursed."

"What curse?" Connor asked.

Dad did a double take in his direction and his brows cranked down. "Nothing."

Yeah, sure. There was a story here and going on the last week he'd spent with these guys, he bet it was a funny one. "What curse?" he asked again, studiously ignoring his father's glare.

Marcus scrubbed a hand over his face. "Uh…"

Danny G jerked his thumb over his shoulder, indicating the registration desk. "I'll, uh, get our room keys." And he made tracks.

"Hey, you're the one with a gaggle of kids," Marcus called after him. "You should know how to field this."

Danny turned, still backing away, and held up his hands. "Not my circus, not my monkey. I still have at least five years before I have to give any of my monkeys The Talk. This is all on Jesse."

Connor rolled his eyes at them. These were grown-ass, kick-ass men, and they were scattering like a bunch of rabbits instead of just coming out and telling him they were talking about sex.

Ugh. Adults. Sometimes he really hoped he never turned into one.

"I know what The Talk is," he informed them. "I've had Sex Ed." And he'd even made it to second base with his girlfriend before he'd been forced to leave Las Vegas, but they didn't need to know that.

"Jesus Christ," Jesse muttered.

"What? Like you didn't know what sex was at my age? I'm almost sixteen, Dad."

"I don't..." He shook his head and pointed across the room to where the recruits had gathered. "Go find Jeremiah Wolfe. You'll be rooming with him this weekend."

Aaand dismissed.

Steaming with annoyance, Connor walked toward the recruits, but as soon as his dad and the others turned their backs, he about-faced and circled around to the other side of the room's giant waterfall centerpiece. Out of sight, but not out of hearing distance.

So call him nosy.

Over the rush of falling water, he could just hear his dad ask, "Curse? What the hell are you two goin' on about?"

"Oh, Cajun thinks a voodoo priestess cursed him on Mardi Gras," Marcus said and thumped Jean-Luc solidly on the back. "He hit on her and wouldn't give up when she told him to get lost, so now he's cursed."

Jesse snorted.

"Hey, voodoo isn't a laughing matter," Jean-Luc said. "I am cursed, f'sure." He pronounced it *fuh shore*. "And she was powerful," he muttered and pulled a small leather pouch on a well-worn cord from his pocket. He stared at it with a frown. "Even my *gris-gris* didn't protect me."

Marcus eyed the pouch. "Dude, you ask me, the curse is a good thing. Seems like your cock drags you into trouble more often than not. About time someone put a muzzle on it."

Jean-Luc gave him the finger. "*Beck moi tchew.*"

Connor mentally flipped through the little bit of Cajun French Jean-Luc had taught him earlier in the week and came up with what he thought was the right translation: *bite my ass.*

Marcus grinned. "Sorry, pal. Already ate."

Jean-Luc muttered something else in another language. The guy knew fifteen—and counting—different languages. How did he have that much room in his brain?

A flash of color to his left caught Connor's attention, and he turned toward it. Schumacher ducked into the alcove by the lobby bathrooms, but not without first glancing toward Dad and the other men by the registration desk. Like he didn't want them to see him go in.

Why not?

Connor waited several beats, then walked over to the men's room door and leaned an ear against it. He didn't hear anything inside. The door was solid, gleaming wood, too thick to allow noise to pass through. So he'd have to open it. He flattened his hands out on the wood and very gently, very slowly pushed it until a crack appeared between the jambs.

Schumacher's voice floated out. "...and she's here." A pause. He must have been on the phone because no other voice responded to him. "No, you're not listening, Briggs. I wouldn't risk calling if it wasn't a fucking problem. We're not prepared to go to war yet—especially not here. You need to pull out and plan B this shit or it's not going to end well for—"

The door creaked under Connor's hands. Schumacher broke off and footsteps echoed on the bathroom tile, coming closer.

Shit. Shit. Shitty shit shit.

He considered his options and came up with nothing good. So he went with his gut and shoved the door open, nearly banging into Schumacher on the other side.

Schumacher's lip curled. "What are you doing here, you little fucktard? Were you listening?"

"To what? You take a dump?" He was surprised at how even his voice was, considering his heart was threatening to bungee out of his chest. "Nasty."

"What are you doing?"

"Since when do I need your permission to take a piss?"

"Maybe not mine, but sure you don't want to ask Daddy? He might want to hold your hand. He does everything else for you."

"Fuck off." He felt Schumacher's eyes drilling into his back as he crossed to the urinal and started to unzip. The guy wasn't moving, wasn't leaving, and he really didn't have to pee. Now what?

He glared over his shoulder. "You gonna watch, you perv? I'm underage. All I gotta do is go tell a cop you touched me in the bad place…" He let his voice trail off.

Schumacher snarled, and it was almost feral. "You're gonna get yours, Daddy's Boy. Just wait."

A second later the door creaked again as it opened. It didn't slam. It was on some kind of soft-close system, which took some of the *umph* out of Schumacher's exit.

Oh man.

Connor slumped forward in relief, bracing his arm against the wall over the urinal and pressing his forehead to his forearm.

That was close.

He straightened and zipped up, then checked the stalls to make sure Schumacher really had been alone. All empty. So definitely a phone call, but who had been on the other end?

And what war were they talking about?

Chapter Eight

Well, he hadn't killed anyone this week. Jesse supposed that counted as a win. All of the recruits, all of his men, and his son had made it through a tough week in the jungle and to their island vacay in one piece. There were blisters and bruises, but nobody had shed even one drop of blood.

He wished the thought relaxed him, but he was still a bundle of nerves. He rolled his shoulders, trying to ease the tension. With how tightly strung he felt, you'd think he was sitting in the middle of an active war zone rather than hanging out poolside around a blazing fire as a salted breeze rolled off the ocean and the moon hung in a lazy crescent overhead. After such a successful mission, Gabe and Quinn were going to be looking hard at him to take up the mantle of XO.

"You scared?"

Jesse jolted as the conversation around him penetrated, and he stared over at Jean-Luc in the seat next to him. The Cajun couldn't possibly know what he was thinking. Or how fucking scared he was that he'd fail them all.

But then he realized Jean-Luc hadn't been talking to him.

Seth, seated across the fire pit, grinned in response. Orange light danced across his face, casting shadows over his scars, making them more prominent. "Nah. Not at all."

"F'true?" Disbelief colored Jean-Luc's question. "*Mais*, you're a brave, brave man. Getting hitched is my second biggest fear."

"Only your second?" Danny asked. The FBI agent had joined them for the exercise for reasons unknown to Jesse. To hear him tell it, his wife had expressly forbidden him from taking the job Gabe had offered a few years back. Maybe he'd wanted to prove he still had his man card and could hold his own with HORNET—and he had done so better than some of the recruits, despite not having any formal training. He would've been a great asset had he joined them.

Right now, Danny certainly looked like he belonged with the rough and tumble group, his dark hair windblown, his jaw covered with a week's worth of beard. He sprawled in the chair beside his best friend, Marcus.

Danny took a long drink from his beer. "So, Cajun, if monogamy is your second worst fear, what's your first?"

"Clowns." Jean-Luc shuddered and tried to catch the straw of his frilly coconut drink between his lips. "*Ech*. Scary motherfuckers."

"It's a wonder you're able to shave in the morning," Quinn said, deadpan. He was seated at Jesse's other side, watching the group over the fire with a small quirk to his lips. "I mean, considering the clown you see in the mirror."

Jean-Luc pressed a hand to his chest. "Quinn. Did you just make a joke?"

Quinn gave him the finger.

Jean-Luc sighed dramatically. "And here I thought your sense of humor was showing."

Everyone laughed. Except for Lanie. She sat directly across the fire from Jesse and she'd been unusually quiet since they'd arrived in Martinique.

Jesse was doing his best to not pay any attention to her, but it was damn near impossible when she wore a red bikini and a gauzy white cover-up that covered-up little. Even with her braids starting to frizz and shadows under her eyes, she was gorgeous. And she never even tried to be. He found it disconcerting. Annoying. Hell, infuriating because his cock had a mind of its own around her. He *knew* she wasn't trying to seduce him by wearing that swimsuit, but every time he looked at her, his body reacted as if she'd crooked a finger and invited him into her bed.

As if sensing his stare, Lanie's gaze lifted from the depths of her barely touched beer bottle. The firelight played up her angled cheekbones, and highlighted the fullness of her lips.

"Well," Quinn said and slapped the arms of his chair before pushing up out of it. "I'm gonna hit the sack."

Read: check on Gabe. They'd all been silently worrying about the big guy ever since arriving at the hotel. He'd excused himself to his room and hadn't been seen since. And while he'd never been the most social creature before he was shot, he'd always been the kind of commander who took the time to bond with his men post-mission, so this was unusual.

Jesse suspected the training mission had taken more out of him than he wanted anyone to know. He'd be getting a house call first thing in the morning. Jesse figured he'd at least give Gabe the evening to relax before the medical poking and prodding started.

He refocused on Quinn. "You're flyin' out tomorrow, right?"

Quinn nodded. "The doc told Mara to stay close to home for the third trimester. She was bummed to miss this"—he swept out an arm, encompassing the resort—"so I promised

I'd fly back early and we'd come down together sometime after the baby's born. Phoebe and Audrey arrive tomorrow."

Meaning Gabe wouldn't be alone for the weekend. Good.

Jesse met Quinn's gaze, nodded once in understanding. Quinn squeezed his shoulder as he passed. It was a gesture of solidarity, of brotherhood. Between the two of them and Audrey, they'd pull Gabe through this trauma.

Jesse felt eyes on him and shifted in his seat, knowing instinctively without looking it was Lanie. He wished he wasn't so damn aware of her all the fucking time. "Go make sure the boss is okay, and tell him I'll be checkin' in on him in the mornin'."

"Oh, he'll love that." A small smiled curved Quinn's lips. "And, not gonna lie, after the way he had you watching me like a hawk, I'm enjoying turning the tables on him."

As Quinn walked away, conversation around the fire trailed off and the mood sobered for a few minutes. Jesse didn't know about the rest of them, but he found himself reliving the moment Gabe was shot followed by the endless hours they'd been trapped together as prisoners. He'd felt so helpless watching Gabe's life slowly seep away and being unable to do anything but the bare minimum for him. It was nothing short of a miracle he'd survived long enough to make it to a hospital.

Danny was the first to break the silence. Maybe because he hadn't been in that snowy airfield in Eastern Europe like the rest of them and didn't understand the significance of the last few minutes of conversation. Or maybe because he did understand and was trying to ease the tension. Which was more likely. Nothing much got by the FBI agent.

Danny leaned forward and stretched a hand around the fire pit to Lanie in greeting. "I know we've been slopping through the jungle together for the last week, but I don't believe we were ever officially introduced. I'm Daniel

Giancarelli. Danny to my friends. I used to work with Marcus in the FBI before he blew me off for these guys." There was a smile in his eyes and his voice. "I solved their first mission for them."

That was greeted by good-natured groans. Someone even threw a colorful drink umbrella at him. Likely Jean-Luc since he was the only one of the group willing to drink the kind of frilly cocktails that came with umbrellas.

Lanie accepted Danny's handshake. "Elena Delcambre. Lanie to my friends. I pretty much solved their last mission for them."

Unlike Danny's statement, hers was greeted with uneasy silence. Lips compressed, she glanced at the men around the fire, then abruptly stood up. "I'm going to bed."

Jesse also rose. Partly because of his upbringing—you always stood when a lady did—and partly because…well, hell, he didn't know. She seemed upset, though he had no idea how he knew it. She wasn't scowling or anything, and she even smiled at Danny as he bid her good night. Something in the way she moved told him she was not okay. Her fluid, graceful step was stilted, her shoulders back, her chin up. If that wasn't a pissed off woman, he didn't know what one looked like.

He opened his mouth to say something before she walked away, but no words formed. He just stood there, jaw hanging, until someone cleared their throat.

He snapped his mouth shut and sat down again.

"What the hell, *mon ami*?" Jean-Luc asked.

He studied the faces in the orange glow of the fire. "What?"

Jean-Luc nodded in Lanie's direction. "You want to go after her, go."

"No. It's not like that."

Marcus snorted. Danny grinned. Seth took a sudden interest in the fire, but his scarred cheek twitched like he was trying not to smile.

"It's *not*. C'mon guys."

"Uh-huh." Jean-Luc stood and skirted around the fire pit. He reached into one of the many pockets in his shorts and dragged out a string of condoms. The foil packets glinted in the firelight. He slapped them into Jesse's hand.

"Oh, Jesus." Jesse glanced around to make sure Connor wasn't anywhere nearby, and spotted his son playing beach volleyball with several of the other recruits. He shoved the rubbers back and squashed down a surge of panic, but Jean-Luc refused to take them.

"Go to Lanie," Jean-Luc said simply. "You don't have to stay out here with us."

"I'm not goin' to—" Jesse glanced at Marcus for help, but only got a nod of encouragement.

"Yeah, dude," Marcus said. "Do us all a favor and get laid."

Danny held up his hands when Jesse's gaze swung in his direction. "Hey, I'm Switzerland here. Completely neutral." He dropped his hands. "I will say, though, you're wound really tight, man."

Jesse scowled. "Switzerland, huh?"

"Just saying. If my wife was here, I'd definitely take this opportunity to blow off some steam."

"If your wife was here," Jean-Luc said, "so would I. Your wife is hot, Giancarelli."

"She is." Danny settled back in his seat and lifted his beer in a toast. "And remind me to punch you for that tomorrow when I have the energy."

With a shake of his head, Jesse set the string of condoms down on his vacated seat and walked away. He had made up his mind to go after Lanie even before the guys started goading him, but he wasn't going to need condoms.

Yeah, all right, he was attracted. Had been for years, way

back when he was too dumb to know what to do with it. But he wasn't going to make a move on her. The last thing he needed was another failed marriage on his conscious, and he knew himself well enough to understand he was a marriage kind of guy. He didn't do flings and had only once had a one-night stand while on leave in Honolulu after his first divorce.

If he slept with Lanie, he'd end up in love with her and want more than a shared bed. He'd want his ring on her finger. Call him old-fashioned or sappy or whatever. It was just the way he was hardwired, and he wasn't about to get his heart broken a fourth time. He honestly didn't know if he could cope with that. One more failed relationship might finally fling him into the blackness of a depression he'd never escape from.

He found Lanie at the tiki bar on the other side of the pool. She was signing something, likely for a credit card or room charge. He stepped up beside her, but didn't say anything until she looked at him.

The corners of her mouth pulled into a frown. "What are you doing?"

"Ma raised me to always walk a lady back to her door."

Her frown deepened. She slapped the pen and receipt for her drink down on the bar with a *thwack* and whirled away.

Okay. So that was the wrong thing to say.

He sucked in a breath and chased after her. "Lanie, wait."

He nearly smacked into her when she stopped short and spun to face him. "Okay, one." She poked a finger at his chest. "We're not teenagers and this isn't a date. Two. I'm not a simpering, helpless female and I don't need a big, strong man to walk me home. I can take care of my own damn self, thank you very much. I think I've more than proved that over the last year."

He blinked at her and backed up a step. The finger she kept shoving at his pec was starting to hurt. "Uh…okay."

"Oh, don't give me that look. I'm not hysterical, either. And if you suggest I'm being overly emotional or PMSing, I swear to Christ Almighty above, I will kick you so hard your future children will feel it."

He opened his mouth. Then decided not speaking was the safest course of action and closed it again without making a sound.

Lanie nodded once and stalked away.

What the hell was that all about?

At a complete loss, he watched her go. A smart man would cut his loses and walk away...

But he wasn't a smart man when it came to her.

• • •

Men.

This week had been an exercise in sexism, and the worst part about it was they—no, *Jesse*—didn't even realize it. It had started as soon as the team touched down in Suriname and unloaded their equipment. None of the men had let Lanie carry anything heavier than a duffle bag—even Gabe had been lifting shit, and *he* should be the one they were all worried about. Then out in the jungle, Jesse relegated her to a glorified lookout while the boys played war. She never fired her paintball gun once all week. And tonight by the fire, when she made the exact same joke Danny had, did she get a laugh? Nope. She'd been greeted with nothing but silence. Forget that it was true and she had saved Quinn's ass last year.

Lanie was used to living in a man's world. Before joining HORNET, she'd been a Texas Ranger—granted, not for long, but it was still a male-dominated field, full of good old country boys who didn't think a woman could do the job. When she went into law enforcement, she'd gone in expecting misogyny, and she'd held her own just fine. She guessed she just hadn't expected that same kind resistance to having a woman on the team from the guys of HORNET.

Stupid of her. These men all had protective streaks as wide as Texas, and they tended to coddle their women. No offense to Audrey or Mara or Phoebe, but she wasn't like them. She wasn't the type to accept coddling.

Which was exactly why she couldn't act on the spark of attraction between her and Jesse, she reminded herself firmly as she left the main path for the smaller one that led to her bungalow. As much as she fantasized about falling into bed with him, the last thing she needed was to be relegated to "girlfriend" status. God. She couldn't imagine how they'd treat her then.

She had to face the facts—they'd never treat her as an equal because she had tits and ovaries. Maybe she'd never find a comfortable spot on this team. Maybe leaving Texas had been a mistake. She'd always had a goal, a clear career path, and not having one now was unsettling.

Footsteps crunched on the path behind her and she glanced over her shoulder at the shadow following her—long, leanly muscled body, wide shoulders, and an ever-present Stetson. She groaned inwardly. Jesse. Of course he couldn't just leave well enough alone.

She didn't bother acknowledging him and let herself into her bungalow with her keycard. She'd hoped the door would shut before he reached it, then she could just ignore him, put on her headphones, and get lost in a book the rest of the night.

He caught the door before it latched and barged into her space like a bull. "What's goin' on with you?"

She snorted and tossed her keycard on an end table. When she first arrived here, she'd been so pleased with the bright, cheerful cabana with its wall of glass facing the ocean and its beachy rattan furniture. But even that didn't cheer her up now. She was pissed off, restless, and just…frustrated with the world at the moment. "You can show yourself out. I don't want you here."

"Hold up a damn minute." He caught her arm. "What the devil did I do?"

She stared at him in utter disbelief. Was he really that clueless? Sure looked like it. His expression showed nothing but genuine confusion. She jerked out of his grasp. "Where do I start? Oh, I know. How about with the fact you've treated me like a helpless damsel in distress all week? Never mind that I'm a better shot than everyone on the team. Barring Seth," she added somewhat grudgingly. But, yeah, nobody was better than Seth.

Jesse scowled. "I have not—"

She held up a finger. "Don't you finish that sentence or I might punch you."

"Go ahead." He tilted his chin up, tapped his cheek with one finger. "You've been spoilin' to for days. Get it out of your system."

"God! You can be such an asshole." She shoved him. Hard enough to let him know he was pissing her off, but not hard enough to hurt him. Or so she thought. But he backed up a step, and when he did, the back of his knees banged the end table. His long legs buckled. He lost his balance, smacked into the arm of the couch, and went sprawling. He lay half on the couch, staring up at the ceiling, blinking in surprise.

Oh shit. Guilt stirred in her belly and she held out a hand to help him up. "Listen, I'm sorry. I know I can be abrasive and pushy sometimes, but—"

He moved fast and she barely registered it until she landed on her back on the couch, her body tucked underneath him. His lips crashed into hers so hard their teeth clicked together. She swallowed a surprised gasp that morphed without her consent into a moan. It had been so, so long since she'd felt a man between her legs, right where his growing erection now pressed...

Wait. What? It was Jesse's weight pressing down on her. Jesse's cock nudging at the vee of her legs.

Jesse.

Lanie clutched two fistfuls of his dark hair with every intention of ripping his mouth from hers and head-butting him.

Except.

Except, God, he had such exquisitely soft hair. The long, silky strands were so at odds with the stubborn man she knew, she just had to run her fingers through them. His lips were soft, too. Even though the kiss carried shades of anger and unwanted passion, his lips felt like velvet.

It would be easy to take what he offered. So easy to have a quickie right here, just to ease tensions a little. Jesse needed the release. So did she.

He yanked up her bathing suit cover, pushed aside the cup of her bikini, found her bare breast, and squeezed her beaded nipple, nudging her over the blurred line between pleasure and pain. She arched into his touch.

So, so easy.

And so wrong.

Not like this. If she ever did allow Jesse Warrick to become her lover, the first time wasn't going to be like this. It wasn't going to be born of anger and frustration. She had more respect for herself than that.

She bit his lower lip. Hard.

Jesse reared back onto his knees and touched the drop of blood she'd drawn, his stare even more dazed now than it had been when she'd knocked him on his ass. His breath heaved in and out of his lungs, shaking his wide shoulders.

Lanie sat up and tucked her breasts back into her bikini top. "You don't want to fuck me. Not really."

Eyes still fogged with the remnants of lust, Jesse gave a

slow shake of his head as if trying to clear it. "No…"

Okay, damn, that hurt, but she'd die a thousand unimaginable ways before she ever let the pain show. She scooted away from him and climbed to her feet. "Yeah, that's what I thought. You're stressed. It's tension."

He seemed to struggle to find his voice. "Lanie—"

"Don't." She drew herself to her full height, threw back her shoulders, lifted her chin. She was strong. Self-reliant. A warrior woman. She didn't need a man, never had, never would. "Don't make excuses. I won't listen to them."

She strode away with every intention of going for a walk on the beach just to get away from him—but no, she wasn't ready to leave it at that. She had a few choice things to say to him first, things he damn well needed to hear.

She whirled to confront him again. "You don't get it, do you? I moved to Wyoming to be part of HORNET. This thing y'all have, it does more good than anything I could have done if I'd stayed in law enforcement. It's something greater than I've ever been a part of, and I want to stay…but I won't if all y'all can't accept that I'm just as capable as any of the men on the team."

"Lanie." He finally moved, closing the distance between them. "Dammit, you *are* capable."

"None of you treat me that way."

He winced. "The guys…they don't know how to act around you." He reached out tentatively, as if he didn't know whether or not she'd accept his touch. She honestly didn't know either until he settled his hands on her shoulders. She didn't move.

"Truth be told," he added softly, "*I* don't know how to act around you."

"Just treat me like one of them!" Exasperation rolled through her. Why was it so hard for him? If he knew she was as capable as the rest of the guys, why couldn't he grant her the respect of equal treatment out in the field?

He was silent a moment and his fingers tightened lightly before he dropped his hands. "I can't do that."

At the resigned note in his voice, she turned toward him and met his gaze. He had the prettiest eyes she'd ever seen on a man. Right now, those eyes were focused solely on her, full of concern and possibly even a hint of nerves.

"Because I have tits?" The question came out far more breathy than she'd planned. Her heart sped up, and heat rose from her belly, flushing her skin. Being close to him always made her body go crazy, but there was a sharper edge to it this time. Longing goaded by exasperation.

His gaze dropped to her bikini top and he swallowed with visible difficulty. The gesture reignited the flame of anger and frustration, but also did something else—made her want his hands and mouth on her again.

He glanced away, and she drew in a deep breath. She hadn't been able to breathe properly with his heated gaze on her. "You're right," he said finally, which shocked the ever-loving hell out of her.

"Of course I am."

He nodded and prowled toward her, his denim blue eyes unreadable. "On all but one count."

Her heart kicked into a gallop and she resisted the urge to back up a step. She wouldn't give ground to him. Ever. "And what's that?" Damn, was that her voice, all sensual and girly?

He stopped short of touching her and whispered next to her ear, "I do want to fuck you, Elena. Have for a long time. That's why I can't treat you like one of the guys. I've never wanted to get any of them naked."

"Oh." *Oh.* He wanted her just as much as she wanted him? A mixture of nerves and excitement fluttered through her belly. Her gaze dropped almost involuntarily to his lips. He had great lips, the bottom fuller than the top, made for being sucked on.

No, girl, don't kiss him.

Kissing him would be a colossal mistake. If she wanted any chance of being seen as an equal, she absolutely *should not* kiss this man.

She kissed him.

It happened a lot like the first time when they were just kids. They both leaned in at the same time and their lips brushed together, innocently at first. If she'd listened with her brain instead of her libido, she'd have ended it there. But, of course, she didn't. He was a bad idea, but she'd always been a fan of bad ideas. She opened her mouth, accepting him in to explore, and the kiss became needy, hungry in an instant. His fingers delved into her hair, tilting her head to better accept his kiss. There was an edge to him, a desperation, and she vaguely wondered if he'd gone as long without sex as she had.

He backed her up until her legs touched the couch. She lowered herself to the cushions and dragged him down with her by the collar of his shirt, knocking his Stetson off his head. Kissing his way down her body, he untied the string holding her top on and found her nipple. Groaning, she arched toward him, pushing more of her breast into his mouth. He used his teeth, again dragging her toward pain, then soothed with his tongue and lips. She'd always known sex with Jesse would walk the line somewhere between gentleness and agony. He was a gentle soul, a healer who cared too much about everyone, but there was also no denying the darkness that plagued his every move. The contrast excited her.

He levered himself up on one arm and reached down to upzip his fly. She batted his hand away and undid the snap herself, sliding down the zipper. He was commando underneath. Like the rest of him, his cock was long, and he was definitely a grower. She wrapped her fingers around him and thrilled as he filled her hand. She squeezed, and watched dribbles of pre-cum leak from his tip.

And she crashed back to reality. The sight of the white stuff was enough to put the brakes on her lust, at least temporarily. If they were doing this, they needed to be smart. She wasn't currently on any form of birth control—hadn't refilled her prescription when the last one lapsed—and she doubted Jesse wanted to risk pregnancy any more than she did.

She looked up to find his eyes closed. His hips rocked into her hand. She forced herself to let go before things got any hotter and they both lost their minds.

"Jesse," she breathed, "we need a condom."

His eyes popped open, and he stared at her for a second before closing his eyes again as if in pain. "Goddammit."

Chapter Nine

"Don't move. Stay right there."

Cursing himself for not taking the offered condoms earlier in the evening, Jesse leaped off the couch and hiked up his jeans. He didn't bother with the button or his shirt, and beat feet to the main hotel. The guys were no longer sitting around the fire. Everyone must have turned in for the night. He went through the glass doors near the bar and took an elevator up to the fourth floor. Two doors down from the room Connor was sharing with Jeremiah Wolfe, he thumped his fist on the door and waited impatiently for it to open. Jean-Luc poked his head out.

"Jess?" He glanced up and down the hallway. "Something wrong?"

"No. Nothin's wrong. I, uh, uh…" He stuttered to a halt. Shit. When he'd bolted out of Lanie's arms, his only focus had been on getting protection and he hadn't considered how awkward this conversation was going to be.

Jean-Luc yawned, scooped a hand through his wild hair, which did little to tame it, then leaned a shoulder against the door jamb. "Then what's up, *mon ami*? You look like you just swallowed a crawfish while it's still pinching."

He tried to see over Jean-Luc's shoulder into the room, but it was dark. "I, uh, didn't interrupt anythin'?"

"Besides my beauty sleep?" He lifted a shoulder. "I told ya. That voodoo lady cursed me. Lost my mojo." His gaze traveled down. "But looks like you found yours finally. Congrats. You might wanna…" He mimed zipping up.

Jesse glanced down at himself. His fly was just barely zipped enough to cover his still semi-hard dick. Thank Christ he hadn't run into anyone during his mad dash across the beach or in the elevator. He hurriedly finished zipping and buttoned up.

"Should've taken the rubbers I offered earlier." Jean-Luc laughed and waved him in. "I gotchu, *mon ami*. I'll hook ya up." He switched on a lamp, and surprisingly, he hadn't been lying about being alone. His bed was rumpled, like he'd been tossing and turning, but empty. He grabbed his suitcase, hauled it up onto the end of the bed, and unzipped it.

"Here, take 'em all." He handed over a full box of condoms. "Someone might as well get use out of them."

Jesse took the box, and although he wanted to run back to Lanie's bungalow, he couldn't when Jean-Luc looked so damn miserable. "Hey, Cajun, you're not cursed."

Jean-Luc zipped up the suitcase and returned it to its spot on the floor before straightening. "I haven't gotten laid in four months."

Well, shit. That had to be some kind of record for the guy. "Really?"

"F'true. Even worse, the few times I had the opportunity, I lost all interest as soon as the woman started stripping." He crossed his arms in front of him. "I've been magically castrated, and I plan to track down the priestess as soon as I get home and make her reverse it."

Jesse gaped at him. "C'mon, pal. You're almost as smart as Harvard. You don't actually believe in that shit, do you?"

Jean-Luc just stared at him, unblinking, for three long seconds. Then he turned away and grabbed the TV remote. "Better not keep Lanie waiting. She might change her mind, and then you'll be in here watching late-night infomercials with me. And although I'm awesome company, I'm not sleeping with you."

"Lanie's not going to—" He couldn't finish the sentence. Jean-Luc was right. If he hung around much longer, she could very well change her mind. Or he could talk himself out of it.

He glanced toward Connor's door and almost started having second thoughts, but fuck that. Now he'd had a taste, he wasn't getting Lanie out of his system until he had all of her. And why couldn't he indulge and take a bit of pleasure for himself? It wasn't selfish to want one night.

He looked at Connor's door again. "Hey, could you, uh—"

"I'll watch your boy, *mon ami*," Jean-Luc said and grinned. "Now go have some fun for once."

He all but tripped on his own damn feet in his haste to get out the door. "Don't tell anybody about this."

"Lips are sealed," Jean-Luc called after him.

Yeah, right. Come morning, all of the guys would know where he'd spent the night. Jean-Luc gossiped like a little old lady at a bingo hall, but he was beyond the point of caring. All he wanted was to get back to Lanie and find solace in her arms.

When he got back to the bungalow, Lanie wasn't on the couch where he'd left her. He skidded to a stop and scanned the floor for her clothes.

Had he lost his chance?

No, he hadn't. Her bikini top was still in a pile on the floor, exactly where it had fallen when he'd pulled the piece off. He blew out a breath in relief, glanced around the cabin, spotted the bottom half of her bikini over by the bedroom door, and turned in that direction. She was going to be naked in there. Ready for him. His mouth went dry. His cock became hard enough to drive a fence post and rubbed uncomfortably against his zipper with each step.

Lanie was on the mattress, propped up on pillows. Still naked, though the details of her body were obscured by the filmy white mosquito net draped over the bed.

He took a step forward, but stopped as a small voice of reason in the back of his brain reminded him that sex with this woman—a woman he admired and cared about—would only end in pain and heartache. Hell, it might be the last push to tip him over into the darkness he always teetered on the edge of. He didn't have it in him to claw his way back from that again.

Did he dare risk it?

She shifted on the bed and let out a soft, sensual moan that sent a jolt straight to his cock. Behind the net, he could just make out the dips and curves of her body and all that lovely dark skin.

Oh Christ, he wanted her. He wanted to touch every inch of her. Taste every inch. Part her legs and get lost in the softness that lay between.

Lanie crooked a finger. "Are you going to stand there all night, cowboy, or are you going to come over here and fuck me?"

Fuck her. Yes, that was all this would be. Fucking. A raw, physical, carnal act that had nothing to do with emotion or love. Other men did it all the time. All he had to do was keep the act separate from his emotions, take pleasure in her without falling in love.

She moaned again and all the blood left his brain.

Frustrated by the mosquito net blocking his view, he stalked forward and ripped it open. He about swallowed his tongue when he spotted her fingers dipping slowly in and out of her sex.

"Lanie." His voice came out strangled as he watched her fingers disappear between her folds. "You didn't wait."

"You took too long."

• • •

He'd only been gone ten minutes, but she'd nearly second-guessed this whole thing. She'd gotten up from the couch after he'd gone, and paced. Worried.

Wanting him as much as she did felt wrong. Selfish, somehow. And more than a little self-destructive. But that didn't stop her from stripping and climbing into bed to wait for him.

And now here he was, staring at her like he wanted to devour her. She opened her legs wider and let him look.

He knelt on the end of the bed, dragging his fingers lightly from her calf up to her knee. "I want my mouth on you."

"Yeah?" She laughed softly, breathlessly. "What a coincidence. So do I."

He settled between her legs, and his breath caressed her sex as he inhaled then exhaled slowly. She groaned and arched toward him. "Jesse. Please."

He nuzzled her, parting her folds with his fingers before his tongue licked out and circled her clit. She shuddered as he alternated between teeth and tongue. He took her to the edge of pain, then he'd soothe her back to pleasure, again and again until she was shaking from the intensity of it. Her body flamed to life in a way it hadn't in a very long time. She dug her fingers into his hair and held him there while he continued his delicious torture.

The orgasm struck like a lightning bolt, leaving her numb down to the tips of her toes. She might have cried out, probably cried out, but she wasn't sure. Couldn't hear anything through the thundering of her heart and buzzing in her ears.

Jesse crawled up the length of her, tracing his lips over her stomach. He stopped long enough to lavish attention on both breasts, teasing until her nipples stood at peaks. Finally he covered her, his bulge pressing rhythmically to the spot between her legs he'd already sensitized. He propped himself up on his arms and grinned down at her as she shuddered.

She reached between them and tugged at the front of his jeans. "Why are you not naked yet?"

"As soon as these pants come off, I'm gonna be inside you, and it'll be over."

She smirked up at him. "No staying power, huh? I'm surprised at you, cowboy."

"It's been a very long time."

"Then you need to practice." In one deft move, she sat up and flipped their positions. It was her turn to prowl down the lean muscles of his body. "Let me help you with that."

She unzipped his jeans and his cock sprang free. She sucked him in, just for a second, swirling her tongue around his tip until his fingers dug into the sheets beside him. Then she released him and tugged his jeans down his hips. She was nearly tempted to leave them on just because he looked so damn good in them, but he looked even better naked. The gangly kid she'd once known had muscled up and filled out, his size finally matching his height. He was probably still considered too thin by most standards, but so was she. And she knew they were going to fit together like they'd been made for it.

Once she had his jeans off, she searched his pockets and found a foil condom packet. She held it up. "Only one?"

"There's a box in the living room."

"Now you're talking." She grinned and ripped the foil open. He reached down and stood himself up so she could roll the condom on. Then she positioned herself over him.

She didn't move slow or easy. It wasn't what she wanted. She took him all in at once, rocking hard against him until they were both panting.

"Goddamn." He gasped and sat up, digging his fingers into her hips, trying to slow her down. "Lanie, I can't—"

His protest was drowned out by her second orgasm. Not as powerful as the first, but it lasted longer, hitting her in waves. Her head dropped back as she rode out the pleasure with rolls of her hips. Jesse scooped a hand behind her neck and nibbled his way up the tendon along the side.

"Fuck me," he said right by her ear. "That was hot."

He flipped them again, and stood, pulling her to the edge of the bed. He dragged her legs up over his shoulders and entered her again. The change in angle produced all new sensations and sent little shocks of excitement tingling through her. He was so much deeper now, moving hard and fast, and the whole bed shook under them. She was surprised to feel yet another orgasm building low in her belly, but knew she wouldn't get there again before him. She was okay with that. She was worn out, wrung out, sated, and she loved watching him move over her. The muscles in his arms and belly flexed and quivered with every thrust. When he tensed with his orgasm, his jaw clenched and his eyes closed. His head tilted back, and sweat-damp hair fell across his forehead.

He was right. Watching him come undone…that *was* hot.

Shuddering, he collapsed on top of her, half on and half off the bed. He pressed a kiss to her collarbone. "Sorry. Told you it's been a while."

She rubbed a hand down his back. His muscles were still quaking. "If you think that was something to apologize for, I can't wait to see what else you got, cowboy."

He huffed out a laugh and levered himself up. His blue eyes sparkled in a way she'd never seen before. "Give me a minute and I'll show you."

Chapter Ten

Some vacay this turned out to be.

Jean-Luc turned off the TV as a ridiculously happy hype man tried to sell him on the virtues of Sauna Pants. Because, yeah, some *couillon* thought it was a good idea to turn your shorts into a working sauna. Who doesn't love sweaty balls?

Merde.

He was going to jump out of his skin if he stayed in this room watching infomercials a second longer. He tossed the remote aside and rolled off the bed. After the intense week of training, the rest of the team was probably asleep, so he wasn't going to have much luck talking any of them into looking for trouble. In truth, he should be as exhausted as the rest of them. Jesse, out of some twisted need to prove himself, had tortured them throughout the week. At times, only the thought of this weekend island retreat—and maybe a chance to break the voodoo curse—kept him going.

And yet here he was, alone in his room watching infomercials. It was like the gazillionth level of hell.

But, c'mon, he was on a Caribbean island. There had to be good times rolling somewhere around here, despite the late hour.

He snagged a clean New Orleans Saints T-shirt from his bag and pulled it on. He'd showered earlier and his hair was still damp. He scooped it up and tied it back from his face as he slid on a well-worn pair of flip-flops. He wasn't usually one to rock the man bun and beach bum look, but tonight he wasn't expecting to impress anyone. Not with the fucking curse following him around like a fart cloud.

No, he wasn't even going to try prowling for a woman tonight. He'd hit up the bar, have a drink or two. Maybe he'd wander down to the nude beach for a night swim. He just needed to move, or he'd spontaneously combust from boredom.

His *mamere* had always said boredom was a dangerous thing for him, which was why she'd encouraged him at age eight to learn a language besides his native Cajun French and English. He'd chosen Spanish and had been fluent within a year. The rest, as they say, was history. The more languages he'd learned, the more he wanted to know.

But Mamere was right about him and boredom. He was well aware it made him reckless, stupid, and got him into trouble more often than not.

"No trouble tonight," he promised her spirit, because he felt her with him as surely as the curse hanging over his head. Hell, she'd probably asked the voodoo queen to magically castrate him. He had fucked his way through the female population of New Orleans in the months after her death. She'd probably been appalled by him.

He rubbed a hand over his face to push back the rush of tears that thought brought to his eyes. He still couldn't believe she was gone. Six months—no, almost seven since she'd died at age seventy-five from a brain aneurysm. Nobody had seen it coming. Edmee Cavalier had been the definition of health—until she wasn't.

He missed her.

And now his mood was even darker than it had been moments before. Maybe he should go back to his room. Exhaustion had made him maudlin and he wasn't fit for public consumption tonight.

He stopped just outside the hotel's side door and scanned the outdoor bar. The place was nearly empty. A few people still hung out around one of the many fire pits, and only one woman sat at the bar. The woman from the lobby, he realized as he approached. The cute blonde who had barely glanced at him before shooting him down.

And, yeah, that had stung. He was still getting used to this whole rejection thing. He didn't like it.

But no meant no. He'd respect her wishes and leave her the hell alone.

He chose a seat at the other end of the bar and flagged the bartender. He was in a coconut kind of mood and hummed the piña colada song to himself as he waited for his drink.

"You're off-key."

His gaze wandered back to the blonde. Focused on the screen of her phone, she wasn't looking at him, but she had to be the one who had spoken because there was nobody else around. "No, I'm not."

"Are, too." She hummed the chorus, proving that, *merde*, he had been off-key.

"I'll have you know I'm an excellent singer."

"Uh-huh."

There was something intriguing about her. She wasn't

qualifying for the Sports Illustrated swimsuit edition anytime soon, but he didn't put much stock in that narrow definition of beauty anyway. All women were gorgeous in their own ways, and she had a clean, au naturel thing going for her. Her face was without make-up and ever so lightly freckled. Her nose had a slight upturn at the tip. He'd noticed in the lobby that her eyes were blue, but more sapphire than the gunmetal-blue peepers he saw in the mirror everyday. Earlier, she'd worn her hair in a ponytail with pieces arranged artistically around her face, but now it was all loose, hanging straight in a sharp bob that ended just above her petite shoulders. Instead of the blouse and skirt she'd had on, she now wore a white tank top, jean shorts, and sandals. All of it very practical, no fuss or frills. She ignored her drink, which had been sitting there for a while judging by the pool of condensation around the base of the margarita glass, and kept checking her phone with a frown. Twice she tried to call someone, but whoever was supposed to be on the other end didn't answer.

After the second time she hung up, she finally reached for her glass and caught him staring. She set the glass down with a *thunk*. "You again."

He held up his hands. "Only here for the alcohol." As if on cue, the bartender returned right then with his drink. "And, apparently, a schooling on the piña colada song.'"

She'd eyed his drink warily. "You needed it."

"This?" He lifted it in a salute before he took a sip. "*Oui.*"

"No, the lesson. You were off-key." She went back to frowning at her phone, but he wasn't ready to give up on the conversation yet. He was enjoying himself for the first time in months.

"Besides," he added, unable to help himself, "I don't hit on women who look like they lost their puppy."

Her gaze snapped up. "I didn't lose a puppy." Back to her phone. Another frown. "It's my partner."

"Partner?" *Merde.* The curse was still in full effect...

"Business partner."

...or maybe not. He knew women, and they didn't make those kinds of distinctions if they weren't interested. Maybe the curse was lifted. Maybe he'd get lucky tonight after all.

He picked up his glass and walked around the bar to the seat beside her. This close, she smelled good, like vanilla and spices. "How do you lose a business partner?"

She bit her lip, drawing his gaze to her mouth. Her upper lip was fuller than the bottom. She probably hated it, maybe even thought she had a duck mouth. He thought it was an interesting feature that made her unbelievably sensual.

"I didn't lose her," she protested. "I just haven't talked to her."

"Why not?"

"I was in Brazil until today. Spent most of my time there out in the rainforest where there isn't precisely a cell signal."

He studied her. She didn't look like the type of woman to go backpacking in the rainforest for sport. She had a shine to her, the elite polish of city-born and highly educated. And although her accent was American, there was something faintly upper-crust British in the way she formed her words.

"Research?" he guessed. It was the only reason someone like her would be traipsing around in the jungle.

"Huh?" The screen of her phone lit up. Distracted again, she picked it up. Frowned. Put it down. "Oh. Uh, yes. Viral epidemiology. I was studying Zika."

Mmm. Sexy and intelligent. Now he was intrigued.

"Here for the conference?" He'd seen a sign in the lobby about the Global Infectious Diseases Summit and Expo taking place in the hotel's convention center starting tomorrow. Or, today, since it was after midnight.

She nodded. "Tiffany was supposed to meet me here this evening, but..." Another puzzled glance at her phone's screen, then she finally slid the thing into her purse. "She didn't show and I can't get through to her. It's not like her."

"Maybe her flight was delayed. There's a hurricane brewing off the coast of Florida." He'd seen a news flash about it while moping in bed. "If she's coming from up north, it's very possible she's delayed."

"Maybe." Again, her teeth sank into her lower lip. Then she seemed to realize she was doing it, picked up her drink, and took a small sip. "The odd thing is she usually doesn't come to these things. She likes lab work and staying out of the spotlight. But her fiancé just called me this afternoon and said she'd had a breakthrough in the lab and she was one her way down. It's just not like her to—" She stopped short, set her drink down. "Why am I telling you this?"

"I've been told I'm a good listener." He winced. "*Mais*, that's not true. I'm a horrible listener. Like the sound of my own voice too much."

She cocked her head to the side. "Are you French?"

"Do I look French?" he asked in the language.

"You look like trouble," she said in the same language.

He grinned. Judging by her easy pronunciation, she was fluent, and he swore he felt his heart melt inside his chest like bananas foster left out too long in the Louisiana sun.

"Ah, *cher*. Run away with me now. We'll grow fat and old together and have lots of babies."

"See, you're trouble." She pointed a finger at him. "And not French. Cajun."

"What gave me away?" Though he knew. Language was his thing, after all, but he was curious how she'd guessed it.

"*Cher*," she repeated, pronouncing it *sha* like he had. "That's a Cajun endearment. Pronounced differently from the classic French word, *chérie*."

Color him impressed. "You know your languages."

"It's a necessity," she said simply. "My work takes me all

over the world."

"Likewise. How many are you fluent in?"

"Counting English, five. You?"

"Fifteen."

She choked on her drink. "Fifteen?"

"F'true." He was enjoying himself, he realized, and he wasn't even buzzing from his drink yet. Somewhere along the way, he'd forgotten that a conversation with an intelligent woman could be almost as stimulating as sex. Almost.

She'd go with him back to his room if he asked her to. He saw it in her eyes. She was as delightfully intrigued by him as he was by her. But when he opened his mouth to suggest they take their conversation somewhere more private, no words came out. Him, Jean-Luc Cavalier, with no words.

Damn that voodoo queen to hell.

The moment passed—and his chance to get laid went with it. He knew it the second she broke eye contact and reached for her phone as it buzzed.

"Oh," she said with a soft sigh of relief. "Finally. She's here. I have to go let her into our room."

Jean-Luc couldn't say why, but his spidey senses started tingling and he knew better than to ignore them. He leaped up when she stood. "I'll walk with you."

She stared at him like he had just spouted a second head. "To my room?"

"Maybe I'll still convince you to run away with me." He shrugged and flashed a smile that usually melted women's panties. All it got from her was a raised eyebrow and a shake of her head as she walked away.

Of all the times to be cursed.

He should let her go. Just give up, go back to his room, and take the loss like a man. But he couldn't ignore the creeping sense that something was...off. A quick study of his surroundings didn't show him anything amiss.

And still.

He dogged her heels and stopped the glass exterior door before it closed in his face. "Have her meet you in the lobby."

Again, she gave that look like she thought he might be an alien. "Why?"

Bad, bad feeling.

And she'd probably start looking at him like he needed a straightjacket if he admitted that out loud. "I can...help carry her bags."

She narrowed her eyes, studied him for a solid fifteen seconds.

He shrugged. "Free labor."

"All right. Fine." She grabbed her phone again and tapped out a text. "But I'm not tipping you."

Whew. Why the hell did it seem like they'd just dodged a bullet? He rubbed the back of his neck, trying to shake off the creeping dread. Didn't help. The air was charged with energy. The way wrong kind. He'd experienced this same feeling a couple years ago in Afghanistan moments before he and the guys were ambushed.

He realized the blonde had gotten nearly half a hallway ahead of him and chased after her. "I didn't catch your name."

"I imagine because I didn't throw it."

"I'm Jean-Luc."

She finally stopped by the elevators and turned to him. "Picard?"

He grinned. Harvard, HORNET's resident genius and fan of all things geek, would love this woman. He'd asked Jean-Luc the same thing when they'd first met years ago. "Nah, I'm more of a Star Wars fan."

She snorted and hit the up arrow to call the elevator. "You would be."

"What's that supposed to mean?"

She didn't respond. Just watched the elevator bank like it

would give her the answers to the universe. When the doors slid open, he went in ahead of her and held the door. She sighed and stepped in. He decided that was a victory. Small one, yes, but he'd take them where he could get them at this point.

"You still haven't told me your name."

"Nope." She hit the button for the lobby. "I haven't. You'd think that'd be your first clue."

He opened his mouth, but again found he had no words. Why did that keep happening?

The doors opened to the lobby, and the woman stepped out. He really should go back to his room before she accused him of stalking or sexual harassment or something...

But there was still that tickle at the back of his neck and until he was sure he was only imagining it, he wasn't going to let her out of his sight.

He scanned the lobby as he followed her toward the front desk. More people here than he expected, considering the time of night. He counted four men, a bellhop, two desk clerks, and a fidgety brunette in a Wonder Women shirt standing beside the water fixture in the middle of the lobby. She fiddled with the handle of her suitcase, and her gaze kept flicking over to a man seated at the computer banks where guests could print off their boarding passes.

The blonde went straight for her. "Tiffany?"

The scared woman straightened. "Claire." Again her gaze flicked toward the computer guy—a big thug of a man with blond hair and a reddish beard. He shifted in his chair slightly, and Jean-Luc glimpsed the butt of an AR-15.

Oh, this was FUBAR.

Jean-Luc reached under his shirt for his knife, thankful he'd strapped it on before leaving his room. A force of habit that had saved his ass many times before, and looked like it would again tonight. He was already moving toward Red

Beard by the time he spotted the second gunman hovering within arm's length of Tiffany.

"*Claire*," the woman choked out and tears spilled from her eyes. "They want Akeso. Run!" Then she shoved her suitcase toward the second gunman.

The man tripped on the rolling bag and his finger tightened on the trigger, sending a wild stream of bullets into the air, the floor, the wall.

Tiffany crumpled. Whether or not she'd been shot, he didn't know, but he had to stop the spray of bullets before anyone else ended up dead. He launched at the guy—a weaselly looking Hispanic man—hitting him hard enough to knock the gun from his grasp.

The guy was about half Jean-Luc's size, but stronger than he looked. He landed one good punch to Jean-Luc's kidney—that was going to suck later—but it was the first and last blow he managed. Jean-Luc blocked the next punch aimed at his jaw, shoving it aside with one arm while simultaneously jamming the knife up into the guy's armpit. The sound he made was more animal than human and his punching arm went slack. Jean-Luc twisted the dead limb, forcing the asshole to face him. Blood pumped from the wound in rhythmic spurts, and Weasel was already half conscious, eyes unfocused. He'd be dead in five minutes, maybe less. Jean-Luc let him drop, and looked around.

The two desk clerks screamed. The bellhop lost control of his luggage-filled cart and it crashed into the fountain. Water flooded across the lobby floor. Two of the Tangos were trying to corral the employees, but Red Beard had gone for the blonde. Claire.

Mais, he'd been hoping for trouble. He'd certainly found it, and more.

He sprinted for Red Beard, sure-footed despite the blood and water slicking the floor, and slammed into the guy from behind. He was much more solidly built than Weasel and it was a bit like hitting a brick wall at full speed. Red Beard fell forward and hit a heavy stanchion chest-first. There was a crack—definitely ribs breaking. He dropped to his knees and bent double, clutching his chest, gasping like he couldn't get a full lung-full of air.

Jean-Luc, still on his feet, jumped over him and grabbed a frozen Claire by the arm. He dragged her into one of the first floor hallways. With two Tangos incapacitated and the other two distracted by the employees, time was on his side. But it wouldn't stay that way, especially if they called in reinforcements.

Stairs. He needed the stairs.

A young man stuck his head out from one of the rooms along the corridor. He was wearing a bellhop uniform.

"How do we get out of here?" Jean-Luc demanded of him.

The kid shook his head, not comprehending. Jean-Luc repeated the question in French and was pointed to a door the very end of the hall. He nodded, grabbed the kid, and asked if there was anyone else in room. Received an answer in the negative and shoved the kid toward Claire. "Take him and anyone else you find along the way, and run. Go out through the pool, onto the beach, and get as far away from the hotel as you can."

"They're after me," she said dully. "They have Tiffany."

"Yeah. Hey." He clasped her cheeks in his hands, made her meet his gaze. "Listen to me, *cher*. You need to go. Whatever these men are after, they're willing to kill for it. Otherwise, they wouldn't have brought assault weapons. Get off this island. Hide and stay safe until I find you."

Another burst of gunshots sounded from the lobby, followed by more screams from the employees still stuck there. The bellhop went white.

Claire flinched, then drew a breath and nodded. "I'll go to—"

"Don't tell me." If he were caught, he wouldn't be able to tell them anything he didn't know. "Just go." He had the strangest urge to kiss her, but that had to be the adrenaline talking. He stepped back and pointed her toward the door. "Go. Now!"

As she turned away, he caught her hand. Why was it so hard to let her go? Especially knowing that every second he kept her here, he put her in more danger. He made himself release her. "If you can get to Cabana 47 safely, go there. Find Jesse. Warn him the hotel is under attack and I'm inside. Have him call me."

The dazed expression left her face, along with several shades of color. She was shaking. The reality of their situation had finally hit home and she was losing her nerve.

"Claire." He ran a soothing hand over her sleek blond hair. "I'm counting on you to get this kid to safety and send in the cavalry. Can you do that, *ma belle*?"

She nodded. Drew a breath. He could almost see the steel infusing her spine as her shoulders straightened. "What about Tiffany?"

He cast a glance down the hallway. Still empty, but the noise from the lobby had died down. No more gunshots. No more screams. Either all the employees were dead, or the Tangos had managed to control them. Going back there was suicide. He looked at Claire again.

Tears glistened in her eyes. "She's like a sister to me."

"I'll get her out of here," he heard himself say and mentally swore in several different languages. He was a sap. A goddamn suicidal sap.

"Thank you, Jean-Luc." Claire took the bellhop's hand and murmured in coaxing French as she guided him out door. He had to stop himself from reaching out for her again.

She was safer outside than in here.

He waited, guarding the door in case any of the gunman found them. Once he was sure they'd had enough time to get out of the building, he looked down at the bloody knife still in his hand. Suicidal or not, he had a job to do. His teammates—hell, his *family*—were scattered throughout this building, and he wasn't about to let any of them get dead tonight.

Chapter Eleven

Lanie woke in the middle of the night to the feel of Jesse's fingers sliding down over her belly, then lower.

"Are you still wet for me, darlin'?" he drawled.

She arched, pushing her hips up to meet his caress.

"Yeah, you are." A soft laugh against the back of her neck sent shivers racing across her skin and her nipples tightened in anticipation. "So wet and ready."

"Yes," she gasped. She was surprised she could still get turned on at this point. He'd thoroughly worn her out earlier, and she'd fallen into an exhausted, sated sleep, thinking semi-deliriously that if she could never have sex again, tonight would be more than enough to tide her over.

But, oh, she'd been wrong. Only a couple hours, and already she wanted him so badly she ached for it.

Jesse's hand left her slit and she heard the crinkle of a condom wrapper. A moment later, the blunt head of his cock was at her entrance, nudging inside. Slowly, slowly.

He set an easy, torturously slow pace and holy God, did he feel good. Just as good as the first time. And the second.

Maybe even better now because she'd always found lazy early morning sex to be insanely hot.

She pushed back against his every slide forward and he groaned.

"Dayam, darlin'. Do you know what it does to me when you grip me like that? Makes me lose my fuckin' mind and want to pound into you until we're both screamin'."

She shifted enough to kiss him. "Then why don't you?"

He made a sound that could only be described as a growl, and pulled her hips up for better leverage. She buried her face in the pillow and screamed out her pleasure when he reached out to rub her clit in time with his thrusts. And still he kept moving, pounding into her until he made good on his promise and they were both screaming.

Sometime later, as they lay tangled together, their sweat raising goose bumps on her skin and their heartbeats settling, Jesse nuzzled the side of her face. "Remember the summer we met?"

The question caught her off-guard. He'd never talked about that summer before. She always thought he didn't remember, or maybe didn't want to remember. "Of course I do."

She'd been fourteen and it was arguably the best summer of her life. Her mother had been going through one of her all-too-frequent "rough patches," and she'd stayed the whole summer at Mara's house. That July, Mara left El Paso to visit her father's family in Wyoming, and she'd invited Lanie along with her.

"I fell in love with your family that summer," she said softly. For so long, it had been just her and her mom, so meeting the Warrick clan had been overwhelming at first. There were eight children—Rebecca, Jesse, Kimberly, Ashley, Scott, Savannah, Dane, and Tyler—and they were a loud, rambunctious bunch. Johanna Warrick was a superhero for raising all of her kids to adulthood without losing her sanity.

Lanie had cherished her time with them. She'd come to think of Becca, Kim, Ashley, and Savannah as sisters, and the boys became like obnoxious little brothers. All except Jesse. From the start, there had always been something else between them. Something *more.*

"I kissed you that summer," he said, and it was the first time he'd ever mentioned it in all the years since it had happened. "After that trail ride at Wind Cave."

She nodded. "I remember." How could she forget? It had been a beautiful day, clear blue skies. Perfect day for a ride — until Jesse's horse saw a snake on the trail and bucked him. She smiled a little at the memory. "That horse was too big for you to handle. You were too skinny."

"Was not," he said, but the defensiveness in his tone was playful. Then he sighed. "Well, shit, yeah, I was skinny, but there's no horse I can't handle. I'm a Warrick."

"And yet." She poked his belly. "You got yourself bucked."

She'd rushed to help him, afraid he'd been hurt when the horse spooked. She'd leaned over him, intending to check for injuries, and he'd sat up at the same time, his lips meeting hers. It was an innocent kiss between two kids not quite teenagers, but it had been her first and she'd never forgotten the soft, secret touch of his lips to hers.

He caught her finger and lifted her hand to his lips. "Did you ever consider maybe I did it on purpose?"

She sat up. "What?"

"I'm a Warrick. We're horse people. I've been ridin' since before I could walk."

Her mouth dropped open. "No way."

He shrugged. "I wanted to kiss you and I didn't know how else to get your attention."

"Oh my God, Jesse. You could've been hurt!"

"But I wasn't. And I got my kiss."

True. Maybe he'd walked away unscathed, but she certainly hadn't. She'd fallen madly, deeply in love with Jesse Warrick that day, as only a preteen girl could. And if she was honest with herself, she'd never fallen out of it. She'd often wondered how kissing him would feel now that they were adults and could explore the act more intimately.

And now she knew it was just as good as she'd expected it to be.

It was silly of her, but after all these years, she still went gooey-kneed when she thought about that summer. What did it say about her that an innocent teenage crush was her most enduring relationship?

They'd drifted apart that winter, IM chats and emails dwindling as each of them got caught up with school, friends, sports. Still, when she'd returned with Mara the next summer, she'd stupidly expected to pick up right where they'd left off. Maybe even take it a step further, since she was a mature fifteen and he'd turned sixteen the previous December. But everything had been different. He'd started dating his future ex-wife, Connor's mother, and she'd gone back to El Paso that autumn completely heartbroken.

"You ever wonder—" He stopped, cleared his throat, and seemed to wage some internal war.

She tamped down the surge of girlish hope. "Wonder what?"

"About us?"

Oh, all the time. She just didn't want him to know that. She scoffed. "C'mon, cowboy. We were barely teenagers and had nothing but an innocent summertime crush."

"*I've* wondered," he admitted so quietly she barely heard him. "You've always been here..." He tapped his temple with one long finger. "In the back of my mind. I can't say I chose wrong goin' with Lacy like I did because that choice gave me Connor and I wouldn't trade him for anythin'. Can't even say I'd do it all differently if given the chance—same reason. But I have wondered."

Her throat closed up. Knowing that after all these years, he'd spent time wondering what could've happened between them opened all kinds of old wounds. She'd thought she'd gotten over him. She'd only been a kid, after all. Half mature and supposedly unaware of what, and who, she really wanted.

But, clearly, she was wrong about that.

For her, it had only ever been Jesse Warrick. She'd known it with all her heart when she was fourteen. Strange that it took until her thirties to figure out why she'd never been good at relationships.

Still. There was too much at stake now. She had her career with HORNET to think about. How would it look if she let herself fall in love with a teammate, let alone the team's new leader? It'd just re-enforce every stereotype ever of women working in a traditionally male profession.

And, okay, maybe she was more than a little afraid of getting her heart crushed by him again.

Suddenly self-conscious, she sat up and dragged the sheet up over her breasts. "Jesse, I—" She stopped short of admitting the truth. Telling him how much he'd hurt her all those years ago seemed too much like admitting a fatal flaw, a weakness she couldn't afford. "This...thing." She waved a hand in the air between them. "It can't be more than...this. It can maybe go beyond tonight if you want, but I can't give more than just sex."

Jesse also sat up against the headboard, and pulled the sheet over his lap. He said nothing for a long time, and she couldn't tell what he was thinking by his closed-off expression. He was almost terrifyingly good at shutting down, locking up, and not letting anyone in.

Which was okay, she reminded herself. She didn't *want* in. Wasn't that the whole point of her little speech just now?

"You're right," he said finally. "This can only be physical."

"Yeah," she said and wondered why him agreeing made her wither inside. Jesus, she had to man up. This was her idea to begin with. "We're good at the physical part. Let's stick to what we're good at, okay?"

• • •

Jesse opened his mouth to reply, but a timely pounding on the cabana's door saved him. Good thing, because every thought running through his head was the exact opposite of what was coming out of his mouth. He didn't want only sex with Lanie. He was halfway in love with her. Hell, maybe he always had been and the sex just brought all those buried feelings back to the surface.

Goddammit, he'd known this would happen, and yet he'd jumped into bed with her anyway.

Beside him, Lanie also seemed glad for the reprieve. As the banging continued, she looked toward the living room. "Who the hell is that?"

"Probably one of the guys bein' an ass." Maybe Jean-Luc, since he was the only one who knew they'd spent the night together. Jesse fell back on the mattress. "Ignore them."

Lanie started to settle down beside him, but froze when the pounding started again and a woman's voice called, "Jesse? Jesse, please open up!"

Lanie raised an eyebrow at him.

"What?" He held up his hands. "I swear I have no idea who that is." This had to be Jean-Luc's doing, too. If so, he was gonna skin the guy for a new pair of Cajun-hide boots.

Lanie pursed her lips and he got the feeling she was trying not the laugh. "Better go find out then."

He swung his legs off the bed and snapped up his jeans from the floor. Took his time pulling them on. If Jean-Luc was pranking him, he wasn't going to hurry. But then as he stepped out into the living area and saw the blood-spattered woman and young bellhop at the verandah doors, he picked up his pace.

This wasn't a prank. Something was wrong.

"Lanie, get dressed. We got trouble," he called over his shoulder as he unlocked the slider. "Ma'am, are you all right?"

The woman shook her head hard, sending her blond bob whipping around her face. He recognized her. The woman from the lobby that had shot Jean-Luc down flat. Beside her, the bellhop was gray-faced and sweating profusely. He babbled something in French, then took off running. The woman shouted after him, but he didn't even look back as he scrambled over the sand dunes, headed away from the hotel.

Jesse watched the kid go. "What's goin' on?"

The woman faced him again. "The hotel is under attack. Jean-Luc's still inside and he needs you to call him."

"Holy shit," Lanie said in what may have been the understatement of the year. She rushed forward and guided the woman inside. "Sit down. Tell us what happened."

Jesse stared at the two women, but his brain wasn't tracking the convo. There was a strange buzzing going on between his ears, and his heart threatened to drum right out of his chest. It took him several long seconds to realize he was panicking and he needed to take a breath or he was going to pass out.

Connor. His son was in the hotel. All the recruits. Gabe and Quinn. Jean-Luc. And he didn't know how many of the others were in the main building.

On autopilot, he walked into the bedroom and grabbed his cell phone, hitting number four to speed-dial Jean-Luc.

No answer. Shit. He tried again, and again got nothing. His imagination started filling in all kinds of horror scenarios. What the devil was going on inside that hotel?

The phone buzzed in his hand. Jean-Luc's name showed on the screen. He answered before the end of the first ring. "Sitrep."

"Four Tangos that I've seen, likely more," Jean-Luc said in a whisper. "They have at least four hostages in the lobby. One Tango casualty, two civilian wounded. Is Claire all right?"

Claire? He must mean the blond woman. Jesse glanced behind him. Lanie had given the frazzled woman a glass of water and taken a seat on the ottoman in front of her. "Affirmative. She's here and safe. What about—?"

"Negative," Jean-Luc interrupted, apparently reading his mind before he was able to force the sentence out through his constricted throat. "I haven't found Gabe, Quinn, or any of the recruits yet."

Jesse swallowed back a rising lump of panic and his fingers tightened convulsively around the phone. "Find my son, Cajun. Get him out of there. Please."

"I gottchu, *mon ami*. I'll find Connor and—*merde!*" There was a scrambling sound, then Jean-Luc cursed in string of different languages, ending with, "Fuckfuckfuckityfuck!"

Gunshots rattled over the line. The shots were short-lived and sounded from a distance. None sounded from closer to the phone—no return fire.

Did Jean-Luc even have a weapon available to him? They'd only had paintball guns during the training mission in Suriname, and all of their heavy-duty weaponry was tucked away on their jet, which Jace Garcia, their pilot, had flown to Washington DC to pick up Audrey and Phoebe.

Surely Jean-Luc at least had his knife—guy never went anywhere without the big-ass thing—and if anyone could prove that old adage about knives in gunfights wrong, it was that sneaky Cajun bastard. But long seconds ticked by, and no sound came from the other end of the line.

"Cajun?"

No response.

"Jean-Luc!"

Nothing. No sound. The line clicked and went dead.

Jesus Christ. Had he just listened to Jean-Luc's death?

Jesse had to make a conscious effort to loosen his fingers from the phone. He closed his eyes, concentrated on breathing through the fear. In and out. In and out. But the yoga breathing trick was doing shit for him right now.

He sensed movement behind him, caught the scent of Lanie's berry shampoo on the air. He whirled. "I never should have brought Connor here. I never should have left him in the hotel alone."

She stepped forward, but stopped short of touching him. "You didn't leave him alone. He was with the guys and the rest of the recruits. You said Jean-Luc was right down the hall."

God. Jean-Luc. What if he was bleeding out somewhere in that hotel?

"We need to go in, get them out."

She stared at his for a solid five seconds. "Jesse," she said finally, very slowly, "go in with what? We have no weapons, no intel. We don't even know how many Tangos we're dealing with here."

"Jean-Luc said four, and he took one out." As he spoke, he was already moving past her into the living room. "He pulled the fire alarm. There's confusion, and we can use that to our advantage."

Claire leaped to her feet as he passed. "Is Jean-Luc okay? Did he save Tiffany?"

He ignored her, snapped up his T-shirt from the floor by

the couch, and pulled in on. He paused long enough to check the kitchen for anything that could be used at a weapon. Nothing sharper than a butter knife. He shoved the last drawer shut and the flatware inside rattled.

Fuck it. He'd go without.

He headed for the door.

Lanie jumped in front of him, blocking his path. "They'll have back up."

"Then we need to get in there before their back up does." He stepped around her, but she caught his hand. When he glanced back, the pleading look in her eyes almost stopped him. Almost. But then he thought of his son, and God, Himself, wasn't going to stop him from getting into that fucking hotel.

"Jess—"

He narrowed his eyes at her. "I'm not leavin' my boy in there."

Chapter Twelve

Shit.

Lanie watched Jesse go, her heart lodged somewhere in her throat, thundering with a noxious mixed of adrenaline and terror. He was going to get himself killed.

"Shit," she said again, out loud this time, because one time didn't seem to be enough. She whirled on Claire. "Tell me everything. Fast."

The woman shook her head. Her blue eyes were too big, glassy with shock. "I-I don't know anything."

Yeah, she did, but she wasn't sharing. Standing around trying to get her to talk was only wasting precious seconds Lanie couldn't afford. "Stay here. You'll be safe here."

She didn't wait for an answer and sprinted back into the bedroom for her phone and the little bit of gear she hadn't left on the plane. Didn't amount to much—a multi-tool, a small set of field binoculars, and a folding knife. She knew Ian and Seth had both opted for the cabanas rather than the main hotel like she had, so she sent them both an SOS text and told them to bring any gear they had. Praying neither of them had shut off their phones for the night, she then dialed the one person who might be able to help them, and bolted after Jesse before she heard the first ring.

Tucker Quentin answered before the end of the second. "Lanie?" There was concern in his voice, and it sounded genuine even though she'd only met the man once before. With the massive number of people he employed, she figured he'd have no idea who she was. "Is everything okay?"

"I'm sorry to bother you, sir." She veered off the path and dodged through a small stand of palm trees to get to the beach faster. "I thought you should know your hotel's under attack."

A beat of silence. In that beat, she sensed his mood change from puzzled concern to barely controlled anger. She could all but feel the chill of it radiate over the line.

"Details," he demanded.

"I don't have any yet. Or not many. It's the main building. Half of HORNET is inside. The recruits, too." Once on the beach, she paused, looking for any sign of Jesse, and saw Seth and Ian running toward her. Ian must have left his dog, Tank, behind. She also spotted footprints in the sand headed toward the hotel. "Jesse's son is inside."

Tuc cursed. "Tell me he's not about to do something stupid."

"I can't, sir."

"And he's supposed to be the level-headed one," Tuc muttered.

Some of her own banked anger ignited at that comment. Even though she agreed Jesse was making all the wrong moves right now, she was compelled to defend him anyway. "Would you keep your cool if it was your kid in danger?"

"I don't have a kid," Tuc said after another beat. "But, no. You're right. Where's my hotel security?"

"I don't know."

"Are you armed?"

"Does a pocket knife and multi-tool count as armed?"

"Fuck me." Tuc said nothing again for a beat, but there was a lot of movement in the background. Whatever he was doing, he was moving fast. "There should be a small stash of arms in the security center down the north hallway off the lobby. I'll send you the blueprints. My men and I are en route, but we're five hours out, at least. We'll use the flight time for intel gathering and send you whatever we find. I'll also do everything in my power to get men there sooner. In the meantime, I'm trusting you to keep my guys from ending up dead."

Lanie huffed out a laugh that was more disbelief than amusement. "That's a tall order with this group."

Tuc sighed. "Don't I know it."

Tuc hung up just as Seth and Ian reached her. They were both carrying backpacks, and she hoped they had more gear than she did.

"The fuck?" Ian said. Concise with words, as always.

Seth translated, "Got your SOS. What's happening?"

Lanie slid her phone into the back pocket of her shorts and gave them a quick rundown, ending with, "...and he's gone after Connor."

"Oh, Christ. Not again." Seth walked several paces away and stared out over the water, his shoulders slumping.

"Hey, Hero," Ian called. "You solid?"

Seth's spine straightened. He rubbed at his face with one hand, then came back. "Yeah, I'm good now. Bad memories. Bad moment."

Ian gave his shoulder a squeeze. "That's not happening again. You're not losing another team tonight."

"Damn right. So." Seth lifted his gaze to Lanie's. "How do we stop this from going sideways?"

She froze, surprised he was looking to her for a plan,

but recovered fast. "First thing, we need to stop Jesse. He's not going to help anyone if he gets himself taken hostage or killed."

Seth nodded. "We better move, then. He's already got a hell of a head start on us."

• • •

The hotel's main building had once been a plantation house. With its wide galleries on each floor and steeply pitched red roof, it looked like it had been plucked from Louisiana and dropped in the Caribbean. Each of the many outbuildings and cabanas had been designed to reflect that same Old World Creole charm, but the main L-shaped building stood out as an architectural jewel among the palms.

And right now, it was as quiet as a tomb.

Jesse slowed to a walk as he neared the edge of the property, then stopped altogether and dropped behind a dune on the beach. From his position, he could see part of the long arm of the building, and the tip of the shorter side of the *L*, where the lobby overlooked the beach. In the middle sat the pool and the fire pits, all dark.

Jesus, what was he doing? Charging in without weapons, intel, or a plan was nothing short of suicide.

He noticed movement on one of the terraces. Squinting, he could barely make out three figures moving from room to room. More shadows joined them on the terrace, streaming out of the French doors in each room. Friendlies or not? Were the three initial shadows taking hostages or staging a silent rescue? He had no way of knowing and wished like hell he had some NVGs.

He sensed movement behind him, and every muscle in his body bunched, preparing for a fight—until the familiar scent of berries reached his nose on the salted ocean breeze.

Lanie.

She'd caught up to him. Dammit. Now not only was his son in danger, but he'd led her right into the line of fire, too. He didn't move, didn't even glance in her direction until she flattened out on the sand beside him.

"You should've stayed with Claire," he said under his breath.

"Claire's safe. You're not," she shot back in a whisper. "And I brought back up."

As she said it, two other bodies joined them behind the dune: Seth on his left, and Ian on Lanie's right. Great. A sniper without a rifle, who was so damaged he struggled to function most days, and a psychopathic bomb tech.

Some back up.

Okay, that wasn't an entirely fair assessment. Of Seth, at least. Ian absolutely was a pyscho, and there was no help for him. But Seth? He was a good man and a world-class sniper. Jesse just couldn't shake his initial reservations about the guy—but he was also self-aware enough to realize those lingering doubts were more a reflection of his own weaknesses than Seth's.

He liked Seth and the rest of the team—even Ian to some extent. In fact, he liked them all too much, far more than he'd wanted to care about any of them when he first started with HORNET. He couldn't separate himself from these guys like he'd been able to do in Delta Force—and God knew he'd tried. As a medic, he'd always had to keep a clinical eye on things, part of him afraid that if he got too close to the guys he treated, he'd be unable to do his job when the situation called for a level head. If something happened to Seth because his PTSD got the best of him during this op, would he be able to save the sniper's life? Or any of their lives, if the situation called for it? He honestly didn't know and the doubt was eating him alive. What if he wasn't good enough anymore and one of these men—his friends—died because of it? What if Lanie died because of it? Or *Connor*?

His hands broke out into a cold sweat. He turned just enough to see Lanie's profile. "I'm sorry I lost my head. You were right. We should pull back, come up with a plan. Goin' in like this is gonna get someone killed."

"Yeah, well, we're here now," she said tightly, still not meeting his gaze. She lifted a small pair of field glasses to her eyes. "And going on the offensive isn't an entirely bad idea. If we're lucky, they're still trying to sort out the confusion and wrangle hostages. We have the element of surprise. Besides, I called Tuc, told him what was going on, and he said there's a room full of arms in one of the hallways off the lobby. We'll need that firepower if we have any chance at saving our guys. So what's the plan, cowboy?"

Jesse felt his jaw hit the ground. He tried to find a reply but all he could think was, *Dayam, girl.* And, shit, she'd been right about something else, too. He'd severely misused her skills during the training mission out of some misguided urge to protect her.

When he didn't respond, she sent him a sidelong glance. "Tell me you have a plan."

He hadn't, but with the new intel, one was starting to form. "Part of a plan."

She sighed softly, shook her head, and lifted the binoculars again. "I can't tell for sure, but I think those people on the second floor terrace are our guys. Looks like they're getting as many guests out as possible. We should clear the closest outbuildings." She indicated to the two buildings closest to the lobby. "We don't want to give them any more hostages than they already have."

"One of those is the fitness club," Ian said. "I was there earlier. This late, it's probably empty."

"The other's a restaurant," Seth added. "Phoebe and I

had a reservation for tomorrow night."

"That's a lucky break," Jesse said. "There's somethin' like fifty buildings on this property. If they have the manpower to clear them all, we're fucked, but I'm thinkin' not. I'm thinkin' they're gonna focus all of their attention on the lobby and the rooms in the attached wings, so that's where you need to focus, too. If Lanie's right and those are our guys out there, you should go help them clear out the hostages."

Lanie scowled. "And what about you?"

"My only priority right now is Connor. I'm goin' to the fourth floor."

Chapter Thirteen

The man that had lived as mild-mannered Paul Jones for the past two years swore as he strode into the lobby.

No. Not Paul. Not anymore.

His real name was Jerome Briggs and he hated that he had to remind himself of it. He'd chosen the most innocuous name he could think of when he took on this mission and at the beginning, he'd thought it fun, like a superhero living under a secret identity while he waited for the scientists to do their thing. He'd enjoyed duping that twit Tiffany into thinking he loved her.

But now it was all going to hell.

Briggs stared in disbelief at the mess his men had made. "What the fuck happened?"

This was supposed to have been easy. Have Tiffany find out what building Claire was staying in, and voilà, they'd have both women and their damn research. Instead, one of his guys was dead, cooling in a pool of his own blood.

So was Tiffany. Not dead. A least, not yet, but with the amount of blood on the floor under her, he didn't give her long. He ignored the little pull in the vicinity of his heart as she reached out a shaking, blood-covered hand toward him. Reminded himself he didn't actually love her.

He'd been acting. She was a job. Nothing else.

He strode past her and the line of hotel employees two of his men were holding hostage. There were also two hotel guards with guns also pointed at the hostages, and Briggs raised an eyebrow at them before turning to his second-in-command.

Melvin "Mel" Kennion was usually a solid operator. The old man was past his prime, but he was sturdy, dependable, if not a little old fashioned and stuck in his ways. Briggs had trusted him with harder missions than this in the past, so what went wrong here?

Kennion straightened away from the reception desk, where he had been leaning with one hand over his chest. He was sweating, his face almost as red as his beard. "Claire had a bodyguard."

"Impossible. None of our intel suggested she's the kind of person to hire a bodyguard."

"Our intel was wrong. Big blond guy. Looked liked a beach bum. Deadly as hell with a knife. He made us right away and dropped Vargas so fast I didn't realize it until we were down one man."

Yeah. Kennion was definitely past his prime. In his younger days, he would've reacted quicker. Maybe it was time to petition for a new second-in-command. Hell, maybe a new team if one guy thwarted four of his supposedly best men with a fucking knife.

Briggs jerked his chin in the direction of the guards.

"What about those guys?"

Kennion coughed, then straightened with a wince. "I offered them money. They took the offer and killed the other two guards on duty."

Briggs pulled his gun and fired two shots, one into each guard's head. The hostages screamed and panicked, but his guys got them under control again fast. "I don't trust bought loyalty." He turned back to Kennion. "Is Claire still somewhere in this building?"

"Believe so. The blond man's still here, and if he's her bodyguard, he's not letting her out of his sight. He keeps popping up, trying to distract us. Think he's trying to get to her." He tilted his head toward Tiffany. "Think he was hired to protect them both?"

Briggs thought of the phone call he'd taken earlier in the day, the one telling him to back off. He swore softly. "I don't think he was hired. We're just dealing with a bonafide hero." He aimed his gun at the hostages, who all cowered back, and grabbed his phone with his free hand. "I'll call in reinforcements and make sure the boss has our asses covered for this. Lock this place down tight. Explosives on any door we can't physically cover. We're going room to room until we find Dr. Oliver. If anyone resists, shoot them."

Chapter Fourteen

Jesse felt naked without a weapon, and he imagined the others did, too. Still, the four of them moved toward the hotel as a unit, fast and quiet, sticking to the shadows.

This was such a bad idea. Any leader worth his salt would turn his team around and take the time to come up with a more cohesive plan that wouldn't get everyone killed. But as much as his brain said that was the right move, his heart kept dragging him forward. He kept picturing Connor—not as he was now, but as a newborn with chubby cheeks and a shock of thick tawny hair. He remembered the awe, the fear, and the overwhelming wave of love when Connor was first placed in his arms. He'd promised that tiny human he'd always take care of him, but somewhere along the way, he'd lost sight of that simple promise. He'd keep it now, though. If it was the last thing he did, Connor would safely walk away from this night.

Lanie held up a fist, indicating they should stop, and they all dropped to crouches behind the foliage ringing a children's playground. "Do you hear that?"

Jesse focused his senses outward, and...yes. He heard it. Beyond the gentle creaking of the empty swings swaying in the breeze was a faint rumble of an outboard motor coming closer. "I'd wager that's not our reinforcements."

Lanie shook her head. "Tuc said it'd be hours before he'd have men here. He'd have called if that ETA changed."

Jesse gazed up at the hotel. They'd backtracked on the beach to come at the building on an angle, out of view of the panoramic windows in the lobby. What he could see of the fourth floor was dark. Connor was probably still sleeping, unaware of the danger he was in. "Then we need to move faster." He broke cover and sprinted across the open playground. Behind him, Lanie and one of the guys were both cursing him out, but the time for stealth was gone. He still had no plan for how to get inside. Figured he'd take a page out of Jean-Luc's book and make it up as he went.

By the time he reached the main building, he found a group of sleepy and confused guests huddled around like a bunch of spooked cattle. Someone in the back of the group called his name.

Danny.

His heart doubled-timed as he changed directions to meet the FBI agent. He found Danny and Marcus playing cattle-dogs to the guests' cattle. "Where's Connor?" he asked first thing.

Both Danny and Marcus looked grim.

Marcus set a hand on his shoulder. "We can't get up to the fourth floor without detection. There's no terrace."

Jesse scanned the group. "That's how you got these people out?"

Danny jerked his chin upward, and Jesse shifted to look up. On the third floor terrace, Gabe, Quinn, and Harvard were lowering people to the second floor, from where they could then take a wide stone staircase to the ground.

But the math didn't add up. It took two people to lower one, so no matter how it worked out, one of the guys would get left behind. "Why aren't you up there with them?"

"Our room's on the second floor."

"So how are they gettin' down?"

Marcus scowled. "I pointed that out to them."

"And?"

"They'd 'find a way.'"

Uh-huh. That sounded like Gabe and Quinn. And he was gonna be right there with them when they did. He pointed back the way he'd come. "Lanie, Seth, and Ian are by the playground. We have incomin' Tangos. Get these people someplace safe." With that, he left them and took the steps two at a time to the second floor. Once he was below Gabe and Quinn, he whistled softly through his teeth to get their attention.

Harvard's head popped out over the railing. "Jesse?"

"Lift me up." He motioned with both hands to make sure he was understood.

"No fucking way," Quinn hissed, his shaved head appearing next to Harvard's. A second later, they lowered another woman. Jesse caught her, and pointed her to the stairs, then refocused on the guys. "You'll work faster with another set of hands."

All he got in response was another set of feet headed in his direction. This time belonging to a thin man with salt-and-pepper hair and a pock-scarred face. Again, he helped the man down and pointed him toward the stairs.

Fuck this. There was no time to convince them of his plan.

Jesse gauged the distance to the third floor. He was tall enough that if he climbed up on the rail, he should be able to stretch and grab the bottom of the railing above. Once he did, they'd have no choice but to pull him up.

He hauled himself up on the railing, and heard Quinn cursing a blue streak overhead.

Gabe's face appeared next. There seemed to be more lines of strain in it than there had been earlier in the evening. "Warrick, don't. That's an order."

"Sorry, boss. I'm gettin' to my son." He straightened slowly, suddenly grateful for a childhood spent playing in haylofts and climbing trees. His boots were steady on the rail.

Two muscular arms reached toward him. Gabe and Quinn. He had a split second to wish Gabe had let Harvard do it—Gabe shouldn't be straining himself—but then he focused. He clasped their arms in a snug grip and used his feet to push up.

And all hell broke lose below him. Gunshots. Screams. People scattered, even as Marcus and Danny tried to keep them calm. He glanced down and saw men in ski masks rounding up the crowd. Overheard, there was a grunt of pain and the dull *thunk* of a body hitting the floor. He looked up again. Two unmasked Tangos had coldcocked Harvard and now held their weapons on Gabe and Quinn.

"Drop him," they ordered.

Gabe gazed down at him, and his grip tightened. "I'm not letting you fall, Jesse. They'll have to shoot me."

Jesus Christ, no. Sickness surged into Jesse's throat as he glanced back and forth between the gunmen and his friends. They were not going to die because of him. He looked down at the ground. The fall was survivable. Probably. But he'd probably break a bone or two or seven.

The gunmen were still ordering Gabe and Quinn to release him, but they were fast losing their patience. It was only a matter of time until one or both pulled the trigger. Another glance at the ground and his heart kicked with panic. Okay, not a good idea. He closed his eyes, sucked in a breath and blew it out slowly. Then he met Gabe's gaze.

"Save Connor."

"Jesse—"

He released his hands. Both Gabe and Quinn hung on, but their grips slipped on his sweat-dampened skin. He used his legs to swing his body, forcing them to let go, and hopefully giving himself enough momentum to hit one of the nearby palm trees instead of plummeting straight to the ground. At least then he'd have a chance of walking away.

Quinn lost his grip first, but Gabe held on, his knuckles whitening, Jesse's skin burning under his palm with each swing.

"Let me go."

"Not a fucking chance," Gabe repeated Quinn's earlier words. But then he didn't have a choice because one of the Tangos finally pulled the trigger.

Jesse fell.

Chapter Fifteen

Briggs swore as the first pops of gunfire echoed outside. This team was useless. Were they *trying* to wake up the whole resort? He had the local authorities contained for now, but there were too many buildings on the property, too many guests, and he didn't have enough men to control them all. He needed the rest of the resort to go on slumbering without a clue. The phones on the reception desk started ringing.

"Shit." He motioned to Kennion, who was looking sallower by the minute. "Watch them. Anyone moves, shoot them."

Kennion sighed and straightened away from the desk. Raised his gun, though his heart didn't seem to be in it.

This whole situation was going to shit. Briggs had to regain control.

The hostages cringed away from him as he strode toward them. He grabbed the receptionist by the arm and dragged her upright. Mascara ran in soupy lines down her brown cheeks and her full, red-painted lips trembled. She said something in a rambling string of French. He didn't have to understand the language to know she was begging for her life.

He dragged her over behind the desk. Turning her toward him, he used the edge his shirt to wipe her face off, then pinched her chin between his thumb and forefinger. "Answer the phones. Tell them everything is fine, but they should stay in their rooms. If you give them any hint that something is wrong, I'll kill you. Nod if you understand."

Her dark eyes bugged, but she nodded. He released her, and she scrambled to pick up the first ringing phone. She spoke in French again but he knew by her tone she was obeying him. Even as her hands shook, her voice was steady, her tone upbeat and reassuring. Keeping one eye on her, he stepped over to the window to check outside. The rest of his team had arrived, and they appeared to be rounding up some more hostages. He'd have to find out who fired those shots and put their whole operation at risk—

The fire alarm screamed. The hostages wailed. Kennion glanced around like he'd been struck by a sudden-onset case of dementia and the whole situation confused him.

Holy fuck. Could anything else go wrong? The receptionist must have triggered it somehow. Briggs swung toward the desk, but caught movement out of the corner of his eye and turned back toward the center of the room in time to glimpse a big blond guy in a New Orleans Saints T-shirt scoop Tiffany up from where she still lay on the floor.

Dr. Claire Oliver's bodyguard.

Briggs lifted his weapon and fired. It was a wild shot, but he was pretty sure it had made contact. The bodyguard didn't even flinch and kept right on running like he hadn't just taken a bullet and wasn't carrying 150 pounds of nearly-dead weight. Tough bastard.

Head pounding from the shriek of the alarm, Briggs took a step to go after him, but the hostages surged forward like they were going to make a run for it and Kennion was doing jack shit to stop them. He swung around, aimed his rifle at the ceiling, and let a stream of bullets drill into one of the wood beams arcing overhead. Splinters rained down, and the hostages fell back, subdued again.

He pointed at the receptionist. "Shut that fucking alarm off!"

Chapter Sixteen

At first, Connor thought the *rat-ta-tat-tat* sound was from the TV. Last thing he remembered before drifting to sleep was Jeremiah Wolfe browsing the channels, looking for something to watch. He had apparently decided on an action movie because the sound of gunfire was loud enough to rattle his bed.

But then Connor opened his eyes. The room was dark. No blue glow from the TV, but still the muffled rattle of an automatic weapon. Disoriented, still not sure he was fully awake, he stared up at the ceiling above his bed.

Who was shooting? Was anyone? Or was he imagining it? Maybe it was leftover from his dreams. Though he couldn't exactly remember what he'd been dreaming about, it was totally possible after the week he'd had that he'd been dreaming of a war zone.

Rat-ta-tat-tat-tat-tat. Rat-ta-tat.

The fire alarm wailed, its shriek piercing the dark.

Wolfe bolted upright, knocking his pillows to the floor between their beds as he did. "What the...? Is that the fire alarm? Shit!" He rolled out of bed, heavy limbs flailing. The guy was all solid muscle, almost the exact opposite of Connor, but he seemed to have the same problem coordinating his body. Instead of the ungainly giraffe Connor was always compared to, he was more like a bumbling bear cub.

Wolfe grabbed his pants and boots from the floor. "What's going on?"

"I don't know." Connor scrambled to his feet. He'd fallen asleep in his clothes and only needed his boots. He was on his way to the door a step behind Wolfe.

"We need to find your dad," Wolfe said and pulled the door open.

Holy shit.

Dad!

Wolfe was right. They had to find him.

Emergency lights strobed in the hallway. The other recruits spilled from their rooms in various states of undress, but Connor ignored them and beelined for his dad's room. He pounded on the door.

No response. Where was he?

Wolfe's large hand closed around his shoulder. "We have to get outside."

"Not without Dad!" His voice cracked, sounding more child than adult, but he didn't care. He tried pounding again, but Wolfe pulled him around.

"Hey. He's not here."

"He has to be!" Panic rose up, fast and hard, nearly choking him. His hands started to shake and he balled them at his sides.

Wolfe tightened his grip on his shoulders. "Man, listen.

I've been training under your dad for a couple months. He's smart. He's tough. If he's not here, he's probably already outside directing people to safety and tending to wounds. You'll see. He'll be taking care of people. It's what he does, and he's damn good at it."

But why wouldn't he come get me first? The question stuck in Connor's throat and brought a coating of bitterness to his tongue. Stupid. He knew why. His dad had a savior complex when it came to strangers, but kept friends and family at arm's length. And double that arm's length for his son. He'd never wanted the responsibility of fatherhood. Why would he start caring about his son now when there were other people to be saved?

Fine. Whatever. It wasn't like he was pining for his father's love anyway. He'd save his own skin, just like he always had.

The fire alarm stopped just as suddenly as it had started. Everyone froze and looked at each other.

This couldn't be good.

Connor turned away from the door and shouldered through the crowd, making his way toward the stairs. Fire alarm or no, he was getting out.

Just as he reached for the push-bar, the door flung open and Jean-Luc staggered from the stairwell, followed by several other people who looked like they'd been through a war zone. They carried a bleeding woman in a sheet. Jean-Luc's shirt was covered with blood, but whether it was his or someone else's was anyone's guess. The moment the final person cleared the doorway, he threw his body weight against the metal door. "Find something to block this with!"

"What about the fire?" someone asked. "We can't stay here!"

Connor didn't hesitate. He'd already figured out there was no fire. He glanced around, spotted a table and chair set-up by the elevator banks down the hall and started toward it.

"Wolfe!"

Wolfe must have had the same idea, because the guy was already one step ahead of him.

"Yeah. Good thinking," Jean-Luc called after them. "We need to block all the exits and jam the elevator. We're going to hold this floor until help arrives."

"But what's happening?" Schumacher asked and was ignored. He looked sleepy and pissed off and not the least bit frightened. The bastard.

Connor wished he could say the same about himself, but his heart was trying to surge up out of his throat. Still he kept moving. He and Wolfe flipped up the long side table that sat against the wall across from the elevator bank and broke off the legs with several well-placed kicks. Jean-Luc grabbed one of the legs, while another recruit—Samira Blackwood—jammed the stairway door at the other end of the hall with another leg. Two other recruits dragged one of the heavy chairs over to jam against Jean-Luc's door, while Wolfe muscled the other chair over to help fortify Sami's door.

While they all worked, Connor considered the problem of the elevators. The easiest way to jam them was to call them and push the emergency stop button when they arrived. He didn't know how smart that would be, though. Someone, somewhere in the hotel had automatic weapons, and judging by all the blood on Jean-Luc, they weren't afraid to use them.

So no calling them. But, like everything else, elevators were computerized nowadays. And Sami Blackwood had been working with Harvard to learn how to hack.

Connor grabbed Sami's arm as she passed. "Can you hack the elevators?"

She looked at the doors and a line of concentration formed between her sculpted brows. "Yeah, but I'd need Harvard's computer. Mine won't cut it."

"What floor is he on?"

Sami pointed down. "Third."

Connor considered the doors again, but shook off the idea taking one down a floor. Harvard might have gotten out of the building. Or he could be dead. But they still had to stop the elevators somehow, and Connor could think of only one way to do it. He jabbed the call button and held his breath as he waited for the ding announcing the car's arrival. The doors slid open...

Empty.

He released his breath, darted inside, and hit the emergency stop button. Then he reached to hit the button again to call the second car.

"Whoa, whoa, whoa, kid!" Jean-Luc plowed through the crowd and tried to swat his hand away from the down button, but was too late. "*Merde*! Your pa's gonna kill me."

"We have to stop the elevators or else blocking the doors won't do much good," Connor explained, trying to sound reasonable despite the terror riding him hard.

Jean-Luc positioned himself between Connor and the still-closed elevator doors. In his hand was a wicked looking blade already dripping with blood. "And they say *I'm* reckless."

"I had to."

"Not saying otherwise, but—" The second set of doors slid open and Jean-Luc readied the knife, but sheathed it when he saw the car was also empty. He exhaled hard, walked inside, and pushed the emergency stop. "Good call," he conceded finally as he dug around in the pocket of his bloodstained shorts. "But no more risks like that. I need to keep you breathing."

He found his phone and cursed in a long string of Cajun French at the spider web of cracks across the blank screen. It wouldn't power on. "Anyone have a working phone?" he called to the group.

"I do," Sami said and disappeared inside the room she'd had to herself. She returned a few seconds later with her phone and slapped it into Jean-Luc's waiting hand. "I should've saved everyone's numbers before we left the training facility. I didn't think—"

"No worries, *cher.*" He tapped the side of his head with one hand while he dialed with the other. "Photographic memory."

Her eyes widened. "Really?"

"What can I say? It's a gift and a curse." He raised the phone and waited through the rings. "Jess, call me back at this number when you get this message. I have your boy. He's safe. All of the recruits are also present and counted for, plus a handful of civilians, one critically injured. We've barricaded on the fourth floor. Christ, Jess, where are you? Could really use some ideas on how to get us out of this clusterfuck right about now."

Chapter Seventeen

Holy fucking chaos.

The bad guys' reinforcements arrived in force and started shooting into the crowd. People panicked and stampeded.

Lanie helped Marcus and Danny guide some of the terrified guests as far as the playground, where Seth and Ian still waited. She'd just passed off a woman with a dislocated arm to Seth, when a lone shot from the hotel had her whipping around. A long, lean figure tumbled from the third floor. She knew that body, had been admiring it quite thoroughly only an hour ago.

Jesse.

No!

The scream lodged in her throat and she had to swallow hard to find a semblance of her voice. "Get the wounded back to my cabana," she told Seth. "I'll be there as soon as I can."

The bad guys had come in hard and fast and had managed to round up some of the guests who had scattered when the shooting started. Bad for those guests, but lucky for her since keeping them from fleeing now occupied the Tangos' full attention. At least, she hoped it did. Or else what she was about to do might end up getting her killed.

She darted across an open expanse of lush green lawn, taking the direct route to where she'd seen Jesse fall, rather than trying to find cover around the edges. She made it across without anybody shooting at her, which was encouraging. A peek over her shoulder showed the bad guys were indeed otherwise occupied, corralling their hostages into the lobby.

"Jesse?" She didn't dare call out above a whisper. There could be more Tangos she hadn't seen yet. "Oh, Jesse, please answer me. Where are you?"

He should have fallen somewhere in this area, but she saw no indication he had. No broken body, no blood on the paved path under her feet. She looked up at the third floor, calculated. If he'd managed to throw himself out, rather than just fall…

She spun and stared at the palms lining the path.

…then he'd have landed in the trees.

"Jesse?" She ducked under one of the low-hanging fronds, and there he was, lying in a pile of fronds he must have dragged down with him. He bled from a gash over his eyebrow, but otherwise looked intact. He was conscious, and pushed himself up to his hands and knees when she knelt down beside him.

"You okay, cowboy?" The question came out light and airy, like she didn't doubt for one second that he was fine, and she was proud of herself for that. Because, holy shit, she was jumping with panic inside. All she wanted to do was wrap her arms around him and press her ear to his chest so she knew for sure his heart still beat.

Blood poured into his left eye from the wound on his head, and he tried to blink it away. Didn't work, so he raised a badly scraped hand to swipe the blood from his face. "Think so," he mumbled. Then winced. "Right ankle's fucked. Might be broken."

She tried to push him back when he made to stand. "Wait, no. Let me see."

He shook his head. "No time. Gotta get you to safety."

Despite everything, she snorted a laugh. "Get *me* to safety? I'm not the one who just fell three stories."

He looked at her with the one eye not blinded by blood. "They shot at Gabe. I don't know if they hit him, but I can't deal with that and the thought of both you and Connor in danger. I just…can't. It might break me."

He cared about her that much? A fist tightened around her throat. "Okay." Now her voice was choked. So much for keeping her poker face firmly in place. She cleared her throat and slid an arm around his waist. "Okay. We'll go back to the cabana, regroup, and come up with a plan to save everyone. Including Connor and Gabe. Deal?"

"Yeah." He swallowed and his throat made a dry clicking sound. Even with her help, he struggled to his feet. "Anyone else hurt?"

He was more injured than he wanted her to know, but that was typical Jesse. Always caring for everyone else before himself. "Nothing you can't fix. C'mon, let's move. I've got you."

Chapter Eighteen

Lanie was right, the wounded civilians mostly had superficial injuries. No bullet wounds. All cuts, sprains, and one woman with a dislocated arm. Jesse couldn't leave her like that, but popping her arm back into place did him in. He could no longer ignore his own pain and limped outside. He needed air or he was going to pass out. Unfortunately, the earlier breeze had died away and the air was oppressively muggy.

Jesse sank down on the cabana's narrow porch and leaned back against its stucco wall. About twenty feet away, Lanie and the guys stood together and seemed to be making plans. He knew he should get up and find out their next move, but he didn't have the energy for it at the moment.

Lanie spotted him and broke away from the group. She walked over and knelt beside him. "How you doing, cowboy?"

Nothing was broken—his ankle had only suffered a bad

sprain—but he still felt like a horse had trampled him. No, not just one horse. The whole fucking Kentucky Derby. "I'm okay."

"Uh-huh." Doubt hung heavy in her tone. She nodded toward the boots he still hadn't taken off. He was afraid he'd not be able to get them back on if he did. "Bet your ankle is swollen up like a balloon. Have you taken anything for the pain yet?"

"No." He ground his teeth. Part of him hated that she knew him well enough to see through his bullshit. Another part of him, the foolish heart that always led him into trouble, fell a little bit more in love with her for her concern.

She shook her head and stood. "I'll get you something."

She came back a few minutes later with aspirin, a bottle of the hotel's water, and his cell phone. She shook out some pills and handed them over, then the water. She only gave him his phone after he'd finished the tiny bottle.

The screen showed a missed call and voicemail from a number he didn't recognize. He accessed his voicemail and sagged with relief as he listened. It was good to hear Jean-Luc's voice. At least the Cajun wasn't dead somewhere in the hotel. And Connor was safe, thank Christ.

He called back, and Jean-Luc picked up immediately. "Please tell me you have a plan, *mon ami*."

"We're workin' on it."

"Work faster," Jean-Luc said. "I'm not looking to relive the Alamo here with a handful of civilians and a bunch of half-trained kids."

"It's not goin' to be the Alamo." At least, he hoped not. "According to Marcus and Danny, the hostage takers seemed to be lookin' for somethin'. Once they realize it's not here—"

"Not something. Someone. They want Claire."

Claire. He'd forgotten about her. He hadn't seen her inside among the wounded, and a quick scan proved she wasn't out here, either. He covered the receiver and asked Lanie, "Where's Claire?"

Lanie shrugged. "The cabana was empty when Marcus and Danny got here with the wounded."

Well, shit. "Claire's gone," he told Jean-Luc. "She took off when Lanie and I were at the hotel."

"*Ça c'est bon.* I told her to get away." There was some shuffling, and a door opened. Jean-Luc grunted softly like he was in pain. "But they're also looking for her business partner, Tiffany. Don't know a last name. We have her. She's our critically wounded civilian. Looks like she was shot. I'm not sure what to do for her, *mon ami.*"

More wounded. Jesse glanced behind him at the injured people he hadn't yet treated. There were so many that they spilled out of the cabana and onto the beach. Lanie had moved off to offer them bottles of water. She must have felt his gaze because she straightened away from a woman with a hastily bandaged head and glanced toward him, concern pulling her brows together. His instinct screamed to go to her, wrap her up in his arms, and tell her everyone would be all right. That *he'd* be all right. It was a ridiculous urge. Knowing her, she'd probably sock him in the gut and tell him to get back to work.

He didn't know why, but that thought steadied him. "Okay, Cajun, are you with the patient now?"

"*Oui.*"

"You need to find the wound, tell me where it is and what it looks like. Even better, can we switch to video?" He waited a moment, but the only response he got was a dull thud from somewhere on the other end of the line. "Jean-Luc?"

More scrambling, cursing, a lot of voices talking over each other. His heart kicked. "Hey, pal. Talk to me. What's goin' on in there?"

"Dad?" Connor's voice sounded tiny and frightened.

It threw him back a decade to the time Connor thought he could slay any monster, including the one under the bed.

He straightened away from the wall and pushed to his feet, ignoring the pain in his ankle. "Yeah. Yeah, I'm here, Connor. What happened? Where's Jean-Luc?"

"He passed out. I-I think he's hurt."

Jesus. Two wounded. "Is he breathing? Does he have a pulse?"

"Y-yes. His face is really white, Dad."

He shuddered at the fear in his son's voice, but somehow managed to keep his own calm. "What about the woman?"

"She's awake. Kinda. She's moaning and mumbling something about Wonder Woman. I-I think she's in pain."

"All right. All right. You're doing great, Con. If the woman doesn't appear to be in immediate danger, let me see Jean-Luc first." Triaging patients when he couldn't see them was a hard call to make, but everyone there was fucked if Jean-Luc died. He was the only one there with real combat experience.

Connor switched on the camera and he caught a fleeting glimpse of his son's stricken face before the lens turned toward Jean-Luc. The big guy was on his side next to the injured woman, his face white, his T-shirt soaked through with blood. "Okay, Connor. Can you hear me? He's losing blood. That's why he passed out. You need to find the wound and put pressure on it to stop the bleeding."

Another set of hands appeared in the frame, small and feminine with a fresh, shiny coat of black polish on the nails. They had to belong to the sole female recruit, the computer girl, Sami. She helped Connor search Jean-Luc until they found the source of the blood. The crazy bastard had been shot.

For a second, Jesse froze. He was back hanging from the terrace, flinching as the gun went off, falling...

And then farther back, stuck in that snowy airfield in Eastern Europe, Gabe's blood soaking through his gloves as he tried to curtail the bleeding.

So much blood…

"Dad!" Connor appeared on the screen, his voice cracking with fear. "What do we do?"

The sight of Connor's pale face and too-wide eyes brought him back to the here and now. He swallowed to ease the tightness in his throat. "Let me see the wound."

Again the camera moved. Sami pulled Jean-Luc's shirt aside, revealing an ugly tear in the skin and muscle of the left side of his stomach. It bubbled blood every time Jean-Luc's stomach moved with his exhale.

"Okay. Connor? It looks bad, but as far as I can tell, the bullet just skimmed the surface. It's not inside him, okay? Biggest concern—and the reason he passed out—is blood loss. Put pressure on it to stop the bleedin', and then bandage it with a clean towel." As he spoke, the camera moved. He caught glimpses of the other recruits standing around, looking shell-shocked. They were all so young and green. None of these kids had seen combat beyond the simulated stuff they'd gone through at the training facility. That had been by design because they hadn't wanted another case like Seth, who still struggled with PTSD, or Quinn, who had hidden his traumatic brain injury until he couldn't any longer. Recruiting from outside the military had seemed like a good idea at the time, but these kids were nowhere near ready for this.

For chrissakes, they hadn't even begun using live ammo in their training yet.

Connor gathered towels from the bathroom and hurried back to Jean-Luc's side. The bleeding slowed almost as soon as Connor put pressure on the wound, which was promising.

"That's it," Jesse coaxed. "That's it. Now keep an

eye on him, and if he doesn't wake up..." Then Jean-Luc was in serious trouble because it probably meant internal hemorrhaging, but he didn't want to scare his son with the worst-case scenario. "Well, we'll cross that bridge when we get to it. Let me see the woman now."

And they went through it all again, Jesse talking them through. The woman, Tiffany, had also been shot. The entry wound was a neat little hole just below her diaphragm, and there was a lot of bruising across her upper stomach, which could mean internal bleeding. She was not in good shape.

He needed to get her out of that hotel, ASAP.

He caught Lanie's gaze again and signaled for everyone to come over. He didn't want Connor or the others to overhear, but as he lowered the phone, Connor panicked.

"Dad! Dad, are you there? Please, don't leave us alone."

He put the phone back in front of his face. "Hey. I'm not hangin' up. You hear me? I *won't* leave you, but I need to talk to Lanie and the guys. I'll be right back."

"What's going on?" Lanie asked as she reached him. Ian, Seth, Marcus, and Danny were right behind her.

He muffled the phone with his hand. "Jean-Luc's been shot. We need to get in there."

"A frontal assault is suicide," Ian said, typical scowl firmly in place. "Didn't we learn that lesson already?"

"He's right," Seth agreed. "We only have a vague idea of how many hostage takers and no idea how many hostages. We don't know what kind of weaponry they have or even where in the building they are. We'd be going in blind."

"Then we need eyes," Lanie said. Everyone turned to look at her, but she was staring down at Tank, who sat faithfully by Ian's side. All gazes shifted to the dog. He thumped his tail, happy at the attention.

Ian's entire body tensed. "What are you thinking?"

• • •

Nobody had liked her plan.

"*No*," Jesse and Ian had said simultaneously when she'd laid it out for them. It was probably the first time the two men had ever agreed on anything. Unfortunately for them, nobody came up with a better idea. Besides, it was hard to argue with solid logic. The Tangos hadn't seen her with the guys, and weren't going to bother with a woman walking her dog down the beach, which gave her plenty of opportunity to recon.

So here she was, walking barefoot in the sand like she hadn't a care in the world, Tank trotting by her side, his favorite ball in his mouth. When Ian had given her the ball, he hadn't wanted to let it go at first, as if his fingers were glued to the thing. Tank had watched them with rapt attention, eyes wide and ears perked.

She'd covered his hand with her own. "I'll take good care of him. I promise."

"Please," Ian's voice had been barely above a whisper. "He's all I have."

She'd be lying if she said he hadn't broken her heart a little with those words. Ian was a mystery to her—insular and stand-offish—but there was no denying he loved his dog.

She gazed down at Tank now. To think that only a couple years ago he'd been an abandoned dog in Afghanistan. He looked like the Belgian Malinois often used in police K9 units. He was obviously a mix—he was too lanky and his coat was too fluffy to be a pure bred—but he had the black erect ears and black mask customary of the breed. His tongue lolled out the side of his mouth around the giant red ball and he trotted along like a regular dog excited to be out on a walk. He appeared to be everything his master wasn't—friendly, sweet, lovable—but she'd seen him in training and he possessed the same deadly intensity that made Ian so dangerous.

With the ocean breathing softly to her left, the moon a sliver crescent in a star-spangled sky, and the barest hint of dawn lightening the eastern horizon, it was a gorgeous night, but she couldn't appreciate it. Any second now, the tangle of palm trees to her right would give way to the manicured resort grounds, and then she'd be exposed.

And there was the hotel, the restored plantation a glittering jewel among the palms. Every light gleamed inside the massive four-story house, but the terraces, and the surrounding grounds were now deserted. It gave the place a weird ghost town feeling, like if she stepped in the wrong place she'd disturb the long-dead slaves that used to work the sugarcane fields here.

A bead of sweat that had nothing to do with the muggy night trickled between her breasts. She'd changed back into her bikini and a pair of shorts to help cement the idea that she was just a local woman taking her dog for a pre-dawn stroll on the beach, but the lack of clothing made her feel even more exposed.

This was a shitty idea.

But it was all they had.

"Tank."

He looked up at her, ears cocked.

She held out a hand. "Ball."

He obediently dropped it into her palm and she gave him the hand signal to sit. Ian had run through some basic commands with her before they left, like "sit," "stay," "attack," and how to call him off. Sure enough, at her raised fist, Tank's butt dropped to the sand. His eyes stayed glued to the ball.

She tossed it into the water. Tank's butt wiggled with excitement, but he didn't move until she gave him the signal. He bounded after it, splashing through the surf, having the time of his life in the waves. After a few minutes, he brought it back and dropped it at her feet. They continued like that for a while—relaxed, unhurried, giving the impression to anyone watching that they were no threat. All the while, she watched the hotel. She saw movement on the bottom floor in the lobby. She'd need to see who was Tango and who was hostage, but she didn't imagine the hostages were doing much moving. The second and third floors were lit up, but silent, the French doors along the galleries smashed and ripped open. She glanced up at the fourth floor where Jean-Luc and the recruits had barricaded themselves. The old plantation house had been built like a wedding cake, with wide galleries rimming the first, second, and third floors. The top floor was the smallest with no gallery, which worked to Jean-Luc's advantage. He only had to defend the floor from an interior attack and not worry about the bad guys coming in through unsecured French doors. Really, the building's architecture was probably the only reason he and the recruits weren't also hostages at the moment.

She again tossed the ball for Tank and laughed when he ran face-first into a wave. He came up sneezing. Silly dog.

She returned her attention to the building and told her heart to calm the fuck down. If it beat any harder, it was going to give her away. Again, there was movement on the first floor. She lifted her small field binoculars, and wished she had NVGs instead. She couldn't see anything. Too far away. She had to get closer.

The next time Tank brought her the ball, she tossed it along the beach and began a nice, easy stroll after him as he chased it. Just a local woman and her dog out for a walk. Nothing more.

Now she had a view inside the large window in the lobby. Not a great view, but it didn't matter. Even from a distance, she recognized the big man the Tangos were moving across the lobby toward the front desk. He was limping.

Gabe.

Oh God. He was alive. Jesse had said he'd been shot at, but he seemed well enough. She squashed down the rush of relief that made her knees want to buckle. There would be time for that later.

She watched in horror as one Tango—the guy who seemed to be in charge of the group—jumped down from his seat on the desk and pointed a gun at Gabe's head. Her heart seized. For a second, everything stopped working. Heart, lungs, brain. She just froze, cold to the bone with terror.

She'd been in that snowy airfield in Ukraine, sitting helplessly by while Jesse worked to save Gabe's life. She'd watched the man's blood leak into the snow, stain the ground pink. And although she hadn't known him well at the time, she'd been terrified that she was witnessing his last moments.

Now...

God, she didn't want to go through that all again. She knew Gabe now. Knew he threw his head back when he laughed, and how the sound boomed through a room. Knew that despite his tendency to be a hard-ass, his wife Audrey somehow always managed to make him laugh that huge laugh every day. She was also one of the only people to know Gabe and Audrey were starting a family—in, like, nine months. She and Mara had been crammed into the bathroom with Audrey when the pregnancy test gave a positive response last week. She had no idea if Gabe even knew yet. Audrey had said she wanted to wait until after the training mission to tell him.

Lanie forced herself to take a breath and move. She gave Tank the stay signal and ran toward the hotel, thankful she was barefoot. She made no sound as she approached the building, hopped the pool gate, and faded into the shadows of the empty poolside bar. Now she wished she hadn't put her bright red bikini back on. It wasn't exactly the most inconspicuous piece of clothing for recon work. In fact, it made her a target.

Drawing in a steading breath, she forged ahead, keeping to the deep shadows cast by the building until she made it to the edge of the lobby window. She couldn't hear anything, the voices inside too muffled by glass, but she now had a very clear view of what was happening. She took out her phone, made sure it was silenced and the flash was off, then started snapping photos.

She counted nine men with guns, some masked, some not. The leader was unmasked and seemed not to care if anyone saw him. He was tall and average looking, his dark hair sprinkled with gray. Good-looking, but not in any sort of memorable way. She wouldn't have thought twice about him had she met him on a street. He currently had one hell of a black eye that shadowed his cheek with deep splotches of purple.

He still held the gun to Gabe's head.

They appeared to be having an intense conversation, but Gabe was calm, which helped steady her heart and her hand. She took several pictures of the leader. If she could get a clear enough photo, Tuc would be able to ID him. At least then they'd have some idea of whom they were dealing with.

She shifted to get a better look at the hostages huddled together near the water fountain. Couldn't get an exact headcount—the cascading water obscured her view—but she guessed at least twenty civilians, plus Gabe, Quinn, and Harvard. The civilians weren't tied up, but Quinn and Harvard were. So was Gabe. The Tangos obviously knew who the dangerous ones were in the group. Made her wonder what else they knew about HORNET. She took a picture.

A body lay face-up on the floor close to Gabe and the leader, eyes staring sightlessly at the ceiling from a wax-pale face. Blood streaked the shiny floor all around him. Too much for just one body. She took a picture.

Way to go, Jean-Luc.

Sometimes she forgot the Cajun wasn't all jokes all the time. He was deadly as hell when the situation called for it.

The leader was getting frustrated. He shoved Gabe's shoulder with the tip of the gun. Gabe's calm expression didn't change. The leader gestured toward the body and appeared to ask a question. Gabe said nothing. Just stared straight ahead, unblinking. Leader motioned with his gun and two of the masked men dragged Quinn and Harvard to their feet, pointed guns at their heads. Leader asked his question again, but Gabe's blank facade didn't crack. No wonder his nickname in the SEALs had been Stonewall.

The leader nodded at his men.

Dear God. They were going to shoot. Quinn, who had a daughter and pregnant fiancée at home. Harvard, who had just turned twenty-five. Hell, he was practically still a kid. Neither of them deserved to die here in a wrong time, wrong place kind of situation. It seemed undignified somehow. An insult to the warriors they were. If any of them were going to die, it should be in a blaze of glory, trying to save the world.

She didn't think. Just acted. She stepped out of the shadows into the pool of light spilling from the window and pounded her hands against the glass.

She clearly heard one of the Tangos say, "What the fuck?" But she didn't stick around to see what else they said. She spun and sprinted toward the beach, praying they'd give chase. And they did. She heard feet pounding the concrete behind her and put on a burst of speed as a bullet zipped by and struck the sand a few feet in front of her. She stepped on it and it burned her foot, but she ignored the pain and kept going. Up ahead, she saw Tank pacing anxiously in the spot she'd told him to stay. His lips pulled off his teeth in a vicious snarl, more like Cujo than the silly dog with his big red ball.

Another bullet struck the sand too close to her feet, startling her. She stumbled and went down on her hands and knees. She couldn't hear the men's footfalls behind her anymore and a glance back showed her why. The two men had reached the beach, and were fast closing the distance between them.

"Tank!"

He stilled, his lean body going taut, muscles quivering. A nocked arrow ready to fly. She gave him the attack hand signal just as the first man reached her. Tank lunged, hitting the man with audible force, his teeth tearing into flesh. The man dropped his gun like his arm had gone numb. Lanie scrambled across the sand, grabbed the gun, and whirled toward the second guy. Her police training was so ingrained she opened her mouth to warn him to drop the gun. Maybe they could end this without bloodshed—but, no, the jack-off was already raising his gun, aiming at Tank.

Yeah. Fuck that.

She pulled the trigger. The bullet hit the guy high in the center of his chest, just below his collarbone. He swayed on his feet for several seconds, blood bubbling from between his gasping lips. With the black mask on, obscuring all but his lips and his eyes, he looked particularly fish-like. Then his knees buckled and he went down.

Terrified for Tank, she spun toward him and raised the gun, but she didn't need to be worried. He still had a death grip on the Tango's upper arm, had dragged the guy down to the sand, and was now shaking his head violently back and forth, the man screaming the whole time. She grabbed her phone from where she'd dropped it in the sand and then scrambled over to the dead man and stripped him of every weapon he had. She couldn't see leaving anything for the bad guys to find when HORNET was already seriously outgunned.

"Tank." She called him back with the hand motion Ian had showed her. He immediately released the bite and ran over to her. "Let's go."

She ran toward the beach, checking over her shoulder to make sure the surviving attacker wasn't watching. He wasn't. He hadn't so much as lifted his head. He'd either passed out from the pain in his ruined arm or he was damn close to it. She scanned for other threats, but didn't expect any, and sure enough, the grounds were clear. The Tango leader seemed like a smart enough guy. He had a limited supply of men— which, hallelujah, was awesome news for the good guys— and he wouldn't risk sending more than two.

Still, that didn't mean she was going to hang around any longer.

At the water's edge, Tank scooped up his red ball and splashed into the surf. She called him to her. "Sorry, buddy. Now's not the time to play."

But he didn't seem to mind. He was happy to gallop alongside her, his bloodstained tongue again lolling around the ball.

She had to get back to the cabana and let the guys know what she'd discovered. Yes, the situation looked grim, but it was not impossible. There had to be a way to rescue their guys and the hostages without anyone dying.

As she ran, the sand giving under her feet, the ocean breeze cooling the sweat on her bare skin, a thought occurred to her and she skidded to a halt.

The boat.

Cut off their escape route.

She dropped the dead man's weapons into the sand and searched until—

Ah-ha. Grenade.

"Tank, stay." She gave him the hand single and he sat,

ball still in his mouth. She ran back in the direction she'd come, but kept going when she reached the main building. With how fast they had closed in on the resort, their boat had to be somewhere nearby.

And there it was, just around the next bend in the beach. Unguarded. Perfect. Grinning, she ran up to it, pulled the grenade's pin, and let it fly. Just as she turned to take cover, she spotted two figures walking hand-in-hand toward the damn boat. She flung herself at the young couple, knocking them to the sand an instant before the explosion rocked the beach.

The woman shrieked. The man shook his head like he couldn't understand what was happening. They both had shiny new rings on their fingers. Honeymooners.

Lanie pulled them both upright and looked the man square in the face. "Get your wife out of here. The hotel is under attack. Leave. Don't pack and don't go anywhere near the main building. Just get as far away from the resort as you can."

"W-what?" he stuttered. He stared at the flaming debris from the boat, and her words finally registered. He grabbed his wife's hand and pulled her to her feet.

Lanie watched until they were out of sight, then inspected her handiwork. Yeah, that boat wasn't going anywhere on the water.

The bad guys were now stuck on this island, just like HORNET.

Chapter Nineteen

"Where are the locals?"

Jesse looked up from pulling glass out of a woman's leg and found Ian standing over him. The woman recoiled, her calf muscle going tense in his hand. Irritation spiked through him, and he released a soft breath to dispel it. He focused on the woman and offered a smile. "It's okay," he said. Even though she didn't speak English, he was careful to keep his voice soft and gentle. He carefully set her leg down and stood, motioning for Ian to follow him outside with a jerk of his head.

Ian stepped over the woman like she was nothing more than a log blocking his path. Jesus.

As soon as they were out of earshot, he whirled. "You need to keep the hell away from my patients. You're scarin' them and they've had enough terror for one night, don't ya think?"

Ian crossed his arms in front of him. In deference to the island heat, his ever-present leather jacket was absent, and his heavily muscled arms bulged under the ink covering every inch of skin from wrist to the sleeve of his white T-shirt. "I'm not the fucking bad guy here."

"Then stop stompin' around scowlin' at everyone."

Seth seemed to appear out of nowhere—the sniper could move like a ghost when he wanted to—and stepped between them. "Guys. C'mon. This isn't helping."

"Stay out of this, Hero," Ian said, knocking aside the scarred hand Seth set on his shoulder.

Seth ignored him. "Hey. I know you're losing your shit about Tank. And you"—he sent a pointed look in Jesse's direction—"about Lanie. They're both going to be fine. They'll take care of each other."

Ian seemed to deflate, the fight going out of him for a moment. There were only two men able to talk Ian down when he got into one of his pissed-off-at-the-world moods—Gabe and, strangely, Seth. It was kind of amazing to watch because Jesse never had any luck talking to the guy.

"Still doesn't change my question," Ian said after a second and straightened his shoulders again. "Where are the locals? Martinique has a police force, and last I knew the French military had a significant presence on the island. So where the hell is everyone? This resort should be crawling with cops, but so far the only two I've seen are Lanie and Danny G."

"Lanie's not a Ranger anymore," Jesse muttered. But, yeah, it was a good question. Not that he would admit it out loud. Ian was the only man on the team he had no interest in getting along with. The guy just rubbed him the wrong way. Had from day one. And he was pretty sure the feeling was mutual. Ian didn't like anyone except his dog. And maybe, occasionally, Seth. The two men had forged some kind of rapport a couple years ago in the mountains of Afghanistan. Though why Seth or anyone else would want to be friends with a volatile asshole who thought blowing shit up was the best form stress relief and torture was a perfectly acceptable means of gathering intel was beyond Jesse's understanding.

Ian grunted. "Once a cop, always a cop."

"Spoken like a man who's had more than his fair share of run-ins with the police."

Ian's lip curled and he stepped forward. "Yeah, well, nobody can live up to the perfection of Saint Jesse."

"Holy fuck," Seth said in exasperation. He shoved first Jesse's shoulder, then Ian's, separating them. "You two need to kiss and make up already because we don't have time for this shit. We have men in trouble and I've already lost one team. I'm sure as fuck not about to lose another because of you two asswipes."

"Are they at each other again?" Danny G's voice sounded from the darkness a moment before he and Marcus appeared on the path. "Are they always like this?"

"Yeah," Marcus said with a heavy sigh. "They're like oil and water. The Sharks and the Jets. Rocky and Creed. Maverick and Iceman. Thor and Loki. Jacob and Edward."

"*Twilight*?" Seth said, one brow arched. "Really?"

"Hey. You caught the reference. What's that say about you?"

"That I have a fiancée, an older sister, and a teenage niece."

Danny clapped Marcus on the shoulder. "Man, you need a woman. You spend way too much time on Netflix and not enough on chill."

Marcus shrugged that off and turned back to the original convo. "Dudes. Seth's right." He waggled a finger between Jesse and Ian. "We have guys in trouble so let's shelf the Hatfields and McCoys shit for the moment, okay?"

They were all right. This stupid rivalry he had going with Ian wasn't helping. He held out a hand, intent on burying the hatchet, at least for the time being, but an explosion thundered through the air.

Everyone froze and looked toward the beach just as a furry, dog-sized bullet shot through the palm trees and all but tackled Ian.

Ian staggered backward, the dog's weight nearly knocking him off his feet until he stabilized himself. He buried his hands in Tank's fur and made a weird, rusty sound. It took Jesse a moment to realize it was a laugh.

Laughter. From Ian.

He didn't think the guy knew how.

"Good boy. You're a good dog, Tanky." Ian pushed the dog down and his smile faded as his hand came away red from Tank's fur. His expression was one of horror before he shut it down, replaced it with an inscrutable mask. "Warrick—"

Jesse wasn't listening. He was too focused on that blood painting Ian's palm, splattered all over Tank's fur. He heard the explosion again so clearly he almost thought there had been a second. His heart rocketed into his throat. "Where's Lanie?"

He didn't realize he'd spoken out loud until a firm hand landed on his shoulder. It belonged to Danny G, and the guy's dark eyes were solemn and kind. He had a way about him, a calming effect that was probably why he and Marcus had made such a kick-ass team as FBI hostage negotiators. Marcus was the buddy, the charmer. Danny, the calm voice of reason.

But Jesse didn't want to be reasonable now. Those bastards in the hotel were already holding his kid hostage. If they had hurt Lanie, too…

The hand tightened on his shoulder, holding him back, and only then did he realize he'd lunged toward the path leading to the beach. Danny was talking, saying something in a fast, urgent tone, but the words didn't compute. The angry red haze that he'd spent so much of his adult life fighting against had enveloped his mind, and all he could think of was getting to his son, finding Lanie, and ripping the people who had hurt them limb from limb.

"I'm goin' to kill them. I'm goin' to kill them. I'mgoin'tofuckin'killthem—"

Danny's grip left his shoulder and was replaced with hands on each side of his face. Soft, feminine hands with golden-brown skin. He blinked once, and again to clear the haze from his vision.

Lanie.

Her lips moved, but the fog hadn't cleared enough to comprehend what she was saying. He raised a hand, touched her check. Yes, she really was here.

All right. She was here. She was safe. The blood wasn't hers.

She leaned into his palm and smiled. "Hey, cowboy," she said in a soft, soothing voice. "You back with us now?"

He had to swallow to settle his heart back in his chest where it belonged, but even then he didn't trust his voice, so he simply nodded. His surroundings were starting to come back into focus. The guys all stood in a loose semi-circle around him with stunned expressions on their faces.

"Whoa," Seth breathed.

Even Ian looked surprised, which was a pretty big deal. Usually his expression came in two flavors—sneer or master poker player.

Danny was rubbing his jaw and for the first time, Jesse noticed the sting in his hand. He glanced down. His knuckles were red and starting to bruise.

"Oh shit. Did I—?"

Danny waved a hand. "No worries. I've taken worse hits. It's fine."

No. No, it wasn't fine. He'd snapped. Lost his cool and had hurt a friend. Which he'd promised himself would never, ever happen again. He was feeling too much, letting his emotions control him again instead of logic and reason. All because of Lanie. And he didn't care. All he cared about right now was that she was okay. He dragged her into his arms, ignoring the sparks of pain the tight embrace set off throughout his body, and buried his face in her braids.

"What happened?"

"They were trying to get Gabe to talk. Were going to shoot Quinn and Harvard. I had to distract them. Their leader sent two guys after me. I got one. Tank got the other. Oh, and I tossed a grenade into their boat."

"Christ, Lanie. You were only supposed to get intel. You weren't supposed to get close enough to engage."

"I wasn't supposed to get close?" she repeated incredulously and pulled out of his arms. She propped a hand on her hip. "How else did you expect me to get the intel we need? I couldn't see shit from the beach."

It had been a stupid risk. He hated that she'd taken it, but at the same time, knew she was right. They needed to know what they were up against.

And still.

"You could've gotten yourself killed."

"But I didn't."

"Lanie—"

"Jesse," she said in the same frustrated tone. "Tell me something. If Marcus had taken the same risk would you be pissed at him? What about Seth or Ian or Danny? Would you be standing here arguing with them about how dangerous it was, or would you be strategizing right now? Hmm?"

"I'm not—" He cut himself off before he finished the thought.

And she jumped right on that. "You're not what? C'mon, finish the sentence, cowboy. You're not sleeping with them?"

"O-kay," Danny said, drawing the word out. "Let's all

take break here, yeah?"

Jesse ground his back teeth and told himself to chill out. He was way too fucking raw right now and should remove himself until he got his shit under control again. Too many emotions seethed right there at the surface and if he let them bubble over again, he might do more than punch someone. He might lose all control and find himself back in that dark, dark hole he'd worked so hard to claw his way out of last time.

Yeah. A break was a good idea.

He limped away from the group without a destination in mind. He just needed a few minutes to center himself before he became completely unhinged. He kept shuffling along until he reached the beach.

The moon was bright and cast a long white streak across the water from horizon to beach. With the way the beach curved, he couldn't see the hotel, but he saw the lights from it over the tops of the palm trees. His son was in there. Every time he thought too much about it, bile surged into his throat, coating his tongue in the acrid taste of fear.

His boy.

His friends.

Somehow, he had to get them all out of there.

Out of the corner of his eye, he caught movement in the water and spun toward it, reaching for a gun he didn't have. Ian. Not a threat, but he still couldn't make himself relax. Tank splashed in the waves while Ian threw his ball in long arcs down the beach in the opposite direction of Jesse. Neither man nor dog had noticed him yet.

He watched the two of them, fascinated despite himself. They functioned like a life-long team, which was downright disturbing. Weren't dogs supposed to have a good sense for people? What the hell did Tank see in Ian that made him so loyal to the psychopath?

Tank finally noticed him and bounded over, happy for

the additional company. Ian turned and his easy smile faded back into his usual scowl. "Are you checking up on me now? Jesus. No wonder your son hates you. I'll be at the briefing on time. Tank had to wash the blood off."

Jesse opened his mouth to retort, but all that came out was a weak, "Connor hates me? Did he tell you that?"

Like with dogs, Ian seemed to connect to kids better than adults. It was entirely possible he and Connor had bonded at some point.

Ian grunted. "All teenagers hate their parents. I sure as fuck did." He flung the ball in a huge arc again and Tank rocketed after it. "But then I had a complete asshole for a father. Connor only has a half asshole. Guess he's lucky."

Jesse surprised himself by laughing. "That might be the nicest thing you've ever said to me."

"Yeah, well. Don't get used to it. I still don't like you."

He suddenly recalled Lanie once asking him what his problem was with Ian. He'd found the question uncomfortable, itchy, and claustrophobic, like a wool sweater against bare skin on a hot summer day, and he never wanted to examine the answer too closely. But here and now, he suddenly knew why. The reason was crystal clear and unavoidable. In Ian, he saw the man he could've been. The man he *had* been for a short time. All that disappointed idealism. All that anger. Ian expressed it by being a psycho. Years ago, Jesse had tried to find a cure for it at the bottom of a bottle. If he'd continued down that road, would he be Ian now? He shuddered to think it, but yeah, that was precisely why he found the man so repulsive. It was kind of like looking in a mirror and hating your reflection.

"Yeah, nothin's changed," he agreed softly, though he kind of doubted it. "Feelin's still mutual, pal." He turned away, intent on going back to the cabana.

"Warrick."

He considered ignoring Ian's call, but in the end, he didn't. He glanced back, but didn't respond.

Ian stood with the moon to his back. It highlighted his skull-trimmed hair and shadowed the sharp edges and valleys of his face, and the effect was altogether eerie. The streak of white across the water seemingly led right to his feet. "Connor will be okay. I'll make sure of it."

With that, he threw the ball again, then ran along with the dog when Tank took off after it.

"He's not the devil you make him out to be," Lanie's voice said softly behind him.

"He's not a saint, either."

"Like you?" she asked.

"I'm not a saint." He closed his eyes and inhaled as she moved closer. Despite everything, she still smelled faintly of berries.

"You try awful hard to be." She set a hand on his back, and he leaned in to her touch. He couldn't help himself. He needed something to ground him right now, and her touch did.

"Jesus, Lanie," he finally muttered and turned to drag her against him. He dropped his mouth to hers, and the meeting of their lips was more a possessive brand than a kiss. She melted, just for a moment, before breaking away.

He cupped her cheeks in his hands. "What you did tonight…"

She gripped his wrists. "I'd do it again. We needed to know what we're up against—"

His thumb strayed over her lips, silencing her. "You are the bravest woman I know and that scares the hell out of me." He could've lost her tonight. He could still lose her. He could lose everyone he cared anything about, and he wouldn't survive it.

His throat closed. "I get what you did, but that doesn't

stop me from bein' so fuckin' scared when you pull shit like that."

Her muscles tensed and he knew instantly he'd said the wrong thing. She deftly extracted herself from his embrace. One minute their bodies touched, the next all kinds of space opened up between them.

"What was that?" she asked.

He dropped his hands to his sides. "What?"

"Jesse…" She dragged both of her hands through her hair, sighed. "I'm not yours to lose. Right? Before all this…" She waved a hand toward the hotel. "That wasn't what tonight was supposed to be about. We agreed—" Her voice caught and she backed up another step. "I'm finally earning the team's trust. I can't jeopardize that."

"Lanie, I—" He stopped short because it was too fast, too soon, to say what he'd been about to confess. But then, why wait? Especially since there was a good chance one or both of them might not make it through the night. They'd both already had close calls. Why the hell wouldn't he tell her what was brewing in his heart.

He took a step forward.

"Jesse, please don't," she whispered. She backed up and held up a hand as if to ward him off. To his surprise, tears welled in her eyes. "We can't go where you want us to go."

"I can't just flip a switch and turn off how I feel." He caught her wrist and pressed her palm to his heart. "Lanie, I love—"

His phone rang.

Chapter Twenty

The explosion rattled the windows of the lobby and made the constant, calming rush of water from fountain stutter. Briggs strode over to the window, and what he saw outside left him cold with a strange mix of fear and rage. The two men he'd sent after the woman were down, and flames danced on the beach from the remains of his team's boat.

"This is fucked," Kennion muttered. The old man was sweating and glassy-eyed, but he was the steadiest of the men. That explosion had shaken all of them. "We should exfil."

"How?" Briggs swung out an arm, indicating the window. "That's our fucking boat. No, we're not leaving until we complete the mission."

The mere idea of failure had Briggs grinding his teeth so hard his jaw ached. He'd lost nearly three years of his life to this. He'd been put in place to watch Claire and Tiffany's research, then take it and quiet them once it was viable.

The women were still somewhere in the building—probably barricaded up on the fourth floor with the blond bastard in the Saints T-shirt—and he wasn't letting them slip through his fingers at the eleventh hour.

He glanced over at the three operators he had bound and gagged. HORNET. Part of Tucker Quentin's ever-amassing army of mercenaries. Briggs was aware of Quentin's reputation and knew the billionaire was making a lot of powerful people very nervous, but he hadn't heard of HORNET until about twelve hours ago. He'd been undercover since before they'd burst onto the private military circuit. Since then, he'd heard the stories about HORNET's accomplishments—dismantling drug cartels in South America, taking out some Big Bad in Afghanistan, exposing massive corruption high up in the military. Ask him, they sounded like a bunch of goody two-shoes with codes of honor and ethics and shit like that. From what he'd seen so far, they didn't live up to the legend. After all, his guys had managed to capture three of them without much hassle and had another trapped on the fourth floor.

Briggs was unimpressed.

You should be, a small voice said at the back of his mind. He may have captured three of theirs, but they had killed three of his.

Maybe Kennion was right about this. Maybe—

No. He squelched the niggle of doubt. He'd never failed a mission and he wasn't going to now.

He walked over to the big man he'd been questioning before the woman interrupted. He pegged the guy as their leader. The way he was holding himself screamed "boss-man" and, Briggs realized, he'd been the wrong one to start with.

He scanned the other two. The one with the buzz-cut hair and gray eyes looked mean as hell, like a starving caged pit bull spoiling for a fight. But the other one in the Star Wars

T-shirt? He was young, skinnier, and smaller than the other two. If they were the heroes Briggs suspected, the young one would be their pressure point.

He strode over and grabbed the kid, hauling him to his feet by his hair. Sure enough, the gray-eyed pit bull tried to lunge and got a kick to the kidney by the man standing guard over him.

Briggs dragged the kid into the leader's line-of-sight and pressed a gun to his temple. "You wanna start talking now?"

Despite the weapon, the kid shook his head hard. "Gabe, don't—"

Briggs pistol-whipped the kid and he sagged to the floor, half conscious. Had to give credit where credit was due, though. The kid was a rail, but he had brass balls the size of an elephant's. "Heroes. The whole lot of you." He grabbed the slumping kid's hair again and dragged him upright enough to return the gun to his temple. "I *will* shoot him. Gabe, is it?"

Gabe's lips twisted into a sneer, but like the good boy he was, he asked, "What do you want to know?"

Briggs tilted his head toward the window. "The chick. She one of yours?"

No answer but mulish silence.

"Hey, if you don't want to talk, I have plenty of hostages. I'll start with the nerd here, and work my way through them all until you tell me what I need to know."

Another long pause. Briggs had just about decided to shoot the nerd to make his point when Gabe said through his teeth, "Yes."

"Yes what?"

"The woman is with us."

"How many of there are you?"

"Ten."

Evenly matched then. Briggs had started with ten men, and HORNET had taken out three. But they had taken three of HORNET's people hostage—well, four if you counted the guy barricaded upstairs. So he had seven men left and HORNET had six.

Briggs let the nerd drop to the floor, motioned for one of his guys to take over holding the gun, and grabbed his cell phone. "I want to talk to your people on the outside. Give me a number."

Chapter Twenty-One

The phone rang again.

Jesse let go of Lanie's wrist and fished the device out of his pocket. He checked the screen and didn't recognize the number, which could be good or bad. The sudden knot in his stomach told him it was bad. His customary greeting was to answer with his last name, but this time he decided to go with a plain, "Hello."

"Are you with HORNET?" a male voice asked. "And think about that before you answer because if you're not, I'm going to shoot Gabe here in the head."

Lanie touched his arm and he realized he wasn't breathing. He sucked air into his lungs and met her gaze. Whatever she saw there—soul-deep fear, a consuming blaze of anger—had her eyes widening in response.

"I'll get help," she mouthed and took off running toward the cabana.

He limped as fast as he could after her. "I'm the medic."

"Good. Good. In my experience, medics tend to be nice guys. They like to be helpful. You want to be helpful, don't you? You like for everyone to live."

He did not like where this convo was going. "Yes, I want everyone to live." Up ahead, Lanie disappeared inside the cabana. A heartbeat later, Danny and Marcus raced out to meet him. As trained negotiators, they'd know how to handle this. Smart woman, sending them first.

Danny made a motion indicating Jesse should put the phone on speaker. He complied just as the hostage taker asked, "What's your name?"

He looked to Danny, who nodded and rolled his hand, silently telling him to answer. "Jesse. And yours?"

"You can call me Paul."

Marcus had a pad of hotel paper and a pen in his hand. He wrote, *Keep calm. Active listening. Empathy. Rapport. Create sense of humanity. Find out demands.* He underlined that last one.

Jesse took a breath. "Okay, Paul. What can I do to be helpful?"

"Well, let's start with some cold, hard facts before we get to that. Fact: I have guns to the heads of three of your men right this very second. Fact: I have another of your men barricaded three floors above me. Fact: I have more manpower than you do and a hell of a lot more firepower. Fact: I have explosive booby traps rigged throughout this building. Fact: I have about twenty civilian hostages. Fact: I will shoot one hostage every hour until you give me what I want. Starting with your friend Gabe."

It was like a cold fist grabbed his stomach and twisted hard.

Danny shoved his shoulder and made bug eyes at him. He realized he'd missed whatever Paul had said.

Wants to know he has your attention now, Marcus scrawled on the paper. *Say yes.*

"Yes," Jesse choked out.

Paul laughed. "And we all know saving lives is what you do. It's the code you live, eat, breathe, and shit, isn't it?"

"Yes," Jesse said again because he wasn't sure he was capable of squeezing a more complex sentence from his throat right now.

"So," Paul continued, "here's what I want. There are two doctors somewhere at this resort. Tiffany Peters and Claire Oliver. Bring them to me, and I let everyone go. Simple as that."

"Everyone except for the doctors, you mean. What if we don't know where they are?"

Both Marcus and Danny started shaking their heads. Marcus flipped back to the first page of his notebook and underlined the word rapport.

"Then you're fucked," Paul said casually. "If you're worried I'll hurt the women, I give you my word I won't."

"Except you can kill a person without hurtin' them."

"Caught that, did you? You're smarter than that redneck accent of yours led me to believe." Paul laughed, but then got serious. "It doesn't matter what I do with them once I have them. All that matters is I'll start killing people if they don't show their faces in the next hour."

"Do you honestly think you're goin' to get away from this island with the doctors? You don't have a boat."

Danny silently smacked his forehead. Marcus tossed the notebook in the air with an expression of exasperation. Jesse ignored them both. No doubt their tried and true negotiation tactics worked in the average hostage situation, but nothing about this was average. They didn't have the time to talk Paul down or wait him out or call his bluff. When he said he was going to start killing people, Jesse believed him.

"Yes. I believe I'm going to walk away with exactly what I want and you're going to help. Otherwise, people you care about are going to die and you hate death, don't you, medic? And if you think the local authorities will intervene before the deadline, you'll be disappointed. They won't be coming to the rescue. You may have Tucker Quentin in your corner, but we have friends in high places, too."

He doesn't know this is Tuc's hotel.

That might be an advantage.

On the other end of the line, Paul made a *tick-tock* sound. "One hour and the clock's already ticking."

And he hung up.

"Well…" Danny said on a sigh. "Fuck."

Jesse gave himself a second to calm down. The smugness in that bastard's voice had sparked his temper, but he couldn't lose control now. Not with so much on the line. He pointed toward the beach. "Get Ian. Is Seth still inside? We have less than an hour to come up with a plan of attack and put it into action."

"So we're going *Full Metal Jacket* on their asses?" Marcus asked. "I thought we all agreed that was suicide."

"You have a better idea? I'm open to suggestions."

Marcus thought about it. "Nope. I'll get Ian." He clapped palms with Danny—it was a thing they always did, like a see-ya-later without words—then ran for the beach.

Jesse pushed through the cabana's door and found Seth offering water to one of his patients. He gazed around at the injured and swore under his breath. "We need to get these people out of here."

Seth looked up at him. "Something happen?"

"Demands. And if we don't comply within the hour, they're going to start killing hostages, starting with Gabe."

"Jesus Christ." Seth's curse was heartfelt. "What about the local authorities?"

"If the Tangos are to be believed, the locals are in their pocket. We're on our own." Jesse again assessed the room. None of his patients were immobile. They could move, and he wanted them as far away from the resort as possible. Shit had a tendency to roll downhill, after all, and if things went south on them in the next hour, he wasn't about to hand more hostages over to the bad guys. "Does anyone here speak English?"

The thin man with steel-gray hair and pock-scarred face he'd helped down from the terrace earlier raised a bandaged hand. "I do. What do you need?" He spoke with a faint German accent, but his English was perfect.

Jesse walked over to him. "What's your name?"

"Dr. Steffan Ostermann."

"You were here for the virology conference?"

He gave a huff that might have been laughter. "I wasn't supposed to be, but my schedule cleared and I jumped on the only available flight here earlier this afternoon."

"Should've stayed home."

He lifted his arm, which was bandaged and immobilized in a makeshift sling. "You're not wrong."

Jesse felt for the guy. To go on a trip you expected to be a work conference and end up in a hostage situation? It'd throw even the most stable man for a loop, but Dr. Ostermann seemed steady enough. Confused, angry, but steady. "The nearest hospital is seven kilometers away." He'd mapped it before arriving on the island. Knowing his teammates like he did, it would've been negligent of him not to know. He swept a hand out, indicating the other patients. "Can you lead these people there?"

"Yes," Ostermann said without hesitation and stood. "Shall I alert the authorities when we arrive?"

Won't do any good, Jesse thought but replied, "Please. We need all the help we can get. Even better—alert the military."

The Tangos couldn't possibly have the entire French military in their pockets as well as the local police. But as the thought crossed his mind, he knew that even if the French stationed on the island were inclined to help, they wouldn't mobilize in time. It'd take Ostermann at least an hour to march his band of wounded into town.

Ostermann nodded. "We'll get help."

Jesse squeezed his shoulder in heartfelt appreciation. "Thank you."

Chapter Twenty-Two

By the time the last of his patients filed out of the cabana, Lanie was huddled together with the guys, discussing their options, tactics. It struck Jesse how right she was with them. She thought she didn't belong with the team, but she did. She'd changed out of her bikini and looked tough, strong, and capable in cargo pants and fitted T-shirt with her braids pulled back in a ponytail. And although he knew she was all of that and more, the thought of her taking part in this probable suicide mission twisted his guts. As the current team leader, he could order her to stay behind…

And she'd accuse him of being sexist.

But it wasn't because she was a woman. He'd known plenty of women who could kick ass and take names, and she was top of the list. But she was also *his* woman and it might break him if she was harmed in any way.

"I called Tuc again," she said as he approached. "Gave him the update."

"What did he say?" he asked as he approached.

"Pissed off is an understatement," she answered. Yes,

she was back in warrior mode, but she was still careful not to meet his gaze. "His team is still at least two hours out."

Bad news. They could sure use the extra manpower before that. Jesse shook his head. "And in the meantime, we'll have lost hostages, includin' Gabe, Quinn, and Harvard. We can't wait for him."

"He knows that, and he's getting here as fast as humanly possible. He said to be careful."

"Does he want us to stand down?" Seth asked. "Because that's not happening."

She winced slightly. "He didn't say it in so many words…"

For once, Marcus wasn't smiling. "Not a fucking chance."

Seth held out a hand and they bumped fists in a show of solidarity.

"If he's worried about his precious hotel's reputation—" Ian started, but Lanie cut him off, slicing her hand in the air in a gesture that shouted "enough!" It was a very Gabe way to quiet the group, and the men all shut up.

Lanie set a hand on one cocked hip. "Tucker's worried about y'all, not his property. He can always build another hotel, but for all his money and talents, he can't raise the dead. He cares about his men—you knuckleheads included." Her tone said they should all be ashamed of themselves. Surprisingly, even Ian appeared chastised when she poked a finger at his face. "I could tell he wants us to stand down, but he knows we won't, so he didn't even ask. Instead, he's going to move Earth itself to find us reinforcements, and until then, he's researching the photos I sent him so we know who the hell we're up against."

Her phone chimed and she reached into the pocket of her cargo pants for it. "And speak of the devil," she muttered after checking the screen. "Tuc just emailed me." She was silent a moment, reading whatever he'd sent, then passed the phone to Jesse.

"The man we're dealing with, the one in charge, is Jerome Briggs," Lanie summarized for the others as he scanned the rest of the email.

"If this is the guy I spoke to, he told me to call him Paul." On screen was a slightly grainy, cropped and zoomed-in photo showing an average-Joe kind of man with a serious black eye. Next to it, another photo of the same man. Except in this one, he had no gray in his dark hair and no black eye. And he looked as mean as a rattler.

"Paul? Really?" She wrinkled her nose. "Maybe you didn't speak to this guy?"

"I don't know, Lanie. I got the feelin' I spoke to the one callin' the shots."

"Then it was him. I snapped this photo before he realized I was there, and Briggs was definitely in charge. But why call himself Paul?"

"So we can't identify him later?" Danny suggested.

"Except Gabe, Quinn, Harvard, and the rest of the hostages have all seen his face," Seth pointed out. "That indicates to me he doesn't plan to let anyone live."

"He did say the hotel was rigged with explosives," Jesse said. "Fuck." The thought that his son and teammates were potentially sitting on a ticking time bomb made him ill and he had to swallow back a surge of bile. For the first time in… he couldn't remember how long, he sent up a quick prayer. If the Big Guy Upstairs was listening, they needed all the help they could get.

"Let Tank and me worry about any explosives," Ian said and gave the dog's head a pat.

Lanie smiled at Ian—which, yeah, irked more than a bit—but then she turned that smile on the dog and her expression went all soft and sweet. Jesse's annoyance faded and he silently castigated himself.

Jealous, now? Really? Dayam. He had to get control of

himself.

Lanie gave Tank an ear scratch that made the dog's leg thump the ground. "Will he be okay?"

Ian looked down at his dog and something that might have been a smile twitched at his lips. "It's what we've been training for. He can handle it."

Lanie turned to Jesse. The whole group did, and he realized belatedly they were looking to him for a game plan. He had nothing, but he was still holding Lanie's phone with the picture of Paul-slash-Jerome Briggs. He passed it around so everyone saw Briggs's picture. "According to Tuc's dossier, Briggs was Army, served in Iraq and Afghanistan, and signed on with Defion Group after leaving the military."

"Defion?" Danny said and scrubbed a hand through his hair, making the dark locks spike up. "Damn, that's who we're up against?"

"You've heard of them?" Marcus asked.

He nodded. "They're a legitimate military contractor with very illegitimate dealings that have only come to light recently. The State Department has been eyeing Defion for an investigation, but there's a lot of money involved. A lot of politics. They've been slow to respond to the accusations flooding in."

"What kind of accusations?" Lanie asked.

"Everything from overcharging the government for paperclips to war crimes. It's believed they've had their hand out to both sides of every war. They don't care which side wins as long as they get paid." Danny took the phone as Marcus held it out to him. He frowned at the picture of Jerome Briggs. "This isn't Defion's typical MO, though. They profit off war, not hostage situations."

Ian barely glanced at the phone when it reached him. Typical Ian. The phone chimed and he passed it back to Lanie. She squinted at her screen, then grinned.

Jesse leaned over. "What is it?"

"Tuc sent blueprints of the hotel. Does anyone have a laptop? Tablet? Something with a bigger screen?" she asked the group.

"Phoebe and I were planning to disconnect for the weekend," Seth said. "I only have my phone so I can keep in touch with her until she gets here."

"I have a laptop, but it's still in the hotel room," Marcus said, and Danny nodded.

"Yeah, my tablet's there too."

"I don't carry any of that shit," Ian said when everyone turned toward him. "That's Harvard's job."

She blew out a breath. "Okay, we can make do." She turned her phone horizontal, and used her fingers to enlarge the image. "You know, this used to be a plantation house. I bet there's a… Yes. Right there." She held her phone up for the others to see the stairs leading to the third floor at the back of the building. "The old servant's entrance. That's our in."

Danny frowned. "They'll have it guarded."

"They don't have enough men to guard the hostages and every exit," she argued. "I saw ten men. Jean-Luc killed one. Tank and I took out two more. That leaves them with seven." She pointed to the blueprint. "They're holed up in the lobby which must be a logistical nightmare to secure with that big window out front. The walls are almost all glass. But unless they want to move all the hostages over to the convention center—"

"Another logistical nightmare," Seth added.

"Exactly. They're not moving. They're dug in, and the only place in the main building big enough for everyone is that glass-plated lobby."

"She's right," Marcus conceded. "If they don't show enough force, the hostages might take their chances with a mutiny, and right now those hostages are their only leverage. They'll focus most of their manpower in the lobby."

"And use explosives to secure the building," Ian finished. "Which won't be a problem."

Lanie nodded. "So here's what I'm thinking, guys. These stairs don't go all the way up, so we'll take them to the third, then take the fire exit to collect Jean-Luc and the recruits from the fourth floor. From there, we fight our way down. They won't expect us to come from above. Especially if..." She trailed off and Jesse's inner alarm started clanging.

"If what?" he demanded. Until now, he'd liked her plan, but he was sure he wasn't going to like the next thing out of her mouth.

She faced him. "If you stay behind and distract Briggs. Make like we're searching for the doctors. Try to get more time out of him. Basically, be exactly what he accused you of being—exactly what you are. A medic with a big heart who wants everyone to survive."

I can't. The thought blasted through his mind with a sizzle of panic. To play that part convincingly, he'd have to open himself up to all the emotions he barely had a handle on. And if he let himself feel everything as deeply as he could, he'd lose his mind. His anger would take control, and he'd say something that would get them all killed.

Marcus clapped his shoulder. "Once again, our girl's right, Jess. Like it or not, dude, you're the point of contact. And you have a bum ankle. You can't go with us. You'll slow us down. If he calls again and you don't answer, he'll know something's up."

"No." He shook his head. Slowly at first, then harder. "No, I'm not sittin' back while—my son is in there!"

"And our teammates," Lanie said softly. "Jesse, you need to trust me."

His gaze caught hers, held. "You're one of the few people

I trust."

"And the rest of those few are standing right here with us," she pointed out.

He gazed over her shoulder at the group. Seth, Marcus, Danny. He trusted these men with his life every time he went out on a mission with them. Ian, too. While he'd probably never like the guy, he knew the volatile bastard would have his six whenever it counted. He returned his attention to Lanie and reached up to trace the line of her jaw with one finger. "It's not you—or them—I don't trust."

It's me.

He didn't say it out loud. He didn't have to. Not with Lanie. She knew his demons, which was probably exactly why she wanted to distance herself from him.

Chapter Twenty-Three

The recruits had all been taking turns watching over the woman and Jean-Luc in shifts while the rest tried to get some sleep. They were all exhausted, but Connor couldn't seem to sleep no matter how hard he tried. He wandered down the hall to Jean-Luc's room, where they'd dragged the wounded, to see if whoever was on duty needed a break. He found Sami on her computer, two cans of an energy drink on the table beside her.

He stepped into the room and stared down at the wounded woman on the first bed. "She doesn't look good." Her skin was the kind of white usually only seen in paper or freshly bleached sheets and her teeth clinked together as she shivered.

At his voice, Sami looked up from her laptop and scooped the longer side of her asymmetrical haircut away from her eyes. She frowned at the woman. "She was restless. I gave her another shot of the pain meds from your dad's kit about twenty minutes ago."

Connor stepped further into the room. "How about Jean-Luc?"

"He's still out. Your dad did say he would be for a while."

"Yeah."

"Do you think we should give him more fluids? I was reading that helps with blood loss."

"I don't know." He wished he did. At that moment, he wished more than anything that he was more like his father. Dad always seemed to know exactly what to do in a crisis. Then a thought struck and he looked at Sami again. "You can get online?" The wifi had been cut off when the hostage situation started, and his phone didn't have an international plan so it was useless.

She snorted. "I always can."

"Are you seeing anything about this in the news?"

She turned her head slightly to one side. "Actually...no. Not a peep."

"So the local police ignored our calls for help and nobody's talking about us? I mean, you'd think there'd be all kinds of police and news reports, but it's like we don't exist. Like this isn't even happening. It's weird."

"What are you saying?"

"I don't know." He sighed and scrubbed his face with both hands. "Maybe I've played one too many Resident Evil games, but this is some Umbrella Corp shit happening here."

"Well, she is a doctor." She nodded toward the woman. "And she does study viruses. She was here for the virology conference this weekend."

A chill of dread prickled across the back of his neck. "That's...not comforting, Sami."

She held up her hands. "Hey, you're the one who brought

up Resident Evil. I'm just telling you what I found out about her."

Connor sat on the end of the woman's bed and studied her pale face. Her eyelids twitched, and a cold sweat broke out across her brow. "You know who she is?"

"Dr. Tiffany Peters. I found her listed on the virology conference's website. She and her partner were supposed to present their research on something called Akeso."

"What's that?"

"The description of their presentation was vague. Maybe some kind of antiviral? They named it after the Greek goddess of the healing process."

A sound from the doorway made them both glance over. Schumacher stood there. "Your shift's up, Blackwood," he said to Sami with little enthusiasm. "I'm taking over."

She frowned. "I thought Wolfe had the next shift."

"He's still sleeping."

"So wake him up," Sami said. "We go by the schedule we agreed on."

"He's sleeping. I'm awake. I don't see what the big deal is." As he stepped into the room, the woman—Dr. Peters—started to thrash. Her eyes were open, but glassy. Her mouth moved as if she were trying to speak. Connor scooted closer, leaned down to hear her words. It sounded like she was saying…sneakers?

Sami rushed to her side and soothed a hand over her head. "Get out, Christian. You're upsetting her."

"I didn't do anything," Schumacher said defensively.

"Then maybe she just doesn't like assholes," Sami shot back. "Get out!"

Dr. Peters continued to thrash around, though she was losing strength. And she was definitely mumbling something about sneakers over and over again, which didn't make any sense.

"Fine." Schumacher raised his hands and backed away. "Whatever. I'm going. I didn't want babysitting duty anyway."

As he stalked away, Connor's gaze dropped to the flash of color at his feet. And the rest of what Dr. Peters was saying clicked. She wasn't just talking about sneakers. She was talking about orange sneakers. Like the expensive high-tops Schumacher was so damn proud of.

"What about them?" he asked softly. "Dr. Peters? What about the orange sneakers?"

"Bad…" she muttered.

"What?"

But she was already drifting back to unconsciousness.

Connor stood. "Are you okay with her?"

"Yes." Sami's voice seemed to have a soothing effect on the doctor. "What was that all about?"

"I don't know, but I'm going to find out."

"Connor." She hesitated. "Don't take any stupid chances."

"I know how to take care of myself, Sami. I've been doing it for a long time." He slipped into the hallway in time to see Schumacher go into one of the empty rooms two doors down. Moving as quickly and silently as he could, he darted forward and stuck his foot in the door before it closed. There was a loud bang from inside the room, like Schumacher had thrown something. Connor held his breath, but seconds ticked by and Schumacher didn't come out and demand what he was doing. Instead, he heard Schumacher talking to someone. A phone call? He eased open the door just a bit more so he could hear better.

"We're fucked," Schumacher said.

• • •

Briggs paced the length of the hotel desk.

Fuck. This should have been a simple snatch and grab

job. They'd had Tiffany, and all they'd needed to do for their big payday was grab Claire. But, no. HORNET had to get involved and fuck everything up. Now they had hostages and they couldn't make a move with the threat of HORNET hanging over their head.

"It's getting close to the top of the hour," Mel Kennion said, sounding out of breath even though he'd only been standing guard over their hostages.

Briggs glared over at the man. Kennion was close to aging out of mercenary work, going both bald and paunchy around the middle. He'd been one of the best operators Defion had at one time, which was the only reason Briggs had approached him about this job three years ago. One last lucrative op before he called it quits. But now the old man was sweating profusely and his face had flushed an unhealthy shade of red. He wasn't cut out for this anymore.

"Losing your nerve, Mel?"

The other man scoffed. "I've been doing this since you were pissing your diapers, kid. I have titanium nerves." Kennion swiped at his forehead with his sleeve. "It's hot in here, is all. What if *they* lose their nerve? Hour's nearly up and we haven't heard from them."

"They won't."

"You're so sure of yourself. That pride's gonna bite you on the ass someday."

Probably, but it wouldn't be today. HORNET's medic would come through for him. They'd trade the women for their guys. He was sure of it. What other choice did they have? He was also sure they'd then try to rescue the doctors, because they were heroes after all, but he had something up his sleeve to squash that.

Although Kennion did have a point. They were cutting it very close. Maybe it was time to light a fire under the medic's ass.

"Mel." He tilted his head, indicating Gabe. "Go point your weapon at his face."

While Kennion shuffled over to their prisoners, he decided they were probably due for a shift change. "Coombs, go upstairs and relieve Armstrong."

"Still say we should blow that door," Kennion muttered.

"And I told you we can't risk hurting the doctors." Plus they couldn't use their explosives until they were well on their way off the island. He'd bribed the police to look the other way and ignore any incoming calls, but that wouldn't last if more shit started blowing up. "We know Tiffany is in there with them. One of you fucktards already shot her and she's probably going to die." He ignored the lump that thought brought to his throat.

Kennion snorted. "Rookie move."

"What?"

"You fell for the target, didn't you?"

Briggs's heart thumped so hard against his rib cage, he was surprised it didn't pop out of his chest. He pictured Tiffany, her dark hair bedraggled, her brown eyes sparkling as she laughed at one of his lame jokes over breakfast. His jokes were lame, too. He'd never had much of a sense of humor, but as Paul he'd made an effort to make her laugh. She had a great laugh.

No. He swallowed back the surge of emotion. He wasn't capable of love and even if he was, Tiffany Peters wouldn't be the kind of woman he'd fall for. "Fuck you, old man. If she's dead, we're not getting paid. Simple as that. Now do your goddamn job and let me do mine."

Grabbing his phone, he speed-dialed the medic, then switched to video mode and pointed the camera at Gabe just as Kennion raised the gun.

Chapter Twenty-Four

Jesse was losing his goddamned mind. Half his team and his son were all in incredible danger. Meanwhile, the other half of his men and the woman he loved were taking on a rescue op with nothing more than a couple of stolen guns and a pocketknife. And what was he doing? Hobbling around the beach, waiting for a call that might never come.

I should be with them.

He stopped and stared toward the hotel, as if concentrating hard enough on the glow of lights above the trees would somehow solve everything. He took a step in that direction—and froze when his phone rang.

Goddammit.

He had a part to play like everyone else, and that was his cue. He sucked in a breath and hoped like hell he didn't fuck this up.

He answered, but only heard distant voices and looked at the screen. It wasn't Briggs calling.

"Connor?"

"Dad." Connor's voice was little more than a whisper and Jesse's stomach cramped with dread.

"Everything okay?"

A pause. "Schumacher's not on our side."

"What?"

"I overheard him talking to someone on the phone this afternoon, and he kept saying they weren't ready to go to war yet. Then again, just a few minutes ago, he reported to the guys downstairs. Then he made another call and said he was out of options and had to get out because things had gone to shit here. I-I think he's here to kill someone."

Fuck. How could that be? They'd thoroughly vetted every one of the recruits. Harvard had run the background checks himself. Had Schumacher decided to switch teams mid-game, or had he been playing for the other side all along?

A Defion plant in their training program.

Holy shit. Had Schumacher infiltrated the program to get close to someone in HORNET? But then why was he reporting to Briggs, when it was likely Briggs and crew had gone rogue from Defion?

"What do I do, Dad?" Connor asked.

"Do not let Schumacher anywhere near Jean-Luc." Though if Jean-Luc had been the target, the Cajun would be dead by now. No, it was someone else. But who?

"We made him leave the room. Dr. Peters doesn't like him."

"How is she?"

Connor hesitated. "I don't think she's going to live much longer. She's really pale."

"How about Jean-Luc? Is he still bleedin'?"

"No. We used the quick-clot stuff from your kit like you said. He looks better, but he hasn't woken up yet."

"He might not for a while." Depending on how much blood he lost, he might not wake up until he had a transfusion. "Listen, Connor. Lanie is on her way up to you with Seth, Ian, Marcus, and Danny. They're gonna get you out of there very soon, and when they do, you need to tell them what you told me about Schumacher. Let them handle him."

"Why aren't you coming with them?" Connor sounded so small, very much like the boy who was once afraid of the monster in his closet and thought his dad was a superhero.

"I…" *Want to be there. Want to hold you the moment you're safe and know you're okay.* But he couldn't manage to say any of that out loud. "I had to stay behind."

"I don't know why I'm surprised." Connor snorted derisively, trying to sound tough, but even over the phone, Jesse heard the emotion his son was battling back. "You were never there when I needed you. Why would it change now?"

Jesse nearly choked on the knot in his throat. "Connor…I didn't stay away all those years because I wanted to. Your mother…" He trailed off, sighed to try and dislodge the ever-tightening knot. This wasn't the way he'd planned on this conversation happening, but he had to make his boy understand.

Just in case things went FUBAR.

"For a long time, your mother didn't want me around you. And I'm not blamin' her," he added quickly. "She was right. At the time, I wasn't fit to be anyone's parent. Hell, I was barely fit to be human. She was protectin' you in her own way. And then, by the time she—" He stopped short, struggled to find the right words.

"When she didn't care anymore," Connor finished for him. "When she had a whole new family and didn't want me around anymore. You can say it."

Jesse winced. He couldn't even deny it. He was ashamed of himself for being too weak to deal with life when Connor was younger, but he was even more ashamed of his ex-wife for casting their son aside when the boy turned out to be too much like him.

"I'm sorry, Connor. Jesus, I'm so sorry. Neither of us did right by you."

Connor said nothing. The silence was the nonverbal equivalent of an eye roll.

This wasn't going well.

Jesse didn't want to point fingers at his ex when he was just as culpable for their failure as parents. He took a minute to sort his thoughts, then tried again. "By the time I was well enough to be a good father to you, the gap between us was already so big. Felt like I was starin' across the Grand Canyon at you on the other side. I wanted to reach you, but I didn't know how to make up for…everythin'. I still don't, but if you'll let me, I'd like a shot at tryin'."

Another long silence, but this one was somehow softer, not as tense. Finally, Connor cleared his throat. "I think…I'd like that."

All at once, his lungs opened up and it was like he could finally breath after drowning for years. "Okay. Okay. This will all be over soon. Lanie's on her way up to you now."

"I like her, too, Dad," Connor said softly. "She's…nice. Just so you know."

He swallowed hard. "I'm glad you think so. I want her in our lives." It was a revelation. A truth he hadn't known until the words were spilling out of his mouth.

Jesus, he should've told Lanie before she left.

The phone beeped to indicate another incoming call. He checked the screen and recognized the number Briggs had called him from before. "Hang tight, Connor. Lanie will be there any minute. I have to go. I love you, son."

Heart cracking wide open at Connor's protest, he ended the call and accepted the incoming video call from Briggs.

Nothing showed on the screen but the tile floor of the hotel's lobby.

"Your hour's up," Briggs said.

Jesse checked the time. "Not yet. We have five minutes."

"You're cutting it close."

"We can't find the women. We think they escaped with the rest of the hotel staff and guests."

"You're lying. You have one of the doctors locked upstairs with your man. He could've brought her down at any time."

The picture lifted to show one of the masked men holding a gun to Gabe's head.

"Do it," Briggs ordered.

"No! Wait! Our guy upstairs is injured. He's unconscious. He can't bring her down."

"Then you should've told those kids in there to open up and let us take her. Do it," Briggs said again.

Gabe drew a deep breath, but he didn't shut his eyes. He unflinchingly stared death in the face—again. But the shot never came. The man holding the gun seemed to falter. His arm dropped to his side as if the gun was suddenly too heavy.

"What are you doing, old man?" Briggs demanded. "Shoot him."

The man coughed up blood and slumped to the ground, the gun clattering to the floor. He wasn't simply defying orders. There was something seriously wrong with him.

"Briggs, listen to me. Your man's in trouble. Do you have a medic?"

"What?" Briggs snapped. He'd put the camera down to help his guy, and now all Jesse could see was the skylight in the ceiling. Too bad they didn't have some tear gas. Drop a canister or two through that skylight and this whole situation would be over pretty damn fast.

"Do you have a medic on your team?" Jesse asked again, shouting to make sure he was heard. "Or a doctor among the hostages? Your guy is sick."

Briggs didn't answer. Instead, there was a grunt, like the huff of air a man made when he was punched solidly in the stomach. The sound of bodies thunking together in hand-to-hand combat. The camera spun as if someone had kicked it, but Jesse could still only see the ceiling. Still, he watched the small screen intently. Gabe, Quinn, and Harvard must have used the moment of distraction to their advantage and launched an attack against the hostage takers.

For one shining moment, Jesse hoped maybe this was the end of it. Gabe and Quinn were professionals. The former SEALs knew what they were doing. They'd gain the upper hand and everyone would finally be safe.

No such luck.

Jesse flinched at the bang of a gunshot followed by screams. Then silence that lasted so fucking long, he thought he might pass out from holding his breath in gut-wrenching anticipation.

Finally, the camera moved. Someone picked it up and pointed it at the group of hostages. One down, blood spreading in a pool around a brunette head. He squinted at the screen, wishing the picture was bigger.

Was that…Harvard?

The camera shifted, and Jesse released his breath in relief. The Tangos had Gabe, Quinn, and Harvard on their knees, hands locked behind their heads. Harvard was bleeding from a gash over his eyebrow, but that was better than a bullet in the brain. Quinn's lip was split and swollen, and Gabe was going to have a massive black eye soon. His lid was already swelling shut.

The camera zoomed in on the dead man. Mid-twenties, maybe. Brunette with blue eyes that stared, glassy and sightless, at the ceiling. His expression was one of frozen shock. Nearby, a woman about the same age had crumpled into a sobbing heap while the other hostages tried to comfort her.

"You have another hour," Briggs said, almost mechanically. Like he, himself, was in shock.

That was the voice of a man who hadn't meant to kill anyone. That was a man having second thoughts. Jesse could use that.

"Briggs. How's your man?"

A pause. "He's breathing blood. How do you think he is?"

"Let me come in and treat him. And anyone else who needs it."

Briggs gave a humorless laugh. "I was right about you, medic."

"Yeah, you were. I hate seein' people die needlessly when I can do somethin' to help them. Let me help your guy, and in return, you'll release one of mine."

Another pause. "Which one?"

"Gabe." Jesse didn't even think about his answer. While his cousin would probably have his head for not getting her fiancé and the father of her children out, he knew Quinn was physically okay. Same with Harvard. Gabe, though, was still on the mend and hadn't been in great shape when he went to bed last night. The video glimpses had been too shaky to make a diagnosis, but Gabe looked a bit gray. He never should have gone on their training mission and he certainly didn't need to be dealing with this. He needed out of there, and Jesse knew both Quinn and Harvard would agree.

"I choose the hostage," Briggs said after another pause. "Not one of your guys."

Jesse gritted his teeth. Told himself to relax. Any hostage release was a good thing. "All right. Fair enough."

"You come in empty-handed. I don't even want to see your phone."

"I'll need a first aid kit."

"We'll find you one. You have three minutes to show.

Take longer, and the deal's off."

Briggs hung up. Jesse gave himself a second to calm his racing heart, then tapped out a fast text to Lanie. The team had to know he'd be inside. He didn't wait for a reply, but tossed the phone aside and started running. Three minutes was barely enough time to get to the beach in front of the main building, not to mention into the lobby, and he couldn't risk showing up even a second too late.

He ran flat out, ignoring the pain in his bad ankle, until he reached the beach in front of the hotel. Only then did he hobble to a stop and check his watch. Thirty seconds left. Heaving in a breath, he ran again, his limp more pronounced with each step. He reached the front entrance just as Briggs held up a phone. On the screen, a timer counted down the last few seconds.

Jesse curbed the impulse to rush inside and stopped on the other side of the glass from Briggs. "I'm here," he called loud enough to be heard through the glass. "Release a hostage."

Briggs's lips compressed, but then he looked at his guy propped against the wall, gasping for breath, and relented. He called one of his other men forward with a hand motion. A moment later, the door opened, and they shoved a woman out. The front desk clerk. She was wide-eyed and babbling in terrified French.

Jesse went to her and grasped her shoulders briefly, telling her, "You're okay now. Run to town. Get help."

He knew she spoke basic English, but he didn't know how much had gotten through her fear and he didn't have time to repeat himself.

Without another thought for his safety, he walked inside and was greeted by the business end of several weapons.

"Search him," Briggs ordered.

He cooperatively raised his hands and locked his fingers

behind his head as two guys slid cautiously toward him. He scanned the room and took stock of the hostages as one man patted him down. The other kept a weapon trained on him, and he made sure not to so much as sneeze. Both of these guys appeared to be nervous, and he didn't want to set off anyone's itchy trigger finger.

From across the room, his gaze locked with Gabe's. The boss didn't look happy with him, but fuck that. He counted at least five serious injuries among the hostages. Gabe looked like he'd keel over at any minute, and he, Quinn, and Harvard were all bleeding from various wounds. Then there was the Tango who most likely needed a hospital.

Gabe lifted his brows in silent question. Knowing he was asking about the rest of the team, Jesse flicked his gaze to the ceiling. He hoped that was enough to convey they had a plan, but he couldn't take the time to make sure Gabe understood. The moment the Tangos finished patting him down, someone shoved a heavy-duty first aid kit at him.

"We removed everything sharp," the guy said in the rough voice of a heavy smoker. "So don't get any bright ideas." He then pushed Jesse toward the downed hostage taker.

"What's his name?" he asked as he knelt beside the man and opened the kit. Thankfully, it was more like his field trauma kit than a typical first aid. Seeing as this was Tuc Quentin's hotel, he shouldn't be surprised. Hollywood took the Boy Scouts' "always prepared" motto to extremes.

"You don't need to know," the heavy smoker said.

Did these guys really still think they were going to get away scot-free? With Briggs found out and Tucker working on the problem back in the States, it was only a matter of time until the rest of their names came out. Their op was beyond FUBAR'd. Obviously they just didn't realize it yet.

Jesse spared a quick thought for Lanie and the guys—it was up to them now—and then got to work.

Chapter Twenty-Five

The old servant's entrance was difficult to find. In fact, if not for the hotel's blueprints, they never would have spotted it on the back side of the building behind the slabs of rock that made up the pool's massive waterslide. No possible way the bad guys could've known about this entrance, and a quick check from Ian and Tank proved the door wasn't rigged with explosives. It took some doing to pry the door open—the hinges had rusted from the contact spray of the waterslide. Marcus and Danny put their combined strength into pulling on the door and it finally creaked open enough that Lanie and Seth, the only two with guns, were able to duck inside. He went left, and she went right.

"Clear," Seth whispered.

"Clear," Lanie echoed.

Holy hell. They'd gotten in without being spotted. They

might actually have a shot at pulling this off.

Marcus stepped in behind them and looked around. The walls on all three sides of the large room were lined with industrial washers and dryers. "Laundry room?"

Lanie consulted the blueprints on her phone and nodded. "Second floor. If we go out that way"—she indicated the large metal doors directly in front of her—"we'll find storage, the kitchen, and eventually wind up in the restaurant. That way"—she pointed over her shoulder at a smaller door on the wall behind her—"to the main hallway. It's more direct, but also more open to discovery. Either direction, we'll find stairs. How much risk do we want to take?"

When nobody spoke, she glanced up. In the light from her phone's screen, she saw the men were all looking at her expectantly. It made her uncomfortable. "What?"

"You got us this far," Marcus said. "And I, for one, trust you enough to get us the rest of the way."

The rest of the group nodded and murmured agreements.

Oh. Wow. That might be the nicest thing any of them had ever said to her. Her throat closed up, but she swallowed down the emotion. She couldn't go girly on them now. Not when they'd put so much trust in her. She studied the blueprints again, and thought back to what she'd seen in the lobby.

"They don't have enough men," she said softly.

"Neither do we," Ian said.

"But they don't have any reinforcements coming and they can't spare men to guard both stairwells. So we'll go to both. We'll split up."

"That never ends well in horror movies," Marcus pointed out.

She looked at him. "You said you trust me. I *know* this is our best option."

Marcus glanced around at the others, then lifted a shoulder. "You're the boss. Point me in the direction you need me to go, and I'll go."

She wondered what she had done to invoke such loyalty. Was it something new that had only just developed tonight? Or had it always been there and she'd been too wrapped up in her own worries to see it? She didn't know, but it hardly mattered now. Fact was, she'd managed to win these guys over and, suddenly, she felt more like a member of the team than ever before.

"Okay," she said because she couldn't think of another reply. "Okay. You, Seth, and Danny go through the restaurant." As she spoke, she sent the blueprints to each of their phones. "Ian, Tank, and I will take the more direct route since we'll be more likely to run into explosives."

"What if we come across one?" Danny asked.

Ian handed him a pair of wire cutters.

Danny winced. "Cut the red wire?"

Ian gave a smile that was just a little bit evil. "It's *never* the red wire."

"Great." Danny's voice came out a bit higher than usual. He slid the wire cutters into a pocket and cleared his throat. "Let's hope I don't need those."

"Be careful," Lanie told them as they turned away as a unit.

"Little hand says it's time to rock and roll." Marcus grinned back at her and gave the "hang loose" hand signal before slipping through the big double doors, following Seth and Danny.

She glanced over at Ian. "Did he just quote *Point Break*?"

He rolled his eyes. "Guy's a walking movie encyclopedia. Haven't you notice the recruits trying to stump him with movies quotes all week?"

No, she hadn't. And why did that thought make her mildly uncomfortable? Because, she realized, she had deliberately been secluding herself from the rest of the team. She'd had her mind made up that they didn't want her, that she didn't fit in with them, so she hadn't really tried to be a teammate.

"I'm sorry."

Ian, already across the room and pulling open the door that would take them to the main hallway, paused. At his side, Tank also froze, instinctively knowing he wasn't supposed to go through the door until his master did.

Lanie shook her head. "I've been a complete bitch, haven't I?"

"Yeah," Ian said in his typical blunt way. "But we, uh, haven't exactly gone easy on you, either."

"God. I was so sure y'all didn't want me on the team, I didn't even give you a chance."

"Well, you're on the team now, huh? All's good." Ian looked as if he'd rather have a root canal with a spoon than continue this conversation. He jerked his head toward the hall. "Want Tank and me to take the lead or—"

Tank's ears pricked and his body went rigid as if preparing for an attack. A low growl rumbled from his throat. Ian made a hand signal and the dog instantly fell silent, but he didn't relax. It was another second before Lanie heard what the dog had picked up—someone was walking up the hallway. If she remembered the blueprints right, that person was headed to the stairs at the end of the long hall, which was precisely where she and Ian needed to go.

"Shift change?" Ian whispered. He didn't move. Still stood with his hand on the door knob, the door half open. If he shut it now, they'd be found out. But if they let the guy go, they'd be making more work for themselves. It'd be much harder to take out two guards.

Shit.

Lanie glanced around, spotted one of the huge rolling laundry bins. Yeah. That could work. "Let the door shut. Draw his attention."

Ian looked back at her in surprise, then nodded when he saw where she was going. Tank was all but vibrating with the need to act, but he sat when Ian gave him the signal. Ian took his hand off the knob. The door didn't slam, but it was loud enough to draw the attention of the guy in the hall.

Just as she expected, footsteps rushed toward the door. The Tango slammed through, and the moment he did, she shoved the rolling cart at him. The heavy bin hit him squarely in the middle and he folded in half. Ian pounced on him from behind, arm barred across the man's throat, while Tank growled and bit at his legs. He made a strangled sound of pain just before his eyes rolled back in his head and he passed out from lack of oxygen.

Ian released him the second his body went slack, and so did Tank. "Good boy, Tanky." He picked up the man's weapon, which had dropped to the floor, and slung the strap over his shoulder. "That's more like it. Now we're both armed." He nudged the man's leg with the toe of his boot. "What should we do with this asshole? I'm all for killing him, but—"

She was already shaking her head. "No."

"That's what I figured you'd say. You're too much like Jesse."

The man was starting to stir. She bent over, fisted her hand in his shirt, and hauled him halfway off the floor. "How many of your guys are upstairs?"

He mumbled something incoherent. She shook him, and when that didn't work, she smacked his cheek hard enough that her own palm stung. "How many?"

"One," he said hoarsely. "J-just one."

She slammed him back to the ground and his head bounced off the floor. The blow rendered him unconscious again. She straightened to find Ian staring at her with lifted brows.

"Not that much like Jesse," she said.

He whistled softly. "Yeah. Noticed that." He waved a finger between her and the unconscious man. "Saint Jesse wouldn't like that."

"Because he's a healer at heart and hates violence. That's why—" She stopped short. She had been about to say, "That's why he struggled in Delta Force," but knowing Ian wasn't Jesse's favorite person, she thought better of it. She doubted Ian was aware of Jesse's history with depression and alcoholism, and frankly it wasn't any of his business. She pulled several zip ties from her pocket and set to work restraining their prisoner. "We need to move or Marcus, Seth, and Danny will get upstairs before us."

Thankfully, Ian let her slide without elaborating further. He walked over to one of the storage shelves lining the room, grabbed a washcloth, and wadded it into their prisoner's mouth, before taping his mouth shut with a strip of duct tape.

He readied his newly acquired weapon and together, they crept out into the hallway. The trip to the stairwell at the far end was tense, but uneventful. They went up one floor and paused on the landing. This was the hard part. Their target had the high ground. If things were going to go sideways on them, it'd happen now.

One floor up, they could hear the guard moving around on the next landing.

Ian made a hand motion, basically indicating they should rush the guard.

Lanie shook her head and pointed to Tank. She knew from experience the dog was as good as a weapon.

Ian looked down at Tank. The dog sat at Ian's feet and stared up adoringly. Ian's lips tightened into a grim line. She knew he was worried for his dog. She imagined it was the same way a parent felt while dropping their child off for the first day of school. He needn't worry, though—she'd seen

Tank in action and she wouldn't send him if she thought he couldn't handle the guard.

She waved a hand to get Ian's attention again and mouthed, "Trust him."

After a pause, he nodded. But still, he hesitated before sucking in a breath and giving Tank the attack hand signal. The dog bolted up the stairs, and the guard let out a scream of pain that echoed in the cavernous stairwell. Ian rushed up directly on his dog's heels, and Lanie was a step behind him. Still, by the time they got there, Tank had the guy on the ground.

Ian called Tank off and pointed his weapon at the guard's face while she kicked his dropped gun away from his reach. The man was pale, shaking, leaking blood from a deep bite high on his shoulder.

"It's over," she told him.

He only groaned in response and she rolled him over to secure his arms behind his back with a zip tie.

Once Ian was sure she had the guard secure, he lowered his weapon and knelt down to ruffle the fur around Tank's neck. "You're such a good boy, Tank. Such a good boy."

Tank's tail *thunked* on the floor and he gave his doggie grin that was no less cute for the blood staining his muzzle.

Lanie went to the door. "Connor?"

No sound came from the other side. She tapped on the door, and called more loudly, "Connor!"

There was some shuffling, then, "I'm here!"

She breathed a soft sigh of relief. "Okay. Back up. We're diffusing the explosive on the door."

She glanced back at Ian, who stood and pulled his pack off his shoulders. She stepped aside to allow him better access to the door. To her, the explosive on the frame looked complicated, but after a quick study, Ian snorted with disgust.

"Amateur hour."

"Is it dead?" she asked.

"Oh, it'll go boom, and it'll cause damage, but there's no finesse here. It's sloppy. Any kid with access to the internet and a handful of household goods could cook this up. It's way below Defion's usual standards."

She watched him work for one minute, and then another. Each second seemed to stretch out into a year. Full of nervous energy, she paced over to the landing to check down the stairs and make sure they were still clear. If the explosive was as easy as he said it was, why was it taking so long? "Ian. We need to hurry."

"Yeah, yeah. Something's...not right about this." His hands worked quickly and agilely as he followed each wire to its source. It was almost like watching a pianist make music.

"Goddammit." He hung his head, gave it a slow shake. "It's the fucking red wire."

Her heart jumped. "I'll text Danny." She hoped to God he wasn't in the process of cutting the wrong wire. Thankfully, he replied right back. And when he did, another text popped up at the same time. From Jesse. She ignored Danny's and read his.

"Oh. Shit."

Ian glanced over his shoulder with a smirk. He was nearly done removing the explosive material from the door. "If Danny cut the wrong wire, don't worry. I was fucking with you. As I said, this isn't advance ordnance disposal here. He could cut any wire and diffuse it."

Scowling, she pointed at him. "Okay, one: you're an asshole."

He shrugged, unapologetic. "It's my default setting."

"And two: I'm not swearing at Danny. It's Jesse. He traded himself for one of the hostages."

Now Ian was swearing. "That altruistic fucker is gonna get himself killed."

"Careful. Someone might think you actually care about him."

"I do," Ian said so softly she wondered at first if he'd actually replied or if she'd heard wrong. But then he added, "Whether I like it or not. He's one of my people now and I don't like seeing my people hurt."

She stared at him for a beat. She'd never thought of him as untrustworthy or deviant like Jesse did, but he *was* volatile and always seemed on the knife's edge of anger. His moral compass didn't always point north. But there was also more to him than that. "You're a good guy, Ian."

"Yeah, well." He shifted from one foot to the other as if the compliment made him uncomfortable. "Don't go around telling people. I have a reputation." Without waiting for a response, he focused his full attention back on the explosive. A moment later, he pulled the door open. She didn't have time to react because a tall, skinny body raced out and slammed into her. Thin arms wrapped around her shoulders and squeezed tight.

Connor.

The hug stunned her, but also reminded her that he was just a boy. He'd been so brave and mature throughout this ordeal, it had been easy to forget he wasn't a trainee or an operative, wasn't even an adult.

"Hey." She patted his back awkwardly, unsure of what to do. Then she thought, fuck it, and wrapped her arms around him in return. He was okay. The overwhelming sense of relief had tears pricking the backs of her eyes.

Over Connor's shoulder, she caught Ian's brief grin before he hid it. He liked the kid, too. Then he shouldered his pack again and stepped through the door into the crowd waiting on the other side. "Where's Jean-Luc?"

She tried to push Connor back, but he wouldn't let go. "Hey. Buddy. We have work to do."

He swallowed hard enough that she felt his throat work against her chest. He was crying, and that's why he didn't want to let go. He didn't want the others to see, and she couldn't blame him for needing to preserve a bit of his dignity. She ran a hand over his hair. "They're gone. They went with Ian."

"Good." He drew back, but instead of the tears she expected, his eyes were dry and serious. "You need to know Schumacher's not on our side. He's working with the guys downstairs, but I also think he was put in the training program for some other reason. Maybe even to hurt someone."

Okay, so not as much a boy as she thought. He was still calm and collected. The kid was too much like his father for his own good.

Lanie frowned down at him. "How do you know all this?"

"He's made phone calls. I've listened."

Smart kid. "Okay. We need to make sure he doesn't—"

A long, raw, primal scream that was more rage than fear sliced through the air, and cut off just as abruptly as it began.

Lanie instinctively pushed Connor behind her and pulled her weapon as she searched for the source of the danger. Up the hallway, several of the recruits were backing away from a room, hands raised. She couldn't see Ian, but Tank's growl would've put Cujo to shame.

"Stay here," she told Connor and shouldered through the wall of muscled recruits. She peeked into the room as she passed and saw Ian holding Tank's collar. The sole female recruit, Samira, was distraught, leaning over one of the two beds. Blood stained the sheets, and it didn't take any medical training to know the woman on the bed was very dead. She'd been shot, twice, execution-style.

"Schumacher," Ian said in explanation. "He has Jean-Luc."

She cleared the doorway and the last of the recruits in time to see Schumacher drag a semi-conscious Jean-Luc into one of the elevator cars. The doors closed before she reached them and she banged a fist against the metal.

"What happened?" she demanded as Ian came up behind her.

"Fuck if I know."

"Shit." She pounded a fist against the elevator door again. She faced Ian and the recruits, first searching for Connor to make sure he was safe. The rest of the recruits seemed none the worse for wear. In fact, she was met with a whole lot of flat, down-to-business stares. Even Samira, eyes wet and hands covered with Tiffany Peters's blood, appeared ready to take up the good fight.

And they were all looking to her for guidance.

When did that happen?

And what the hell did she do now?

"We've lost our element of surprise, and now they have two more of our guys as hostages." As she spoke, she took out her phone to text Marcus, Danny, and Seth, telling them to go back to the restaurant's balcony, which overlooked the water feature in the lobby. Seth didn't have his sniper rifle, but she had no doubt he'd be able to make a shot with the weapon he had if the situation came to it. Plus, having eyes up above the action was never a bad thing.

"Two?" Connor asked.

She looked him square in the eye. He'd find out soon enough so there was no sense in beating around the bush. "Your dad traded himself for one of the civilian hostages."

Connor went white. "Dad did what?"

"He'll be okay," she assured, and reached out to squeeze Connor's thin shoulder. At least she'd managed to keep her own fear out of her voice. Hell, she even sounded sure of herself, which was damn near a miracle because inwardly, she was floundering. She caught Jeremiah Wolfe's gaze and flicked hers pointedly at Connor. Wolfe nodded once and looped an arm around the kid. "C'mon, pal. Let's get out of here."

Connor shrugged him off. "I'm staying."

"No, you're most definitely not, young man. You're going with Wolfe to safety." Lanie didn't know where that "mom voice" had come from since she never had a mother who was mom enough to learn it from. Maybe it'd been born from the bone-deep fear of picturing Connor caught in the crossfire of what was sure to be a nasty standoff.

Of course, Connor got that mulish Jesse expression on his face. The one that said he was about to dig in his heels and would only be moved by an act of God. Save her from Warrick men.

"Connor, please." She went with instinct and pulled him into her arms. She hadn't meant for her voice to crack on his name. "I can't do my job unless I know you're safe."

Truer words had never been spoken, she realized. She wouldn't be able to concentrate unless she knew Connor and the rest of them were safely out of the hotel. She released Connor and studied the group. Her gaze found Ian's, and he gave a small nod. He was thinking along the same lines. "All right. Everyone, follow Ian. He's going to lead you to the door we came in. If you have a weapon, take it with you."

"Hang on." Sami ducked into her room and came back a second later with her laptop bag slung across her shoulders. "What?" she said defensively when she noticed her teammates' stares.

"That's not a weapon, Geek Girl," one of the guys pointed out.

She hitched the slipping strap back onto her shoulder. "Harvard says it is, and I happen to agree."

"Oh, Harvard," Wolfe teased in a falsetto. "You're so smart and handsome and I hang on your every word."

Sami crossed her arms over her chest and fumed. "Keep

that up, Wolfey, and I'll send your browser history to your mother."

Wolfe shuddered. "Low blow, Geek Girl. Low blow."

"That's enough," Lanie said mildly and then wondered when she became the adult in the room. Surreal. She herded the group toward the door Ian had already gone through. "Move fast and keep quiet."

As the recruits got serious and filed out, Connor fell into step beside her. "Dad's going to be okay, right?"

"Jesse knows what he's doing." She hoped. But she also knew he could become so focused while helping others that he didn't always watch out for himself.

Connor said nothing in reply. He stayed silent while Ian led them back to the old servant's entry in the laundry room. The Tango they had tied up was still there. Not that it mattered. Schumacher would expose them the moment he got to the lobby.

Ian held open the door and the recruits streamed outside, blinking against the early dawn light. "Go down to the beach," he told each of them as they passed.

Finally, only Connor remained. He stepped toward the door, but hesitated and turned back to face her. "Dad loves you, you know? He didn't say it when I talked to him earlier, but he never does, does he?"

By some miracle, she didn't swallow her tongue in surprise. "Uh...no. No, he doesn't. Talking about stuff like that is hard for him."

"I kinda get it now. He's afraid. He went through a bad time when I was little, didn't he?"

She glanced at Ian, who at least had the grace to pretend he wasn't listening. Stepping forward, she gripped Connor's shoulders. "Your dad loves you very much, but you're right. He struggled and he had a hard time coming back from it. Now he's afraid of his emotions overtaking him again, so he shields himself by keeping his distance. So our job, as the people who love him most, is to show him he doesn't need that distance."

Connor nodded. "I think you're good for him, Lanie."

"I think you are, too." She ruffled his hair and sent him out.

Ian watched him go. "He's a good kid."

"Yeah," she said softly. "He is."

Ian pulled the door shut and took his weapon off his shoulder. "So let's go save his dad."

Chapter Twenty-Six

As soon as Jesse got a good look at the downed Tango—
"Kennion" he'd heard one of the other guys call him—he
realized the guy was in serious trouble. He was coughing
up blood and had decreased lung sounds on one side. An
examination of his chest showed a circular bruise just to right
of center.

"Did something hit you?" he asked as he strapped an O2
mask over Kennion's face.

He nodded and pointed to one of the stanchions near the
registration desk. The circular tip was the exact same size as
the bruise on his chest. If he hit that with enough force to
cause a pulmonary contusion, he was lucky it hadn't thrown
his heart into a fatal arrhythmia. A few inches to the left, and
it probably would have.

Jesse looked up at Briggs, who hovered nearby. "He
needs a hospital."

Briggs pressed his lips together, glanced at the hostages. "He has you. Do what you can for him."

Jesse considered the first aid kit. "His lung is damaged. Without my trauma kit, I can't do anythin'."

"Where is it?"

Jesse kept his gaze focused on Briggs, careful not to give any indication that he was also speaking to Gabe, Quinn, and Harvard. "In my room. On the fourth floor."

Translation: the cavalry is coming from above.

Briggs's lip peeled off his upper teeth in a sneer. "Exactly where we have your friends trapped. Convenient. What else do you have up there?"

"Nothing but my trauma kit. Think about it. If I had weapons in my room, our friends wouldn't be trapped."

Briggs said nothing. Just stood there, staring down at Kennion.

"Do you want him to die?" Jesse demanded. "Because that's what'll happen without immediate medical attention."

"People die all the time."

"Hope you're gettin' paid well. That money will be a real comfort when your buddy here drowns in his own blood." Feigning annoyance—though, honestly, he didn't have to try too hard—Jesse began packing up the first aid kit. It was stocked better than most. Almost as good as his trauma kit. It had everything from QuikClot to…morphine in auto-inject syringes. The two knuckleheads who had searched the kit had completely passed over the auto-injectors because they weren't obviously sharp.

Their mistake.

Jesse palmed the three morphine pens, and caught Gabe's gaze as he stood. Gabe nodded slightly. Help may be coming, but they weren't going to wait for a shootout. If they could end this now, they'd take the chance. He flicked his gaze over to Briggs and wiggled the pens down at his side.

Again, Gabe nodded.

Just as Jesse moved into position next to Briggs, a small bell announced the elevator's arrival and everyone jumped— the hostages and the hostage takers. Which, given all the frayed nerves in the room and the twitchy trigger fingers, was a recipe for disaster.

Everyone shifted to face the elevator bank and guns came up. Jesse slid one of the injectors into his pocket and readied the other two. Maybe this was the help he'd promised, but more likely, this was someone throwing a wrench into the works. He wanted to be ready in case things went to hell.

And they did the moment those doors slid open.

Schumacher stepped out of the elevator, dragging a semiconscious, barely coherent Jean-Luc with him. He had a gun to the Cajun's temple.

"What the fuck?" Quinn and Briggs said at the exact same time. And, ironically, for the same reason. It was a kick in the balls when a man you thought you knew decided to pull a Benedict Arnold on his trainers, then turn around and *Et tu, Brute?* his own teammates.

How had they not realized this guy was so dangerous?

Jean-Luc's eyes weren't focusing and as Schumacher dragged him forward, he slurred something in a language that was not English. In fact, it didn't seem to be any one language, but a mix of several.

Jesus, did the Cajun have head trauma? Connor hadn't mentioned anything about Jean-Luc sustaining a blow to the head. Or maybe he was just delirious from blood loss? Either way, this was really fucking bad.

And where, for the love of God, was Connor?

If Schumacher had Jean-Luc, did that mean Connor and the rest of the recruits were—

No. As his stomach twisted with horror, he couldn't even finish the thought.

Briggs held up a hand to his three remaining guys, who all had their weapons trained on Schumacher. They relaxed a little, but didn't completely lower their guns.

"What are you doing?" Briggs demanded.

"Following orders," Schumacher said.

"Whose?"

"Your former employer's. They're unimpressed with your performance and asked me to fix the situation." Without any other warning, Schumacher pulled his gun away from Jean-Luc's head and shot Briggs directly between the eyes.

Briggs didn't fall right away. He stood there, blinking in shock as blood dripped off his nose from the neat little hole in his forehead. Then his eyes glazed over and his knees buckled. The silence in the wake of the gun blast was so deep that the *thunk* of Briggs's body hitting the floor echoed.

Schumacher, his arm still banded around Jean-Luc's neck, easily spun and pointed his weapon at Jesse. "And this is 'cause I don't like you or your little shit of a kid."

That old saying about your life flashing before your eyes in the moments before your death? Yeah. It wasn't so much his life, but his mistakes. And, boy, there were many. His relationship with Connor and the way he'd left things with Lanie chief among them. He had a moment to wish he'd done it all differently before—

Jean-Luc straightened and jabbed his elbow backward into Schumacher's gut while simultaneously shoving the gun aside. The bullet missed Jesse by several feet and cracked the glass of the lobby's front window. Another gunshot cracked from somewhere over their heads, and opened a gash across Schumacher's cheek. If he hadn't been wrestling for control of his weapon with Jean-Luc, if he hadn't moved his head in the instant before the bullet struck, it would've gone into his skull.

Jesse looked up. If they had another shooter to worry

about, he wanted to know where the hell the bastard was and—

Oh. Nope. It was the good guys. Seth lay flat on his belly, rifle pointed between two balusters of the second floor balcony, ready to take another shot at Schumacher. He didn't get it. Schumacher shoved Jean-Luc hard enough that the Cajun, in his weakened state, lost his balance.

And then Schumacher turned to run like the coward he was.

Yeah, fuck that. Until Jesse knew his son was safe, that asshole wasn't going anywhere. He lunged after Schumacher and caught him around the middle. They hit the marble floor hard, jarring every ache and pain in his body, but he ignored the discomfort and held on. They slid several feet and skidded into a potted palm tree. Schumacher twisted in an obvious attempt to get the gun up near Jesse's head and pulled the trigger. The bullet burned past his cheek. Too close. Way too close. Jesse closed a hand around Schumacher's wrist and knocked his hand against the potted palm until the gun clattered to the floor.

Schumacher swung a sloppy fist, all anger and no finesse. It glanced off Jesse's chin and snapped his head back. He'd taken harder blows and recovered, but a simultaneous kick to his bad ankle had him seeing stars. His grip loosened and Schumacher squirmed free. He was gone before Jesse's vision cleared.

Jesse pushed up on his hands and knees, and stared at the now empty hallway. He heaved out a breath, then limped to his feet and let the two empty syringes drop from his hand. Schumacher wasn't getting far with two doses of morphine in his system.

At some point during the chaos, Gabe, Quinn, and Harvard had all reared up and used their zip-tied wrists as garrotes to neutralize the three remaining Tangos. Hostages screamed. Some scattered, racing toward any door they could find. Some cowered, adding to the noise and chaos. Danny and Marcus came down from the restaurant's balcony and worked at directing people outside to safety.

Jesse snapped up the first aid kit and hobbled to Jean-Luc's side. "Hey, Cajun. How you doin'?"

"Oh, you know," Jean-Luc said in a reedy voice. He pulled his hand away from his side to show the fresh blood staining his palm. "Just bleeding all over the damn place like a stuck pig. I'm gonna pass out again, f'true."

"Go ahead. It's over now. I got you."

"Good. Nobody else I'd trust to save my awesome self." And his eyelids eased closed.

Jesse snorted. "Glad to see your ego's intact, pal."

Chapter Twenty-Seven

"Looks like we missed the party," Ian said and lowered his gun.

Lanie scanned the lobby, counting heads. Only when she saw all of her people accounted for and whole did her heart rate slow to something below jackhammer. Ever since they'd heard the gunshots, she'd feared the worst, but her first priority had been to get Connor and the rest of the recruits out of the hotel to safety.

"What happened?" she asked nobody in particular.

"FUBAR happened," Harvard said as he walked by with a stack of sheets. He had a bit of a limp, a split lip, and his Star Wars T-shirt was torn and spattered with blood, but otherwise he seemed all right. As he filled them in on what went down, he draped a sheet over one of the dead men on the floor, then continued on to the next in line.

In all, she counted four bodies. One had definitely been a hostage, judging by his clothes. Another was the man Tank had bit—teeth must've hit an artery. The third was another of Briggs's crew, the guy Jean-Luc had neutralized. And the fourth was Briggs himself.

"Well, shit," she said softly and motioned to Briggs with the tip of her weapon. "How did that happen?"

Harvard glanced over his shoulder at the body. "He was fired. Schumacher gave him his pink slip."

She whistled softly. "That's one way to handle HR."

Harvard cracked a smile, which must have stung like hell because of his lip. "Don't give Gabe and Quinn any ideas."

She smiled back at him. It was impossible not to when he used that awkward, nerdy charm of his. "Where's Jesse?"

He motioned to the sweeping expanse of windows. "Outside tending to the wounded. Where else? Tuc called. Back-up should be here any minute."

"About time. Thanks." She squeezed his shoulder as she passed. She'd intended to find Jesse and let him know Connor was safe, but as she neared the window, she saw the cavalry had indeed arrived in the form Tucker Quentin and a convoy of large trucks and vans. The beach and parking lot were full of people. Somewhere in the distance, police sirens finally sounded.

A little late, guys.

Still, she was glad to see them.

At the hotel's front entrance, she paused to watch Jesse and Connor. If the emotional reunion had already happened, they sure weren't acting like it. Jesse was sorting the wounded into vehicles, while Connor sat sullenly with Sami and several of the other recruits. Jesus. Those two. After everything, they were still being stubborn, neither wanting to break down first.

"'Scuse me, Lanie." Marcus came up behind her carrying Jesse's well-worn medical bag. "Jesse needed his kit," he explained as she stepped aside to let him pass.

"Hey," she called after him. "Earlier you quoted *Point Break*. The first one. The good one."

He flashed a grin over his shoulder. "Nice catch."

"'Shall we play a game?'"

He didn't turn back, but snapped his fingers. "*WarGames*, 1983. You need to do better than that if you want to stump me."

"Oh, it's on, Deangelo."

Now he did turn and crooked his hand in the Neo "bring it" wave from *The Matrix*.

She laughed and stepped through the door, enjoying the rush of cool morning air against her skin. The sun wasn't quite up and the humidity hadn't yet cranked to unbearable levels. For the first time all night, she felt like she could finally breathe. She closed her eyes and savored the feeling of oxygen flowing freely in and out of her lungs.

From somewhere over by the vans, she heard Jean-Luc's voice. "Hey, Quentin. The resort is top rate. Gorgeous views, friendly staff, excellent food, and bonus points for the crew of homicidal mercenaries. Who doesn't want a bit of adrenaline with their Caribbean vacation? Five stars."

Then Tucker's wry reply: "You're welcome back anytime."

"Yippee," Jean-Luc said with zero enthusiasm.

Laughing softly to herself, she opened her eyes and glanced over in time to see Jean-Luc being loaded into the back of one of the vans on a stretcher. He was still ghostly pale, but he was joking around, so she had no doubt he'd be fine.

They were all okay. Her guys would all be okay.

Tucker Quentin stood at the back of the van, consulting with some of his men. She should go thank him. Without his help, they wouldn't have gotten into the building in the first place.

She started toward the group, but changed her mind and detoured when she spotted Danny sitting on one of the resort's beach loungers, a rifle balanced across his lap. He stared out across the calm water at the rising sun on the horizon, but she had the feeling he wasn't seeing Mother Nature's gorgeous painting of pinks and oranges.

She sat down on the lounger beside him and dragged her hands through her hair. Her braids were falling out and her hair frizzed wildly around her face. The way she had to keep scooping it back, she felt like a sheep dog and wondered not for the first time if she should buzz it all off and just go natural.

But Jesse liked her hair. And, honestly, so did she. It was a lot of work to maintain, but she liked her hair long. Her one vanity.

God, that was a girly thought. She sighed at herself and drummed up a smile for Danny. "You okay?"

He didn't answer for a long moment, then blinked and looked over at her like he just realized she was sitting there and had spoken. "Huh?"

She knocked her shoulder into his. "You look a bit shell-shocked."

He gave a half laugh. "Guess I am. That was... Seeing the guys in action... It wasn't like the training exercise. Jean-Luc taking on Schumacher like that when he could barely stand? Man. And then Jesse lunging after him? And Gabe, Quinn, and Harvard? They moved like one person when they decided to attack." He shook his head. "I've never seen anything like it."

"I know." She smiled, remembering her first encounter with HORNET. "I felt the same way the first time. Shocked, but also—"

"Exhilarated," he finished.

"Yeah. Exactly."

He looked back out over the horizon. "I was just thinking about my wife. Leah didn't want me coming here. We don't fight about much, but we fought about this. She wants me to stay with the Bureau until I retire, but..."

"You want more."

His gaze dropped to the weapon on his lap and he picked it up. "HORNET does a good thing. They help people, which is all I've ever wanted to do. But more and more, with all the politics and red tape in the Bureau, I'm not helping anyone. I feel...useless."

"Oh, I get it." Lanie scooped up a handful of sand and let it run through her fingers. "Last year, I was in the same boat. I'd worked my entire life to be a Texas Ranger like my dad was. I finally got there, and I wasn't satisfied. When I met HORNET, I thought, *this is where I belong.*"

Her smile faded. At the time, it had seemed like such a clear-cut thing. It was as if she'd been in a dark tunnel and someone had handed her a flashlight. Now she wasn't so sure. Maybe she'd won over the respect of the other guys tonight, but Jesse would never see her as a teammate. To him, she'd only ever be a lover.

God, sleeping with him had been a mistake. She wished she could chalk it up to temporary insanity, but she knew better. She'd wanted Jesse ever since he'd shown back up in her life last year. And as much as she knew she should, she couldn't regret any of it.

"I told Gabe I want in," Danny said in a rush, then pushed out a breath. "But I'm not looking forward to having this conversation with my wife."

"Hey." Lanie again knocked her shoulder into his. "I'm not usually all that great at girly stuff, but I do know one thing. If she loves you, she'll support any decision you make."

Behind them, a heavy foot crunched in the sand and she glanced back, hoping to see Jesse, but unsurprised to find

Marcus approaching. She raised a hand in greeting, and a flash of light from the roof of the building behind him caught her attention. A dull, perfectly round glint...like the rising sun reflecting off a lens.

Sniper.

"Get down." Her voice came out a croak. She tried again. "Get down! Sniper!"

Marcus didn't hesitate and dropped so fast that at first she was afraid he'd been shot.

Danny lunged to push her out of the way, but they were both too late. Too slow. Heat stripped her side and she heard a faint *umph* from Danny. Then more heat and wetness soaking through her shirt and...

Blood. So much blood, seeping out all over her hands as she rolled Danny to his back.

"Jesse!" Her shout was ragged, and not as loud as she'd wanted it to be. "Jesse, help! Danny's shot!"

She tried to stop the blood from pumping out of the ragged hole in Danny's chest while he gasped for oxygen and his face lost all color.

Oh God, it was like Gabe all over again, just in the sand this time instead of snow. This was going to destroy Jesse.

Footsteps pounded all around her and big, hard, male bodies crowded in.

"Where is he? Where's the sniper?" someone asked. She didn't know who, didn't care. She pointed at the building without looking up.

Marcus scrambled over on his hands and knees. He drew up short when he saw the damage and his complexion also lost color. "Oh fuck. Dan, hang on. Jesse's coming. He'll fix you up. Just hang on." He gripped Danny's hand and used his other to help put pressure on the wound.

Breathing hard, Lanie backed away. A tremendous pressure crushed her chest. Danny wouldn't die. Jesse would do everything in his power to make sure of that.

The guys had surrounded Danny, formed a human wall. All of them—Gabe, Quinn, Harvard, Seth, Ian, and Tank—putting their lives on the line to protect him. Even Jean-Luc had pulled himself out of the van and stood guard with them, scanning the rooftops.

Danny was protected. She should go to Connor, make sure he was safe. Jesse wouldn't be able to do his job if Connor was in danger. She ran in the direction she'd last seen Connor, but skidded to a halt when she spotted movement on a nearby rooftop.

In the distance, Tucker Quentin called out orders and his men raced across the parking lot toward another building, guns drawn. She was pretty sure they were headed in the right direction—except the movement she was seeing now was on the roof of the convention center.

Jesus. Were there two shooters?

Bullets sprayed the sand half way between her and the guys. She dropped to the ground. The guys huddled in tighter, closing ranks around Danny. Tank showed his teeth and let out a growl that rumbled across the sand.

Not another sniper, then. A sniper would have been more precise. This attack was sloppy, but it was still an attack.

Despite the growing pressure in her chest, she picked herself up, found her weapon in the sand, and ran toward the convention center. There were four flights of stairs to the roof, and each step seemed higher than the last. By the time she reached the roof door, she dragged in huge gulps of air, but still wasn't getting enough oxygen. It was like breathing underwater, drowning, but she didn't dare stop moving. If she stopped moving, she wouldn't get back up.

Lightheaded and woozy, she hit the push bar and staggered out onto the roof. Goose bumps lifted on her skin and she shivered, suddenly so very cold despite the hot rays of sunshine spilling across the water and lighting up the beach like a yellow spotlight.

And there was Jesse zigzagging down the beach toward Danny and the guys, medical bag in hand. He was magnificent. Racing to help with no thought of his own safety. A healer down to the very core of his being.

And flattened against the roof in front of her was Christian Schumacher, drawing a bead on him with a rifle.

No.

She raised her own weapon. "Christian, put the gun down and get slowly to your feet."

He glanced over his shoulder and smirked. His eyes held a glassy, unnatural sheen. "You're bleeding."

She suspected as much. The pressure in her chest was almost unbearable. She ignored it and kept her aim steady. "Why did you shoot Danny?"

"I didn't." He pressed his eye to the scope. "Though I wish I had, just to watch them all scramble."

"Who's the other shooter?"

"Fuck if I know. Your boys have made enemies. Funny how the sniper showed up with Tucker Quentin, though, isn't it?"

No. Tucker didn't have that in him. And, sure, she didn't know his men well but they had to be good guys, too. "So Defion didn't think you could handle the job and sent someone else?"

He tensed. She'd obviously hit a nerve. Without warning, he pulled the trigger, spraying the beach below with bullets.

She flinched and searched for Jesse. He'd hit the ground as the bullets zinged by, but he was already on his feet and running again. He was going to save lives today if it killed him.

She loved him for it.

And she'd protect her man so he was able to do what he

did best. She raised her weapon and fired before Schumacher could take another shot.

Schumacher grunted at the impact, but didn't drop his gun. In fact, the wound barely seemed to register. He just glanced at it like it was little more than a bee sting. "We're both bleeding now." He rolled and pointed the business end of his rifle at her. "Who do you think has the faster trigger finger?"

She shook her head. "Don't make me kill you. It doesn't have to end this way."

"I'm already dead. I failed Defion. I let this whole shitstorm of a situation spin out of control, and then I had to blow my cover to clean it up. You think Defion will take me back after that?" He laughed bitterly. "No. That sniper is coming for me next."

"We can protect you."

His eyes darted. His pupils were so constricted, they were little more than black dots. He shook his head hard, stabbed a finger in her direction. "Bullshit. Bullshit, bullshit. That's such bullshit. You woke a sleeping giant. You don't know anything about them, but they know everything about all of you. They know everything about everyone. You won't even be able to protect yourselves when they come for you. They're going to rip your little team and your fucking trainees apart piece by piece."

Her vision started graying around the edges. She blinked and tried to stay upright even though her knees wobbled. "What does Defion want?"

"To destroy Tucker Quentin and crush HORNET like the bug you are." He raised his weapon. "I should kill you. Maybe they'll take me back. Maybe— Yeah. One less busy little bee flying around, making an annoyance of herself. They'll take me back. They'll have to. They'll have to." Again he aimed the gun at her.

He might have pulled the trigger if she'd given him the chance. It wasn't exactly a kill or be killed kind of situation. He was high on something and any bullet he fired might not have even hit her. But her strength was fading fast, and she couldn't let herself pass out without knowing the threat he posed was neutralized.

Her bullet struck him in the neck. He gagged and dropped the rifle, tried to staunch the blood with clumsy fingers. It was no use. She'd hit an artery. Within seconds, his arms went limp and his head lolled back.

He was gone.

Lanie's legs gave out and she dropped to her knees, then sat back on her butt and stared at the body. She didn't realize she was crying until the tears dripped off her chin. She'd done what she had to do. Now Jesse would help Danny and all would be okay.

Everything would be okay. She could rest now. Just... rest.

Her vision began to darken.

You woke a sleeping giant.

No.

She shoved herself upright and staggered to her feet. Felt like she was moving through pudding and she couldn't catch her breath, but she had to warn her guys. And she had to tell Jesse...something important. Her brain fuzzed and she paused on one of the landings to shake her head.

No, not just something. She had to tell him she loved him. She needed him to know.

Chapter Twenty-Eight

Not again. Not again. Not a-fuckin'-gain.

The words repeated on a loop in Jesse's head as he raced across the parking lot and out onto the beach. Out of the corner of his eye, he saw Tucker Quentin and his men race toward the building where the shots originated. He wanted to call out to their medic, Rex, in case he needed a second set of hands, but it probably wasn't a good plan to draw the shooter's attention to the fact that a team of serious badasses were bearing down on him.

A stream of bullets came from somewhere and buried in the sand less than a foot from him. He hit the ground on instinct, then bounced back up before the sound of the shots even reached his ears.

His own team had formed a human wall around their fallen man, every one of them looking dangerous, pissed off, and spoiling to shoot someone. Even Jean-Luc, hunched and pale-faced, but with a gun in his hand all the same.

Jesse had to remember to give him an earful about that later.

He slid in between Jean-Luc and Ian and got his first look at his patient. Shit, this was bad.

Danny was conscious, his gaze ping-ponging anxiously all around as he breathed in rapid, shallow pants. His complexion was too white, and his skin was clammy to the touch.

"Where were you hit?" Jesse tore open his kit and got to work, looping a blood pressure cuff around his arm. Damn. BP was low and sinking fast.

"Back," Danny said between gasps.

Jesse grabbed an ambu bag and placed the mask over Danny's nose and mouth. "Marcus. Hey, I need your help, pal."

Marcus looked up at the sound of his name, tears streaming from his too-wide eyes. He didn't seem to be tracking the conversation. "Jess, you gotta help him."

"I will." Jesse guided his hand to the bag and squeezed. "Nice, easy rhythm. Squeeze, wait five seconds, squeeze again. Can you do that? Help him breathe."

Marcus nodded and took over the bag, squeezing it with blood-stained hands.

Jesse set up IVs for fluids and pain meds. He cut through Danny's shirt, then log-rolled him to check the entry wound—a tiny hole just to the left of his spine. Jesus, the bullet tore through his chest at an angle. There was no telling what all it damaged without opening him up. But that had to come later. Right now, it was all about getting him stabilized enough to transport to the nearest local hospital.

There wasn't a lot of blood from the entry wound, but he covered it with a clotting agent-treated square of gauze anyway. Gently, he laid Danny flat again and internally winced at the ragged exit wound on his upper right chest. The bullet had tumbled as it passed through. Probably damaged the lungs, and maybe the heart. He couldn't find his stethoscope in his bag, so he bent over and pressed his ear to Danny's chest. Decreased breath sounds on the right side.

Shit. Tension Pneumothorax? Made the most sense. Air was leaking into his chest cavity, constricting the right lung, causing the breathing difficulty.

Jesse tore through his bag until he found a chest dart. He didn't have time to second guess, or for the nerves that had been plaguing him for so long. All of that just disappeared. A familiar sense of detachment settled over him. He didn't see Danny, his friend and teammate. All he saw was a list of medical conditions that needed immediate treatment or the patient would die.

He was glad for it. Once again, he felt calm, steady, in control of everything from the steady beat of his own pulse to the continuing beat of Danny's.

A splash of Betadine turned Danny's chest orange. Jesse walked steady fingers down from the clavicle until he found the right spot between the second and third ribs and inserted the dart. Blood arced from the tube and splashed across Jesse's arms and chest.

Not tension pneumothorax then. Hemopneumothorax. Blood and air was filling the cavity and compressing the lung.

Danny started breathing better almost immediately as the blood evacuated the space and relief filled his eyes. "Thank you."

"All right," Jesse said and left the catheter to drain the blood while he rechecked vital signs. Still not good, but improving. Wouldn't last, though. He'd sprung a leak somewhere in his chest and without exploratory surgery, there was no way of knowing where or how to stop the bleed. "You're gonna be all right, Danny. We'll get you to a hospital, and they'll patch you up as good as new."

"He'll be okay?" Marcus asked.

He wished he could say Danny was out of the woods, but

judging by the hemopneumo and the look of the exit wound, he doubted it. There was so much more damage they couldn't see. "I bought him time. He needs surgery to repair the bleed or his chest cavity is goin' to keep fillin' up with blood until he runs out of it. We have to move. Now."

"Can't," Gabe said over his shoulder. He and the rest of the guys still stood guard. "Tuc and his team haven't found the sniper yet."

"He's not gonna start taking shots at us with Tuc's guys after him," Marcus snapped. "He's long gone. You heard Jess. Danny needs a surgeon."

"I'm okay," Danny whispered, voice soft and reedy. "I feel okay. I'm warm. I was so cold, but…I'm okay now."

No, he wasn't. Not even close. And just then, gunshots ripped through the air. Everyone tensed, but Jesse ignored the noise.

"Goddammit." He had to find the source of the blood and clamp it off or Danny wasn't going to make it to a hospital. Jesse grabbed a scalpel and scissors. "Someone hold him down." Even with the morphine pumping into his system, this was going to hurt like a bitch.

Ian, of all people, knelt to grip Danny's shoulders. He met Ian's gaze in surprise.

"Do it," Ian said. "I got him."

All right. Here goes nothing. Jesse pushed out a breath, then sliced open the side of Danny's chest, used the scissors to cut through layers of muscle and fat. Danny screamed and tried to thrash, but Ian held him still.

Jesse stayed focused on his task, looking for the bleed. It was here somewhere. Had to be here…

He ignored the sweat dripping into his eyes, ignored the gunshots thundering around him. Finally, Danny passed out, and the screaming stopped. "Marcus, keep with the bag." He didn't have time to intubate if Danny stopped breathing.

Danny's heart beat sluggishly. Blood had filled the sac around it, compressing the heart with each beat. Jesse used a needle to evacuate as much of the blood as he could…

And it filled up again.

He had to find the damn bleed.

And there it was. Yes. He clamped it off, drained the sac again, and watched the heart resume a normal beat…

For a minute.

The sac filled again. The heart itself was bleeding. He took a closer look and…yeah. The percussion of the bullet had turned Danny's internal organs to mush. The heart was damaged beyond repair.

Sick to his stomach, Jesse stopped what he was doing. He didn't need to recheck vitals to know Danny was deteriorating. Too much blood loss and still bleeding. Too much internal damage.

He covered the incision with a bandage, more out of a sense of decency than medical necessity. He stripped off his gloves, and found a space blanket in his bag to cover Danny's shivering frame. He could see Danny's body shutting down one process at a time, all of it by-the-book. Bluing lips and nail beds. Purple splotches appearing on his hands, and a check of his feet showed the same. Each breath he exhaled rattled in his throat.

Danny was dying. And, goddamn it all to hell, there was nothing more he could do to stop it. It was Gabe getting shot all over again, except this time, he really had failed. Danny wouldn't live to see his wife and kids again.

"What are you doing?" Marcus demanded. "Why are you stopping?"

His expression must have betrayed him because Marcus shook his head in denial. "No. Don't say it."

He didn't have to. Marcus knew what was about to happen as well as he did.

Danny was already coming back around to consciousness. Man, he was strong. If Jesse hadn't seen for himself the incredible damage done by the bullet, he'd almost think Danny could beat this. But he couldn't. Nobody could live with a destroyed heart.

Danny groped blindly at the air. "Marcus..."

"Hey, buddy. Relax." Marcus clasped his hand and leaned down. "You're going to be fine. Hang on a bit longer, okay? You'll be just..." His voice cracked. "Fine."

"I don't think—" Danny wheezed in a labored breath, let it out with a soft rattle. "We're going surfing today."

"We'll go tomorrow, yeah? Once we get you to the hospital, you'll be back out on a board in no time."

"You'll...take care of Leah?"

"You know I will, man, but don't talk like that. Don't talk like—like that."

Danny's gaze drifted over to Jesse. "Lanie...okay?"

Lanie.

He froze, for the first time realizing she wasn't among the group. He'd been so focused on his patient, it hadn't left room for any other worries. And then he remembered the blood. There had seemed to be a lot of it, but very little of it had come from Danny until after the needle entered his chest.

Because it had come from Lanie.

He scanned the area, spotted her staggering across the grass in front of the convention center. She collapsed before reaching the beach. He grabbed his med kit and bolted toward her.

"Jess!" someone shouted and gunfire popped behind him, but he ignored it all. He didn't care about the sniper, didn't care about his own safety. He had to get to her.

She was unconscious, bleeding, her shirt soaked through. Her injuries mirrored Danny's, except there was no exit wound—the bullet must have entered his left back, exited his right chest, and hit her left chest. Even without his stethoscope he could hear her uneven breath sounds. Her pulse weakened by the second, and her blood pressure was dropping.

God. Was she bleeding into her chest? Was he going to lose her, too?

His hands shook as he fumbled through his bag for another chest dart. His heart hammered, and he couldn't find the damn thing.

Where was it? Where was it? Where the hell—

He finally found the dart right in the pocket where he always kept them. Christ. He needed to focus, but his hands shook so badly he couldn't get the sterile packaging open.

He was losing his cool, the calm detachment he worked so hard to cultivate cracking around him like huge sheets of glacial ice in the summer sun. He was too frantic. Too scattered. Too goddamn scared. He'd lost all objectivity and that was why Danny was dying. That was why Lanie would die.

A sob ripped free from his throat as he struggled with the dart.

"Dad."

Okay, now he was hearing things because Connor couldn't be here. He was safely tucked behind the van, out of the line of fire, away from the blood and carnage. Exactly where Jesse always wanted him to be.

"Dad!" His son's hands wrapped around his, stopping his struggle with the packaging.

Panicked, he gazed up into eyes so very much like his own. "What are you doin'? You were supposed to stay behind the van! Connor, Jesus. I can't lose you."

"Dad," Connor said with a grave kind of wisdom no kid his age should ever possess. There were tears in his eyes, but he didn't let them fall. "Dad, breathe. You got this."

"I-I can't—what if I fail again? I saved Gabe with pure

luck. Now Danny's dying. What if I lose her?"

"Dad, I've seen you work," Connor said firmly and squeezed his hands. "You got this."

"I love her," he said softly. He didn't know why, but it suddenly seemed important to say out loud.

"That doesn't mean you're going to fail her. You think it does, but it doesn't."

"I love you. I failed you."

Connor shook his head. "No. I get you now, Dad. I know why you tried so hard to keep your distance. You thought you were helping me, keeping me away from all this." He waved a hand at their surroundings as gunfire continued in the distance. "But keeping me away, it hurt me. It'll hurt Lanie too if you stay all bottled up. Use what you're feeling. If you love her, use that to help save her. You can do this."

The certainty in his son's voice settled something inside him. Like a switch flipped, the panic drained away and he went into the zone again. It had always been a cold, objective place, a place he'd strived to maintain even in his day-to-day life. That detachment. That clinical observation. But Connor was right. Staying there, locked up inside himself, wasn't working for him anymore. It caused nothing but distress and panic when he slipped up and lost his cool, and his distance only hurt the people he loved.

So he opened the doors on that cold, clinical place, and let the love and fear and all of the messy emotions flow in. Amazingly, they didn't detract from what he knew he had to do. He was still in the zone. Only now, there was a driving sense of urgency, a sense of importance he'd never felt before.

He clasped his boy's cheek in one hand. "How did you get to be so brilliant?"

Connor's lips twisted. "I'm told I have a smart dad."

Jesse got to work. He cut open Lanie's shirt and handed Connor the bottle of Betadine. "Sterilize the ribs on her left side."

When Connor was done, he ripped open the dart and trailed his fingers down Lanie's chest, counting the ribs, looking for the slight depression between the second and third. There. He pushed the needle in and felt it pop as it broke through to where it needed to be. Air rushed through the catheter. Not blood. Her chest expanded fully and her eyelids fluttered.

Connor released a relieved huff of air, followed by a laugh. "She's okay!"

Jesse checked her vitals. The bullet was still inside her and would need to be removed, but everything was stabilizing. Blood pressure, pulse, lung sounds—all good. The bullet had lost so much velocity by the time it tore through Danny and hit her it hadn't caused the same kind of damage.

Thank God.

Her eyes opened, focused. "Jesse?"

He leaned over so she didn't try to sit up, and pushed her wild hair back from her face. "Welcome back."

"Where…did I go?" she asked on a breath of sound.

"Nowhere. You're not goin' anywhere."

"Okay. Good." She groaned. "I have a bone to pick with you."

He grinned. Here she was with a bullet wound and a recently re-inflated lung, raring to tell him off. Yup, he was completely head over heels, crazy in love with her. Hell, maybe he always had been. "I can't wait to hear about it."

"Dad stuck a huuuge needle in your chest!" Connor exclaimed, the wise old soul suddenly a kid again. "Like this long!" He held up two fingers to demonstrate. "It was kinda cool, and I'm pretty sure he saved your life. He loves you. He won't tell you himself, but you should probably kiss him anyway."

Lanie's lips curved. "Yeah," she said softly. "Or he could

kiss me."

Heart in his throat, Jesse leaned down and pressed his lips to hers. Soft. Gentle. He wanted to kiss the hell out of her, scoop her up in his arms and hold her tight, but he was wary of hurting her.

Later.

Yes, later, when they were safe and she was healed, he was going to hold her. And he might not ever let her go.

Chapter Twenty-Nine

Lanie wished he'd hold her. She knew it was a stupid and girly thing to want, especially after railing so hard against being coddled, but whatever. She was a contrary bitch on her best days, so he'd have to get use to it.

But Jesse pulled away.

She viciously squashed the disappointment. Of course he backed off. This wasn't exactly the best place for a make-out sesh. Defion was gunning for them, and an unknown sniper had shot—

"Where's Danny?" She tried to sit and sucked in a breath at the incredible pain. Jesse planted a hand on her shoulder and kept her still. Only then did she notice the needle Connor had mentioned sticking out her chest. Oh, okay. That was disturbing. She suddenly felt like she might be sick all over Jesse's boots.

"Shh," Jesse said and soothed a hand over her head. "You need to take it easy."

"I really don't like needles."

"I know. But that one has to stay put for now."

"Oh God." She lay back again and closed her eyes. "Is Danny safe? He pushed me out of the way."

When he didn't answer right away, she opened her eyes again. "Jesse?"

"Let's worry about us first, okay?" Regret flashed across his face before he could hide it, which told her far more than his non-answer.

Tears blurred her vision. "Is he okay?" she demanded, voice cracking. But she already knew the answer. An affirmative wouldn't put that much sorrow in her man's eyes.

Jesse moistened his lips. "No, darlin'. He's not."

No. She struggled to sit and made it upright this time, but dizziness swamped her. Jesse's hands settled on her shoulders.

"Hey, whoa. Lanie, lay down."

"Where is he? I want to see him."

Jesse looked at Connor and opened his mouth as if about to say something, but stopped before uttering a sound. He winced, but said, "Con, help me get her up? It's safer over there anyway."

As she gazed back and forth between them, following some kind of unspoken conversation, she realized something had changed for them. Jesse wasn't shutting his son out anymore and Connor wasn't purposely needling his dad. As soon as she could think more clearly, she'd ask Jesse about it.

When the two lifted her to her feet, pain fuzzed her mind and she regretted her request to go anywhere. She swayed and tried to talk her stomach out of expelling the coffee she'd drank last night.

Jesse scooped her up into his arms. "We have to hurry. We'll be exposed. Con, grab my bag."

She wanted to protest. She wasn't a damsel in distress, thank you very much. But at the same time...

Yes. This was right. This was exactly what she had wanted, and his arms felt so incredibly good around her.

"Do you think the sniper is still up there?" Connor asked.

"No," Jesse said. "He's long gone, but until we get the all-clear, we're goin' to act like he's still there. We're not takin' any chances, so run as fast as you can, okay?"

Connor nodded and took off like a bolt.

"Good boy." Jesse readjusted her in his arms. When she winced, he pressed a kiss to her forehead. "I'm sorry. This ain't goin' to feel good."

"I'm fine," she said through gritted teeth and wrapped her good arm around his neck. "Get moving, cowboy."

"Hang on." And he followed right behind his son.

By the time he made it behind the wall of men protecting Danny, she had tears streaming from her eyes, but she refused to make a sound in pain. Jesse would hate hurting her and she didn't want to lay that burden of guilt on him. From what she could tell, he was already struggling with enough of that.

He gently set her down in the sand beside Danny and she caught her breath at the sight of the man. He looked nothing like he had only minutes ago. It was as if the big, happy man who only wanted to help people had wilted. Blue tinged lips stood out against the waxy whiteness of his face. His eyes were half open but clouded and unfocused. He was still breathing—barely. Deep gasps followed by long periods of stillness. Death breathing. She reached for his hand, found it cold and limp.

"Jess—" Her voice broke. "Is there anything…?"

He shook his head when she trailed off. His features pinched, and she knew he was trying not to cry. "The bullet significantly damaged his heart. I tried to buy him time to get to a hospital, but…it wasn't enough. I couldn't do enough. He just keeps bleedin'."

"Jesus," one of the guys muttered from the circle. Someone else sniffed hard, but they all still had their backs to the dying man, still scanning, sweeping the area with their weapons.

This could be her right now. If Danny hadn't lunged at her, knocking her out of the way, the bullet would have hit her first. She'd be the one drawing her last breaths now.

Danny exhaled one last time with a soft rattle, and then his chest stilled. Jesse didn't move at first, then slowly reached out to check his pulse. A full minute ticked by with Jesse's fingers pressed against Danny's neck. She stared hard at him, silently pleading he'd find a heartbeat or some sign that it wasn't over.

At last, he sat back on his heels, shook his head slightly, and looked at his watch. "Time of death—" His voice cracked. "0614."

The sound Marcus made was more animal than human. He bent over and gathered his best friend's limp body up in his arms.

She blinked and more hot tears trickled down her cheeks. "Danny gave his life for me. He saved me."

Marcus looked at her with bleary red eyes. "He does that. All he wants is to save people. All he ever wanted...was to save people."

But they hadn't been able to save him.

The sentiment went unspoken, but not unheard.

She gazed up at Jesse in time to see the anguished look cross his face. In a lot of ways, Jesse and Danny hadn't been so very different. They were both healers, saviors. This had to be tearing out his heart. "Marcus, Jesse tried—"

"I know." His voice wavered, but when he gazed up at Jesse there was nothing but sincerity in his eyes. "I know if you couldn't fix him, nobody could."

Jesse swallowed hard. And she saw it—the flash of guilt again. The kind of guilt that gnawed at you, twisted you up. He was going to blame himself for this for a very long time, and she wished she knew how to help him.

Chapter Thirty

If you couldn't fix him, nobody could.

Marcus's words played on repeat in Jesse's head as they watched the team's jet, affectionately called the Hornet's Nest, land at the airport shortly after noon. Right on schedule.

If things had gone according to plan, they'd all be soaking in some tropical sunshine today. Gabe and Seth would have reunited with Audrey and Phoebe here at the airport before going on to the hotel. Quinn would've headed home to Mara. Connor and the recruits would've bonded over volleyball and trips to the beach. He and Lanie would have spent the day in her cabana discovering each other.

And Marcus and Danny would be surfing.

But things hadn't gone according to plan. At all.

If you couldn't fix him, nobody could.

A lie. He'd never felt more like a fraud in his life. Danny could've lived. He'd started declining the moment Jesse had cut him open and gone searching for the bleed. If he hadn't done it...maybe Danny wouldn't have bled out before he reached the hospital.

If ifs and buts were pots and pans...

He could almost hear his mom's voice repeating her favorite idiom. And, as always, she was right. He had to stop thinking about it, stop torturing himself with everything he did or didn't do, or else he was going to fall into that hole he'd clawed so desperately out of a few years ago.

The Hornet's Nest came to a stop on the tarmac and a few minutes later, the door opened. Audrey came running out of there so fast her feet barely touched the ground. She took a flying leap into Gabe's arms and he dropped his cane, catching her despite his bad leg. Audrey was crying. The two kissed, held each other in a tight embrace, and kissed again.

Phoebe was only a few steps behind, and Seth met her halfway across the tarmac. More kissing, more hugging.

Jace Garcia, HORNET's pilot, appeared next. He took one look at the group of them and shook his head. "You *cabrones* always have all the fun without me."

Normally, a comment like that would have elicited jokes and jabs at Garcia. But nobody was much in the mood for joking, and when Garcia spotted the coffin waiting to go home, his smirk faded.

"Who?" But then, he didn't need anyone to answer. He had eyes and could see who was missing. "Danny." He swore in Spanish and if Jesse wasn't mistaken, the usually inscrutable bastard actually had tears in his eyes. "It's always the good ones."

"Which is why we'll all live forever," Tucker Quentin muttered to nobody in particular as he stepped up beside Jesse and swiped a sleeve over his sweating brow.

"Did you find the sniper?" Jesse asked.

"No. He got away, but not before he winged one of my

guys. The asshole's a good shot."

"Why Danny?" He was just thinking out loud and didn't really expect an answer, but Tucker went very still beside him. Before that moment, he'd never seen the man look less like the billionaire Hollywood heartthrob he was, and more like a straight-up killing machine. "What's wrong?"

"I don't think the shot was meant for him."

"Then who?"

Tuc released a long breath. "While you were working on Danny, Lanie found Schumacher on the roof of the convention center. He was taking potshots at us, but he didn't pull the trigger on Danny. He said Defion has it out for us. They must have put Schumacher in our training program as a plant to keep an eye on us. They're HumInt's biggest competitor and they were probably worried about what we were up to out there in Wyoming."

HumInt, Inc. was HORNET's parent company, the private military contractor arm of Tuc's empire, Quentin Enterprises. Jesse hadn't thought there was any group on the PMC circuit as big or well-connected as HumInt. "Is Defion a threat?"

Tuc waved a hand in the general direction of the hotel and the look on his dirt smeared face said *duh.*

"No shit," Jesse snapped. "But they were there after a very specific target and shit went sideways on them. I mean, are they a threat to us? To HORNET and you?"

Tucker looked at the coffin, sleek and black in the sunlight. Like an oil spill. "I don't know," he admitted and rubbed both hands over his face. All at once, he looked exhausted. "I don't know what their end game is. I fucking hate not knowing, but I'll find out. I always do." He dropped his hands, sighed. "I'm sorry for Danny's loss. I was prepared to offer him a job. He'd have made an excellent addition to HORNET."

"He'd have taken the job."

"Mm." Tucker hummed an agreement, then turned and clapped Jesse's shoulder. "I'm going to need you now more than ever."

"Me?"

His gaze traveled over the pavement to the happy couples still holding each other. "Gabe and Quinn are out of the field permanently. They'll still do the behind-the-scenes work and run the training center, but I can't ask them to put their lives on the line anymore. HORNET needs a strong, stable leader."

It's not me, Jesse wanted to say. If Tuc only knew how unstable he really was, always teetering on the edge, always one spark away from an explosion he might not come back from. If Tuc knew, he sure as fuck wouldn't be getting a job offer now. "I'm not the right man."

Tuc's brow arched. "Then which of the men do you suggest I offer the job to?"

He spotted Lanie walking across the parking lot. She was supposed to be on bed rest, but he'd had a hell of a time keeping her there when there had been so much damage control to do. She was moving slowly, painfully, but she was in surprisingly good condition considering she'd had air in her chest, crushing her heart and lungs, less than six hours ago. But once he'd drained the air and re-inflated her lung, her bullet wound had proven to be very non-fatal. He'd been able to remove the bullet with tweezers and close the wound with a couple stiches.

She was an amazing warrior. Brave, strong, and stubborn.

He watched her sit down beside Marcus and wrap her arms around him. Yes, she was a warrior, but she also possessed a softness the rest of them lacked, a kind of all-encompassing empathy that even the best men he knew weren't capable of.

She was so afraid she didn't have a place on the team. But she did. She was their heart.

He turned back to Tuc. "Who said anything about a man?"

• • •

Lanie felt like shit. Not only because she'd been shot, but also because watching all the happy couples reunite only served to drive home the fact that Danny gave his life for her. He'd shoved her out of the way, and because of that, he'd never have a happy reunion with his wife.

To make maters worse, her own happily ever after seemed to be slipping farther away with each passing minute. Jesse had distanced himself again. Okay, true, he'd had a lot to do in the last few hours, but now that they were getting ready to go home, he still hadn't spoken to her. He stood over there with Tuc Quentin and hadn't spared her a glance.

Okay, girl, enough with the pity party.

She turned away from him and spotted Marcus over by his best friend's coffin, watching all the happy couples come together on the tarmac. God, she'd never seen him look so defeated. Marcus was one of those guys with a bigger-than-life personality. He lit up every room he walked into, and was always quick with a joke and that charming mega-watt smile of his.

Now, he was just…broken.

She walked over and set a hand on the coffin. A knot rose in her throat. She hadn't known Danny long, but she felt his loss as sharply as a knife through her heart. She couldn't imagine what Marcus was feeling. "Are you okay?"

He didn't speak for a long time. So long, she almost turned away, figuring he didn't want the company.

Finally, he sucked in a sharp breath and looked at her. Tears spiked the thick lashes rimming his blue eyes. "Lanie. I don't know what to do."

No, he didn't need solitude right now. He needed a friend. She sat down beside him, careful not to jostle her wounded side. "What would Danny have done if the situation were reversed?"

"He'd take me home to my mom."

She placed a hand on his knee and waited until he looked at her. "Then take him home."

He shook his head. "It's all wrong. It *should* be reversed. It *should* be me in that coffin. I don't have a wife, kids..."

"You have a mother. I know you're close with her and she'd grieve if it had been you."

He bent double and buried his face in his hands. "Oh fuck. What do I tell his wife? I don't know what to say to Leah. She's going to blame me and she'll be right. This is my fault. He never should've been here. I convinced him to come. He never should have been here."

At a loss, she pulled him into her arms and held him while he cried. What else could she do? Her own eyes teared up and she again glanced toward Jesse. Tomorrow wasn't guaranteed. Hell, she wouldn't have had a tomorrow if not for Danny.

Jesse might break her heart again. Being with him might impact her future with HORNET. But not being with him when her whole heart and body demanded it, seemed like an insult to Danny's sacrifice.

Both Jesse and Tuc looked her way right then. They seemed to be intently talking about her, which wasn't a comfortable thought. Maybe her career with HORNET was already over. If that was the case, what was stopping her from pursuing something more with Jesse?

She held Marcus for a few minutes more, and cried a few tears of her own. "I wish I'd known Danny better."

"He was impressed by you." Marcus gave a watery laugh. "He also called Jesse a few names for not snapping you up."

She laughed, too. "I think we would've been really good friends."

"Yeah." Marcus finally pulled away and swiped at his

eyes like he was angry with himself for the tears. "He was a—a great friend. The best."

"He was more than that. He was your brother." She leaned in and kissed his forehead, then cupped his beard-stubbled cheeks in her palms. "And please don't think you need to be a tough guy right now. You're allowed to cry."

A large shadow fell over them and she gazed up at... everyone. Jesse, Gabe, Quinn, Seth, Harvard, Ian, Jace Garcia, and Tucker. Even Jean-Luc had been brought over in his wheelchair by Rex, the medic from Tucker's team. The women, Audrey and Phoebe, stood off to the side.

One by one, they each embraced Marcus, then paid their respects to the coffin. Gabe and Quinn both pounded a pin into the lid—their SEAL tridents. Jean-Luc murmured something in another language, then lay his *gris-gris* on the coffin between the pins. Tucker stood with his hand on the coffin for a long time, his expression torn between devastation and rage.

When it was Ian's turn, he held onto Marcus a bit longer than everyone else. "I'm sorry," he said in a broken voice. He turned away without looking at the coffin as if he couldn't bear the sight of it.

They were family.

Having come from a very dysfunctional family herself, their bond was a beautiful thing to witness. And, God, she wished she didn't still feel like such an outsider.

"It's time to take him home," Gabe finally said.

Marcus nodded and took hold of one of the coffin's handles. Jesse, Harvard, Quinn, Seth, and Tuc took up positions around the coffin. Together, the group lifted it and moved silently across the tarmac to the plane.

The others, including Tuc's men, all saluted as the procession passed.

Chapter Thirty-One

"Jess, you have a minute?"

Jesse stopped and cursed silently. Now that everyone was safely onboard the plane, his only goal was to make sure Lanie was okay and comfortable. He'd been on his way to her bunk, but that was Gabe's voice calling to him from the conference room. If it were anyone but Gabe, he'd tell them to fuck off. He wished it were anyone but Gabe. Unfortunately, it was the boss-man and he respected the guy too much. He backtracked to the door and peeked inside.

A few years ago, Tuc had remodeled HORNET's jet to include several bunkrooms, a prison cell, and this conference room. There was a wide array of technology on the walls meant to help plan missions, and a table that sat ten.

"Have a seat." Gabe was in his usual spot at the head of the table. He waved a hand, indicating Jesse should sit. A laptop sat in front of him. Harvard must have given it to him—Gabe was good at a lot of things, but technology was not one of them. Not to mention, it had a Star Trek sticker on the back, which certainly wasn't Gabe's.

Jesse jerked his thumb over one shoulder. "I was actually on my way to check on Lanie…"

"This won't take long," Gabe said.

So much for getting out of this. Not that he really thought the excuse would work, but it had been worth the shot. Steeling himself for whatever was about to go down, Jesse stepped inside and shut the door when Gabe indicated he should. He took off his Stetson and placed it on the table, but didn't sit down even though his ankle, now in a plastic air cast, was throbbing. "If this is about the field commander position, I already talked to Tuc."

"I know."

"And?"

"And we're discussing your suggestion." He waved that conversation aside like it was an annoying bug. "That's not why I called you in here." He pinned Jesse with his gaze. "You need to stop treating me like I'm going to break."

Okay, that hadn't been anywhere on Jesse's radar for this convo. "W-what?"

"I'm not dead," Gabe said very evenly, "and I'm not dying anytime soon."

"With all due respect, boss, you nearly *did* die."

Gabe's jaw tightened, but then he inclined his head in acknowledgement. "Yes, I'm aware, but that has nothing to do with why I'm getting out of the field. Audrey's pregnant, and I intend to be around to help her raise our baby."

"Oh. Wow. Congratulations." Now Jesse sat. Or more, collapsed into the chair. It felt a bit like Gabe had dropped a bomb on him. Though he knew Gabe wasn't taking a dig at his parenting failures, he still couldn't help but think of how much he'd missed of Connor's life.

"Thank you," Gabe said, and the big man all but shone with happiness for a second before he shut it down and slid seamlessly back into badass commander mode. "I'm not taking a step back because I'm broken. I can still do the job."

"You tire too easily," Jesse pointed out.

Another slight incline of his head. "You're right. I'm not at full strength. Yet. My doctor assures me I'll get there. I'm alive and I'm healing and that's because of you."

"No. I didn't do anything—"

"You think I got lucky?" Gabe interrupted. "That it was a miracle I survived?"

"Yes. By all accounts, you should have died."

"No, that's only by *your* account. You think you did nothing, but everyone I've talked to about the hours after I was shot says differently. Including Lanie, and she was right there by your side through the whole thing."

Jesse said nothing to that. He didn't know what to say.

Gabe grabbed his cane, pushed back from the table, and stood. He motioned to the computer. "There's someone here who has been wanting to speak to you for some time." He limped out, pausing only to squeeze Jesse's shoulder as he passed. "Whatever you decide, we're behind you."

Jesse sat in silence for a whole minute once Gabe was gone, staring at the back of the computer. Finally, a voice with an accent somewhere between British and Indian said, "Hello?"

Jesse got up and walked over. He recognized the thin, spectacled man on the screen—Dr. Jayesh Bhatt, the surgeon who had handled Gabe's initial surgeries in the UK, and one of the most revered trauma surgeons in the world.

Jesus. He should've taken some time to clean up in the last few hours. He still looked like he was in war zone. He tried unsuccessfully to brush down his out of control hair, then took the seat Gabe had vacated. "Dr. Bhatt."

Bhatt smiled warmly. It creased his cheeks and crinkled

his dark eyes behind his glasses. "So you're the medic who saved Gabe's life."

"Oh no. That was your doin'. I just kept him alive long enough to get him to you."

"No easy feat, given the situation and the damage done. I know of maybe five, ten others with that kind of talent, and most of them are doctors. I can assure you if anyone but you had been on the battlefield with him, he wouldn't be alive today to share the joyous news of his impending fatherhood. Absolutely no question in my mind."

"It was luck." Jesse's throat tightened and he cleared it. "I'm not as good as you think I am. I lost one of our men today."

"I'm sorry to hear that. What happened?"

"He was shot in the chest by a sniper. Hemopneumothorax. I made the decision to open him up right there, try to clamp the bleed, but once I got in..." He trailed off, remembering the pulpy mess of muscle that should have been Danny's heart. "His heart was destroyed."

Bhatt sighed, took off his glasses. "I'm about to tell you the hard truth of medicine, Jesse. One I still struggle with even after nearly thirty years of practicing. You can't save them all. You'll lose ones you thought were stable, and you'll save ones, like Gabe, you thought were not long for this world. If you weren't able to save your man today, I'm sorry to say there's likely nobody who could've. It's a hard truth, like I said, but it's one you need to learn to live with if you want to practice medicine." He paused and stared into Jesse's eyes for a beat. "You do want to become a doctor, don't you?"

Again, his throat tightened, and his heart started banging hard enough to put a rock concert to shame. "More than anything. It's all I've ever wanted, but I can't get into med school."

Bhatt replaced his glasses and sat back. "Are your

university marks bad?" His smile said he already knew the answer to that, but Jesse replied anyway.

"No. I worked my ass off in my undergrad classes and rocked the MCAT, but I don't have an honorable discharge from the Army, and I've been to therapy for depression and anger management. Nobody's willing to take a chance on me with my past."

Bhatt sat back in his chair. It was evening wherever he was, orange-pink sunlight spilling across his face from a window somewhere off screen. In the background, a call to prayer sounded over loudspeakers.

Bhatt looked toward something to his left, then refocused on the screen. "I won't be back in London for another week, but when I get home, I'll send a letter of recommendation to any university in the world. Your choice."

Jesse half rose from his seat in shock. "Sir?"

Bhatt gave his eye-crinkling smile again. "I'm willing to take a chance on you."

Chapter Thirty-Two

It was a long while before Lanie was comfortable enough to find sleep, and not because the jet's bunks were uncomfortable. Tucker Quentin hadn't skimped on creature comforts during the jet's remodel. But her side hurt, and her heart hurt, and she couldn't shake the feeling that Jesse was avoiding her.

She finally fell asleep somewhere over the Atlantic. When she woke, the plane was over land. She groped around under her pillow for her phone and the time. She'd slept for six hours. They had to be close to home now.

She rolled over and realized for the first time she was no longer alone. Someone had claimed the other bed.

No, not just someone. Her someone. Her only one.

Jesse was propped against the wall, long jean-clad legs hanging over the edge of the bunk. He'd traded one of his boots for an air cast, and she was glad to see it. About time he took care of himself instead of everyone else. His Stetson tipped down over his face like a cowboy in an old Western and judging by his lolling head, he was sound asleep. He'd wake up with one hell of a neck ache.

She swung out of her bed and grabbed her pillow. She stuffed it between his shoulder and the wall and gently pushed his head toward it.

He woke with a start, then winced and rubbed his neck. "Ah, damn."

God, he was cute sometimes. "Why didn't you lay down?"

"I didn't mean to fall asleep," he said and yawned. "I came in to see how you were doin', sat down, and that's the last I remember."

"How long were you out?"

He checked his watch. "Twenty minutes."

Not nearly long enough, she thought. Exhaustion lined his handsome face and carved shadows under his eyes. She reached out and gently traced one of those lines with her fingertips. He caught her wrist, turned his lips to her palm. The tender brush of his lips sent bolts of desire right down her center.

She stepped toward him, letting her intent show clearly in her eyes. He didn't try to stop her. She climbed up onto the bed and straddled his lap. Kissing him, the man she'd loved for more years than she cared to admit, felt like a trip down the rabbit hole, where reality and unreality collided. But this time she let herself fall, because whether or not this was real, she needed it. Needed him. She'd put on the tough act for the benefit of the guys, but in truth, her nerves were shot. Jesse knew it, too. That was why he was sitting here, watching over her, when he should be resting himself. He knew her. He knew that without him, without this kiss, she'd be lying in her bunk, sobbing, trying to pull herself back together so nobody saw how much the last twelve hours had destroyed her.

Oh God, she wanted him.

She surged forward and sealed her mouth back to his. He groaned, a rumble of need from deep in his chest. His hands moved from her hips to her spine, pressing her closer. She broke contact just long enough to pull off her shirt. He tensed up underneath her at the sight of her bullet wound and played his fingers over the edge of the white gauze bandage.

"Don't. I'm okay. We both are." She stopped his hand, and instead guided it up to her breast. He cupped her, molded her into his palm. She loved watching him explore her body, loved the contrast of his tanned skin against her darker. He traced light circles around her nipple until it puckered so hard it ached. Only then did he dip his head and suck it into his mouth, simultaneously relieving some of the delicious pressure building inside her and igniting it.

She bowed back, giving him better access. "Jesse, I need you. Do you have—"

He was already pulling a condom from his pocket. She lifted herself enough to finish undressing. Watched him unzip and roll the condom on. There was something undeniably sexy in the careless way he handled himself. She prowled back onto his lap and settled over him again, but he caught her hips before she could sink down his length.

"Lanie, wait. Are you sure you're well enough to do this?"

She leaned in and nipped his bottom lip. "Yes. I need you."

"Thank God." He filled her in one deep thrust. Her body ached from the beating it had taken, but she ignored it all, rolled her hips and focused on the heat and sensations only Jesse had the power to stir within her.

Each time their bodies came together, she felt more alive. Although they both may have come close last night, neither of them was dead yet.

She came fast in a long sweep of pleasure that left her bones rubber and her muscles liquid. But no, she wasn't ready for it to be over yet. The connection was too intimate, too perfect. Everything she needed. She slowed the roll of her hips until she was barely moving, instead using her inner walls to stroke him.

Jesse's entire body coiled tight. His head fell back against the wall, and his hands tightened around her waist. The tendons in his neck popped as he fought to hold back his orgasm. Even now he was fighting, always so afraid to lose his grip on his control.

She leaned forward, nuzzled his neck, kissed his ear. "I love you, Jesse."

She tightened around him again. His fingers dug into her back and his hips bucked upward as he finally let go.

"Oh, Jesus," he breathed and leaned into her, pressing his forehead to her chest. His breath cooled the sweat on her skin.

She smiled and tangled her fingers into his hair. They'd knocked his Stetson off. "Helluva long night," she murmured.

And, like that, the deep, strong bond she thought they'd just forged together snapped.

"Yeah." Groaning, he picked her up, set her aside, and stood to deal with the condom. He came back a moment later, zipped and buttoned. A sure sign he wasn't looking for a round two. He stared at her for a long moment, and she got the feeling he was rehearsing some kind of speech inside his head.

Oh yeah. He was definitely going to break her heart again.

And, still, she didn't regret it.

He picked up his Stetson. Knocked it against his thigh like it was dirty. "My head's fucked right now. I keep replayin' Danny's...and then Connor and you and—" He stopped, seemed to regroup. "I'm gonna need some time, Lanie."

"Okay," she said slowly. She climbed off the bed, found her underwear and tank top, and pulled them on. Whatever was coming, she was sure it wasn't a conversation she wanted to have naked.

"I'm gonna need some time," he said again, and she wondered if he was trying to convince himself or her. "Unless you still want our relationship to be only about sex?"

"You know I don't. Honestly, I never wanted to stop there. I was just…afraid." She drew a breath. If she was going to tell the truth, it was now or never. "You broke my heart when we were kids."

"I know," he said softly. "I feel awful for that. I didn't know what I was doin'."

"I loved you, Jesse Warrick. I guess I never stopped."

"What I feel for you… Christ, it scares me." He put the Stetson on and gazed down at her from under the brim. "But I've been down this road three times before. Every time I thought I was in love, and I thought the woman I loved was in love with me, through thick and thin. And every time, I got my heart stomped on. I don't want to get hurt again, but more than that, I have to think about Connor. I've spent way too little time thinkin' about what's best for him and I need to make that up to him." He lightly traced her cheek with the tips of his fingers. "So give me time to sort out all of my shit. Can you wait for me?"

She nodded and he bent down to kiss her very gently on the lips. Then he was gone.

She touched her lips. Yes, she'd wait for him. Hell, she'd already waited nearly twenty years. What was a few more?

Chapter Thirty-Three

The call from Gabe hadn't been unusual in itself. Lanie had taken many calls from him in the past. What was unusual was the formal nature of his request to meet him at Quinn and Mara's house. He sounded stiff, even for him.

After he hung up, she stared at the phone for a long moment.

They were going to fire her. It was all she could think. She'd killed Schumacher and didn't follow protocol and now they'd decided she wasn't working out for the team and—

Whatever.

She set the phone aside and stood. Glanced around her little house. Dammit, she liked her home here, with its wood-burning fireplace, claw-foot bathtub, and the rustic reclaimed wood she'd chosen for the cabinets in the kitchen. In fact, it was the first place she'd ever owned that felt like hers, the first place she'd considered a home. She'd hate to leave it, but if HORNET fired her, she had no reason to stay in Wyoming. Jesse certainly hadn't given her a reason. In fact, he hadn't given her anything in the weeks since returning from Martinique. Not even a freaking text.

He said he'd needed time, but she was starting to suspect by "time" he'd actually meant "never."

As in, "I never want to see you again."

Which hurt like a bitch, but she'd get over it. Maybe. Well, probably not, but she'd survive. She'd soldier on. The same as she'd always done.

On her way out the door, she passed the gray barn cat that had wandered over from the Warrick ranch and inexplicably adopted her as his person. His given name had been Lucifer, though she'd taken to calling him Lunchmeat out of spite of his adoration for her. She didn't even like cats, but as she stared down at the furry lump of fat stretched out in the morning sun on her front porch, she realized she'd miss him if she left. A lot. They had a routine. He'd wake her up ungodly early for breakfast, and she'd threaten to make a sandwich out of him. After breakfast, they'd mutually ignore each other until he was ready for dinner, and the process repeated. Sometimes there was some sneaky cuddling that neither would admit to under oath. The whole arrangement worked for them. Actually, it worked better than every single one of her past relationships.

Maybe Lunchmeat should go with her, wherever she ended up.

She gave the cat a belly rub. He promptly curled up and bit her hand. It was another routine she'd miss if she left him behind. "Pack your litter box, buddy. If they give me the boot, we're not sticking around."

She decided to walk the half mile to Quinn's house. It was shaping up to be a gorgeous summer day, the sun bright in a cloudless blue sky, giving everything a golden glow. Plus, walking gave her a few more moments to enjoy the life she'd been building here. Was it perfect? No. But it was worlds better than the lonely life she'd led in El Paso.

God. She didn't want to leave.

All too soon, she found herself at Quinn and Mara's house. Their cat, Hawkeye, was stretched out in a patch of sun on their porch much like Lunchmeat had been on hers. He was blocking the top step, and she was forced to step over him as she passed. The one-eyed beast lifted his head and seemed to glare at her.

She glared right back. "Lunchmeat is cuter."

Hawkeye flicked his tail—she figured it was the cat equivalent of the middle finger—and went back to his nap.

"Stop antagonizing Hawk," Mara's voice said from inside.

She pushed open the screen. "I wasn't antagonizing him. We have an understanding. A relationship based in mutual dislike. It works for us."

Quinn and Mara's dog, B.J., nearly keeled over in excitement at having a visitor, hopping around on her three legs. Her curled, bushy tail was nothing but a high-speed blur of tan fur. Grinning, Lanie bent down to pick her up. She was not the brightest pup in the litter, but boy, was she sweet.

She had to fend off dog kisses as she carried B.J. into the living room. Mara sat in one of the recliners, a sundress stretched tight over her big belly, her swollen ankles propped up on a pillow on the footrest.

She fanned herself with a magazine. "Ugh. Get this kid out of me."

Lanie set B.J. down and smirked at her best friend. "Girl, you'll get no sympathy from me. You did this to yourself."

Mara grinned. "So worth it."

"You won't be saying that when you're trying to push that kid out. You'll be threatening to cut off Quinn's balls."

"He says I did threaten that and worse last time."

Lanie *tsked*. "And yet you let him do this to you again."

She rubbed her belly like she was already stroking her baby's cheek. "Still worth it."

"I hope so." Audrey Van Amee-Bristow came out of the downstairs bathroom with one hand pressed to her belly. She looked genuinely green. "Because right now I'm wondering what the hell I've done to myself."

"Not going to tell you it's easy," Mara said as Audrey flopped down on the couch. "But you'll forget all the discomforts when your baby is placed in your arms."

Audrey splayed her hand over her still flat stomach. "I hope she has Gabe's eyes. He has such pretty eyes."

Gabe Bristow, the man who could glare an oil stain off a driveway, had pretty eyes? Lanie tried not to snort at that, but didn't quite succeed. When the two hormonal women frowned at her, she covered her gaffe by asking, "How do you know it's a she? Isn't it, like, the size of a pea right now?"

"I just have a feeling." Audrey shrugged, then frowned. "Is that weird?"

"Not at all. I knew this one"—Mara tapped her belly—"was a boy long before we saw the ultrasound."

"Bianca looks so much like you. I bet he'll look just like Quinn," Audrey said, and that set the two women off talking about babies and cribs and breast milk and other things Lanie didn't understand.

The love the women had for children they hadn't even seen yet made something wrench loose in the middle of her chest. Would she ever know that feeling? Probably not, if Jesse didn't want her. He was the only man she wanted, the only one she might consider doing the whole pregnancy and parenthood thing with.

Suddenly, she very badly needed to escape the living room. Even the idea of getting fired didn't disturb her as much as the ones going through her head now.

"I, uh..." She fumbled. "I need to go. I have a meeting."

"Yes, you do," Mara said. "They're waiting for you in the office." She was usually very expressive but her face gave nothing away this time.

Lanie crossed the room to the double doors of the office. Instead of finding Gabe, Quinn, and Tucker Quentin gathered around the desk plotting a deadly op or world domination, she found the three of them sitting on the floor coloring with little Bianca. Like any sane female, Bianca was thrilled to be surrounded by three handsome men and basked in their attention. She babbled, but her baby gibberish was starting to sound more like English each day. She demanded Tucker use the pink crayon to color in the sun, and he caved like he wasn't one of the most powerful people on Earth.

More with all the happy family stuff. They sure knew how to kick a girl when she was down.

And, okay, that wasn't fair. They weren't happy and secure in their relationships to spite her. She was just being mopey.

And, besides, as far as she knew, Tucker didn't have a pregnant wife waiting for him at home. He was as single as she. Though, he didn't seem to be as bothered by it. At one time, she hadn't been either. When had that changed?

She cleared her throat to draw the men's attention. "You wanted to see me," she said to nobody in particular.

"Lanie. Hey. Yeah, thanks for coming." Gabe closed the coloring book he'd been working in and used his cane to lever himself up to his feet.

Quinn scooped up Bianca. "Give me a minute." He walked out with his daughter, a handful of crayons, and her coloring book.

Lanie waited, but neither of the other two seemed inclined to speak until Quinn returned. The quiet was driving her nuts. It was bad enough waiting for the anvil to drop without adding an uncomfortable silence to the equation.

"I just heard the news," she blurted. It wasn't exactly true—she'd known Audrey was pregnant before he had, but she wasn't going to tell him that. "Congrats."

Gabe looked at her for a moment like he was trying to figure out what she was talking about.

"The baby," she prompted and watched his face light up with a genuine smile that reached all the way to his eyes. And, okay, she saw it now. When he smiled like that, his hazel eyes were pretty.

"Thanks. We'd been trying for a while before..." He waved at himself like that was explanation enough. And it was. She knew exactly what he meant.

Before he was shot.

She noticed he never completed that sentence, never said it out loud. That couldn't be healthy.

"So yeah," he finished. "We're excited it finally happened." Even though it was technically Quinn's desk, he took a seat behind it like he owned it. Quinn wouldn't mind, though. In their little realm, Gabe was king.

And if Gabe was king, Tucker Quentin was God.

She wasn't entirely sure what he was doing here. He gathered the rest of the coloring books in a neat stack and set them aside as he propped a hip on the corner of the desk. In his perfectly fitted jeans and an open-collared white dress shirt with the sleeves rolled up, he looked like he belonged on the cover of *GQ*. In fact, she thought she might have seen him there once or twice before.

He gave her his magazine-worthy smile. "How have you been, Lanie?" Either he was a good actor or that was genuine concern in his voice. Having seen the movies he'd starred in as a teenage heartthrob, she knew he wasn't a good actor. His concern loosened the knots of tension bunched up along her spine.

"All healed." She held out her arms to prove it. "All's good. Well, okay, not really. Honestly, I'm wondering what I'm doing here. Are you gonna fire me for killing Schumacher?"

Another flash of a smile. "We'll get to that."

Quinn returned and closed the door behind him and the atmosphere in the room shifted from casual small talk to let's-get-down-to-business.

She drew a breath and steeled herself. Here it comes. But if they were going to fire her, would they be so relaxed? And no way Mara, her best friend, would let her walk in here without warning her.

"We have a lot to discuss, so let's get to it," Gabe said and drew a thick file from one of the drawers. He passed it across the desk to her. "Tuc's men handled the interrogation of the surviving Defion operatives from the situation in Martinique. They claim they were hired by Bioteric Pharmaceuticals to steal research from Doctors Tiffany Peters and Claire Oliver. For the last several years, the women have been working on a panacea drug that's supposed to cure any and all viruses. Needless to say, Bioteric is very interested in getting their hands on it."

"And they weren't opposed to making the doctors disappear to get it," Tuc added. "Lucky for us, Defion's team picked the wrong time and place to try."

"I wouldn't say Tiffany Peters is feeling very lucky right now. Or Danny." Lanie spoke before she thought better of it and all eyes shifted in her direction.

After a heavy moment, Tuc inclined his head. "You're right. I worded that wrong. We lost a good man and an innocent woman, and I never meant to make light of that. But we did keep Defion from their goal, which is a win for us. Do you know who Bioteric is?"

She nodded. "Who doesn't?" With the way their drug commercials played constantly on TV, they were a household name. "They're the biggest drug company in the world."

"And if they got their hands on that research, they'd control the entire pharmaceutical industry. It'll give them the power to decide who lives and who dies."

"The power to play God," Lanie said and whistled. "That's bad."

Gabe nodded. "Which brings us to our next problem. Jean-Luc."

She looked from one man to the next. "What's wrong with him?"

"He's gone." Quinn rubbed his temple like he had a headache. "He went against our direct orders and took off in search of Claire Oliver. He thinks she's still in danger."

"Well, if Bioteric and Defion are after her, I'd say it's a good bet he's right."

"We agree," Gabe replied. "But we don't have enough intel yet to launch a rescue op. I told Jean-Luc that. He didn't like hearing it. Now we're gonna have to find him, too."

Lanie set the file down on the desktop without looking at it. "While this is all interesting, I don't get why you're telling me."

Tuc spoke up first. He nudged the file toward her again. "I'm prepared to offer you a job."

She opened her mouth. Closed it without making a sound. Of all the things she'd expected from this meeting, a job offer hadn't been anywhere on that list. "I, uh, already have one…" She glanced between Gabe and Quinn. "Don't I?"

"You absolutely do," Quinn said. "The guys told us how you handled yourself in Martinique. Hell, you handled everything. Whether or not you accept Tuc's offer, you'll always have a spot on the team."

"But this"—Tuc tapped the file with two fingers—"is more."

Slowly, she reached for it, picked it up, opened the cover.

Inside was a contract like the one she'd signed when she first started with HORNET, except the job description was much, much different. Her head snapped up so hard she gave herself whiplash. "Field commander?"

Tuc motioned to the other two men. "Gabe and Quinn will no longer go on ops. They'll work behind the scenes from now on, stay here and beef up the training program. So we need someone with a level head to take command."

Again, her mouth was doing the fish thing. Open, shut. Open, shut. The folder wobbled in her hands. "And you picked *me*?"

"In all honesty, we picked Jesse first," Quinn admitted. "But he turned us down and suggested you. After seeing how you handled things in Martinique, we had to agree with him. You're the best choice for the job."

"Even better than Jesse," Gabe added, "since his goal always has been and always will be a medical career. What's *your* goal?"

She thought of Danny then, sitting on the beach, staring out over the water, and she heard herself repeating his words: "I want to help people." Then she laughed. "And kick bad guy ass. If I can do both at the same time, that's my dream job."

"Yeah," Quinn said and grinned at the other two men. "This is gonna work. So you're in?"

She folded the file against her chest. She wanted to say yes, but...there was something she needed to do first. "Can I sleep on it tonight?"

Chapter Thirty-Four

"Dad, look!"

At the sound of Connor's laughter, Jesse set aside the saddle he'd been cleaning and stuck his head out of the tack room. Half Pint, the only pony in his stable, nuzzled Connor's side, searching the pockets of his lightweight jacket. His son looked absolutely thrilled, like a five-year-old told he was going to Disneyland. "She knows you have a treat for her."

In the two weeks since their return from Martinique, Connor still grumbled about his chores in the barn, but now he actually came home from school and did them with little other fuss. He'd fallen for the horses—every single one from sweet gelding Almonds, to the temperamental mare Dixie Diva, to quiet Old Lady Ophelia, and even Tasmanian Devil, a.k.a. Tazzy, the occasionally fractious stallion. But Connor had a particular soft spot for Half Pint, the Shetland pony with spiky black hair and a fuzzy, stocky tan body. He'd taken to bringing her a sugar cube every afternoon before he started his chores.

"You want your sugar, huh?" Connor said to the horse.

She nickered and shook her head in an emphatic up-down of agreement. Connor dug the sugar cube out of his pocket, watched her eat it out of his hand, then produced an apple—Jesse was pretty sure it was the one he'd put in Connor's school backpack yesterday—and also gave that to her.

Amused, but trying not to show it, Jesse shook his head. "You spoil her."

"Only the best for my girl." Connor ruffled Half Pint's spiky mane, the strode over to greet Diva, who pranced back and forth in her stall, throwing her head in exasperation that Half Pint was getting attention and she wasn't. "Oh, and Dad? Someone's here for you," he added a little too casually. "Out front."

Jesse's suspicion radar went on red alert. "Who?"

Connor only shrugged and grabbed a bridle before opening Dixie's stall door. He was good with the horses. A natural. But that wasn't a surprise. He may not have been raised around them, but he had Warrick blood in his veins and Warricks always were and always had been horse people.

Which made Jesse wondered about the decisions he'd recently come to. With ranch life so thick in his blood, was it wrong to want more for himself and his son? He didn't know. But something had to change.

He considered ignoring his visitor. He had a pretty good feeling he knew who it'd be, and he knew his asked for time was up. But in the end, he walked out of the barn and finally faced the woman he loved.

Lanie leaned against the hood of her car, long legs crossed at the ankle. When she spotted him, she straightened and gave a tentative smile. Which just wasn't right. Lanie wasn't a tentative woman.

"Hey," she said softly. "Haven't seen you around."

He stopped a few feet from her. "I told you I needed

some time."

"I get that. What happened to Danny..." She trailed off. Drew a breath that moved her shoulders. "Well. It shook us all."

"Yeah."

Silence stretched between them, so long it became awkward.

Lanie shoved her hands in the back pockets of her jean shorts and rocked on her feet. "You, uh, know it wasn't your fault, right? The autopsy showed he could've been shot in a hospital surgical suite with a full trauma staff on stand-by and he still would've died."

"I know." It had taken many sleepless nights replaying the scenes over and over in his head, analyzing and reanalyzing his every move, before he'd finally accepted that there had been no other possible outcome.

But he still couldn't shake the thought that if he'd had more knowledge, maybe Danny would have survived. He wanted to learn more. He wanted to be better prepared. He wanted the MD after his name.

Lanie didn't look convinced, but he wasn't yet ready to talk about the decision he'd made regarding his future with HORNET. Not when he still wasn't sure what *their* future held. Or even if they had one together. He certainly wanted one. He could admit that now. He'd only sworn off women in the first place because of her. He'd convinced himself that if he led a monk's life, his feelings for her would disappear.

Yeah. He was an idiot.

"How's Marcus?" he asked, because it seemed safer than anything else he could've said.

She lifted a shoulder. "He hasn't been around. He went back to California to be there for Danny's wife through the funeral and he hasn't come back yet. Gabe told him to take as much time as he needs."

"And Jean-Luc?"

She winced.

"What's wrong with Jean-Luc?" The Cajun had needed a transfusion and some stitches, but his prognosis had been good. Jesse couldn't imagine what had possibly happened to change that in the past weeks.

"He's gone rogue."

"Oh shit."

"Uh-huh. He wanted to find Claire Oliver. Gabe and Quinn told him we didn't have enough intel to go on and he shouldn't be in the field until he was medically cleared, so he told them to do something anatomically impossible and took off. Nobody's seen or heard from him since."

"Jesus. That reckless bastard is goin' to get himself killed."

"That's the general consensus, yes."

More silence. They'd run out of the safe small talk.

Lanie took her hands out of her pockets, but then seemed to not know what to do with them and shoved them back in. "So," she said after another beat. "I just left an interesting meeting with Tucker, Gabe, and Quinn. They said you suggested me for field commander. They offered me the job."

His mouth twitched with a smile. "Did you accept?"

"I haven't given them an answer yet. I..." She hesitated. "I need to ask you something first. Why did you suggest me?"

He finally closed the distance between them, catching her face in his palms before she could turn away. "I told them to consider you because I believe with all my heart you're the best person for the job. And they must agree with me or else they wouldn't have extended an offer."

Her gaze dropped to his lips, then shied away. "I don't want to be accused of sleeping my way into the position."

Yeah, he figured. She was so sensitive to others' perception of her. "I may have a bit of pull with Gabe and

Quinn, but not with Tucker Quentin. The only person who influences Quentin is Quentin himself. So did you sleep with him?"

She reared back in shock. "What? No! Of course not. He's not my type."

"Then I don't see how anyone could accuse you of sleepin' your way to the top." He traced a finger along the sharp line of her jaw. "They made the offer because you're good at what you do. You're a natural-born leader. You deserve this."

Her hand came up and loosely circled his wrist. "What about you? They offered it to you first. Don't you want it?"

"No."

"You're not just saying that because—"

He kissed her to both stop whatever question she'd been about to ask and because he just plain wanted to. It had been too long since he'd felt his lips against hers and he missed it. He missed her. "I've done a lot of thinkin' these past weeks and I realized somethin'. I'm not cut out for this life. I'm not sure I ever was, and it's been slowly eatin' away at me. I live every day in fear of goin' back to the darkest days of my life, and yet every op, I put myself in the same conditions that led to them the first time around. I can't relive them. I won't survive it a second time. I need to think about Connor."

She drew back enough to gaze into his eyes. "What are you saying? You're quitting?"

"Not yet. I won't leave the guys without medical care. God knows this group needs me. I'll go on ops when I'm needed, but I'll start trainin' a new medic. Jeremiah Wolfe has shown promise. Soon, though, I want to leave HORNET and go to medical school."

He wasn't sure what kind of reaction he'd expected from her, but her complete non-reaction wasn't it. She withdrew from his embrace and crossed her arms in front of her. "So you're quitting. Where does that leave us?"

He dropped his arms to his sides. "I hope in a better place than we were a few minutes ago. If I stay, you'd be my commander, and I wouldn't be able take you to bed and do the kinds of things I want to do to you."

She released a shaky breath and all the steel went out of her spine. "You still want me?"

"Oh, Lanie." He again gathered her close and held her against his chest. She didn't resist. Her arms wound around his waist and held on while he breathed in the scent of her shampoo. "Of course I do. I've spent a good chunk of my life wantin' you. I'm sorry I kept you at arm's length these last few weeks. Danny's death…it woke me up. I needed to figure everything out before I brought you into my life. But I do want you in my life. I love you."

She swallowed hard. "I won't hurt you. I support whatever decision you make. If going to med school is what will make you happy, we'll make it work. Whatever happens from here on out, I'm here for you. I stick."

"I know." He grinned. "Like a burr."

"Hey!" She playfully smacked his chest, then fisted her hands in the front of his sweaty shirt. "I love you, cowboy."

And she dragged him in for a kiss that knocked his Stetson off his head.

Epilogue

"It's not just reckless," Gabe said and sat in the chair behind his huge desk. The leather squeaked as his big body settled back. "It's dangerous."

Dangerous? Jean-Luc snorted a laugh. "Since when has that stopped us?"

"Suicidal," Jesse corrected. The cowboy took off his battered Stetson and dragged a hand though his dark hair. "Jesus, Cajun. You're barely back on your feet."

And languishing in bed had almost killed him as sure as the bullet that tore through his stomach last month. He'd hated the forced inactivity and the overwhelming sense of helplessness it had brought on. And then there had been the dreams. Crazy stuff, peppered with images of his *mamere* in her kitchen, whipping up her famous *étouffée*. She'd scolded him for being a selfish *coullion*, for never doing anything that didn't benefit him in some way.

Mais, Mamere, I'm trying to do good.

For once in his life, he wanted to do the right thing and he was facing nothing but opposition for his trouble. He wished he could be as blasé about this as the rest of the team was. Some mornings, he'd wake up and tell himself Dr. Claire Oliver's safety was technically none of his concern.

And then he'd go to bed the following night and dream of Claire. Of her blond hair tucked back in a neat little bun and a tongue as sharp as her eyes were blue. Of the fear in those eyes last time he saw her. Of the promise he'd made her to protect her friend…and hadn't kept.

Which brought him back to the original reason for this meeting. "I know my intel's good. Claire was spotted three weeks ago in Morocco, and again a few days later in Cote d'Ivoire."

Lanie gave him an apologetic smile. "But we've also had reports of her from Tunisia, Croatia, Madagascar, Sri Lanka, Myanmar… She's not staying in any one place for more than a few days, sometimes only a few hours. Even if she was still in Cote d'Ivoire, she'd be long gone before we got to her."

He couldn't explain how he knew this time was different. Yes, Claire had been bouncing across the globe, just as he'd told her to. Every place they'd traced her to had been completely random. No rhyme or reason to her destinations, which had been smart of her, but now she was moving in a distinct direction. Croatia to Tunisia to Morocco to Côte d'Ivoire. She was on her way somewhere in Africa, and if he'd figured that much out, then so had Defion. Big money funded their hunt for her, and they weren't idiot rent-a-soldiers. They were well-trained, battle-hardened operatives on a mission.

Aaaand there was that sense of helplessness again, winding around his chest like a boa, choking the air from his lungs. "She's not safe."

Lanie set a hand on his shoulder and light glinted off the simple white-gold band on her ring finger. Jean-Luc looked down at it, then up at Jesse. Well, fuck him sideways. The slow-poke cowboy could move fast when he made up his mind about something. Smart man.

Lanie squeezed his shoulder, drawing his attention back. "We *will* find Dr. Oliver, but—"

"But going off half cocked on three-week-old intel won't help," Quinn finished, speaking for the first time since Jean-Luc walked into the office.

He shrugged off Lanie's hand and paced to the big bay window overlooking the rolling Wyoming plains. In one direction was the training center, a blocky concrete building where their dwindling group of trainees were supposed to be learning how to pull off a successful op. Half a mile in the other direction, the frame of Gabe and Audrey's new house was just about completed. Surrounding it all, the Tetons loomed in silent guard. Sometimes he wondered if the mountains were meant to keep bad guys out or to keep him in.

God, he missed Louisiana. He missed humidity so thick that breathing was more like slurping pudding. He missed the quiet of the bayou near his *mamere's* house, and the pungent earthy scents of moss, peat, and brackish water, the symphony of cicadas lulling him to sleep every night. He missed the color and flash of New Orleans, too. The bayou had his soul, but that city had his heart. He was more than a little sick of this dusty, rugged place, where the nearest bar was a honky-tonk forty miles away in Idaho.

He spun back to the group. "It's better than sitting here in Bum Fuck, Wyoming, with our thumbs up our asses."

Quinn merely raised an eyebrow. "Explain how getting yourself killed somewhere in Bum Fuck, Africa, will save her?"

Merde. This convo was going nowhere. After leaving on his own intel-seeking mission last week, he shouldn't have returned here. The moment he traced Claire to Africa, he should've hopped on a plane. Yeah, it was a big continent, but he couldn't shake the feeling that if he didn't start looking now, Defion would find her first. Hell, they might already know exactly where she was. He could already be too late.

Weird how that thought made his stomach ache.

He told himself it was the freshly healed bullet wound that hurt, nothing more.

"Why don't you give the information you have to Harvard?" Lanie suggested after an uncomfortable silence. "See what he can find. Once we have more intel, we'll come up with a plan. I promise you we won't leave Claire out there unprotected, but we need to be smart about this. Nobody wants a repeat of what happened in Martinique."

A fist closed around Jean-Luc's throat at the reminder. They had never lost a man until Martinique, and, okay, yeah, he understood their need for caution. But Danny's death, so close on the heels of his *mamere's* passing, was precisely why he wanted to tell them all to fuck caution. He couldn't take anyone else dying right now.

So, okay, he was being selfish. A tiger can't change his stripes and all that.

He reined in his frustration. As annoying as it was, Lanie had a point. If Claire had left a trail, Harvard would find it, and that knowledge was the only thing keeping him from tearing out of here and jumping on the first plane to Africa. "Yeah, I'll give what I have to Harvard."

Jesse nodded, and if Jean-Luc wasn't mistaken, the fleeting expression crossing the medic's face was relief. "We'll find her, pal."

"*Oui*, I know." As he turned to the door, he felt weirdly deflated, and more than a little exhausted. Maybe he wasn't at full strength yet, but it didn't matter how he felt. He wasn't the one in danger of dying right now.

He stalked out of the office, his bad mood following like a storm cloud, charging the air around him. On the front porch, he paused and drew in a breath of the hot, dry summer air. It did nothing to ease the aching tightness in his chest.

He hated this.

Hated feeling useless. Hated the inactivity. Hated that he cared so fucking much about the welfare of a woman he'd had only one conversation with.

"They're not telling you everything."

Marcus's voice caught him by surprise and he stumbled on the last step of the porch. He straightened and glared. "You scared the piss outta me. Warn a guy next time, yeah?"

A smile ghosted across Marcus's lips as he stepped out of the shadows cast around the porch by the early morning sun. He didn't smile as often or as brightly since Danny's death, which was a real damn shame. Jean-Luc had been with enough people to say with certainty that Marcus Deangelo had the most beautiful smile of anyone he'd ever met, man or woman.

Another smile whispered through his memory. Claire's. He'd spent their entire conversation at the poolside bar in Martinique trying to get her to smile. She never gave him a full one, but rather an uncertain twitch of her lips, like she hadn't wanted to but couldn't help it.

"Well, aren't you Mary Sunshine this morning," Marcus said.

"Okay, one, it's morning. When have you ever known me to be a morning person?" He ticked the points off on his fingers. "Two, I haven't been laid in over five months."

"Still think you're cursed, huh, Cajun?"

"I don't think. I know. And three, I don't like being lied to. What the fuck do you mean they're not telling me everything?"

Marcus glanced over at the house, then tilted his head toward the training center, indicating they should walk. Jean-Luc fell into step beside him and waited impatiently for an answer. He didn't get one. With every step they took, anxiety tightened its fist around his stomach. He slid a glance in Marcus's direction. Guy wasn't right, hadn't been since they put Danny in the ground, but he was pretending all was A-okay. Walking beside him was a bit like standing next to a rumbling volcano. You didn't know when it'd erupt, only that an eruption was coming.

Halfway across the field, Jean-Luc couldn't take the silence. He stopped short. "Talk, *mon ami*."

A few steps ahead, Marcus also stopped and turned back to face him. "They know where Claire is. Or at least have a better idea than they led you to believe."

The words landed like a physical blow. All the air left his lungs in a huff. Questions spitfired through his mind—why would they lie? How long have they known? How could they betray him like this?—but the one that made it past his lips was the most important: "Where is she?"

Marcus reached into the back pocket of his jeans, pulled out a piece of paper, and held it out.

Jean-Luc slowly took the page and opened it. It was a printout of a BBC news article about an outbreak of Hantavirus in Nigeria. Normally another virus outbreak in Africa didn't make Western headlines until it reached epidemic level or killed off a few white people, but this one was apparently newsworthy because Hantavirus was a Euro-Asian virus and hadn't ever been seen in humans in Africa before.

A thrill chased through him and he crushed the paper in his fist. "She's there." He didn't know how he knew it, but he was as certain as he was of his own name. "She's in Nigeria."

It made sense, given the southward trajectory of her recent travels.

Marcus nodded. "That's what Jesse thinks."

"How do you know?"

"Overheard him talking to Gabe and Quinn about it this morning. They all agreed to investigate it further, but not tell you until they had something more concrete. Jesse doesn't think you're ready for active duty yet."

Betrayal left his mouth tasting bitter. "But here you are, telling me anyway. Don't *you* think I'll get myself killed over there?"

Marcus gazed out over the grounds. He was looking toward the training center, but Jean-Luc doubted he was actually seeing it. He had that thousand yard stare of a soldier who had seen too much. *Oui*, that explosion would happen, and probably sooner rather than later.

Then Marcus shook his head, drew a sharp breath. "Danny died trying to protect this woman and her research. The bosses are being overabundantly cautious and it's making them slow to react. If Dr. Oliver dies before we get to her and her research falls into the wrong hands, then Danny's death was for nothing. I can't—" His voice broke and he cleared his throat. "I told his wife his death meant something. Told her he helped save millions of people. It gave her some comfort, and I don't want to be made a liar." He met Jean-Luc's gaze again, and his lashes were spiked with moisture. "So I'm coming with you and we're going to make sure your woman stays alive."

A quick spurt of panic sent his blood racing. "She's not my—"

"Yeah, right. Keep telling yourself that, buddy." Marcus held out a hand. "Do we have a deal?"

Jean-Luc looked back toward the house. Jesse and Lanie were just leaving, climbing into Jesse's old beater of a truck.

"This might get us thrown off the team."

Marcus didn't even blink. "I don't care."

Neither did he. His only hesitation was Marcus—if not for the other man, Jean-Luc would already be on his way to the nearest international airport. But Marcus was a grown man. If he wanted to put himself in danger, that was his own choice.

Jean-Luc accepted the out-stretched hand. "Pack a bag, *mon ami*. We're going to Nigeria."

Acknowledgments

I owe my thanks and maybe a box of chocolate to the following awesome people:

Elizabeth Thayer and Nicole MacDonald for helping me name this book.

Jackson D'Lynn for her blurb writing talents.

My editor, Heather, for her endless patience, and the entire Entangled team for all the work they do. You're all superheroes.

And finally, The Boyfriend. You're my rock. I wouldn't have made it through the last crazy year without you, and this book certainly never would've been finished without your nagging—er, I mean, support. I love you.

About the Author

Tonya Burrows wrote her first romance in eighth grade and hasn't put down her pen since. Originally from a small town in Western New York, she suffers from a bad case of wanderlust and usually ends up moving someplace new every few years. Luckily, her two dogs and ginormous cat are excellent travel buddies.

When she's not writing about hunky military heroes, Tonya can usually be found at a bookstore or the dog park. She also enjoys painting, watching movies, and her daily barre workouts. A geek at heart, she pledges her TV fandom to *Supernatural* and *Dr. Who*.

If you would like to know more about Tonya, visit her website at www.tonyaburrows.com. She's also on Twitter and Facebook.

Discover more Amara titles...

Hard Run
a Delta Force Brotherhood novel by Sheryl Nantus

Ever since ex-Delta Force Operations Specialist Finn Storm's life was shattered when someone close to him was killed by drugs, he's been focused on taking out those preying on the weak. So when Skye Harris shows up on the Devil's Playground doorstep asking the Brotherhood for help with a gang taking over her hometown, Finn's the first out the door. He'll protect the town and rain hell down on the drug-dealing gang. But nothing prepares him for the effect Skye has on his soul.

Temptation and Treachery
a Dangerous Desires novel by Sahara Roberts

Andres "Rio" Rivera became his ICE profile years ago. Cold and calculating, he never promises anything beyond right now. But when he ends up with a cancelled flight and a shared hotel room with the secretive Celeste Patron, the fire behind Celeste's buttoned-up exterior melts every barrier. He may only have her for one night, but that's long enough to make her every fantasy come true.

Disavowed
an NYPD Blue & Gold novel by Tee O'Fallon

NYPD Detective Dom Carew hasn't let a woman under his skin since his lover was killed in Afghanistan fifteen years ago. That is until one incredible, hot and steamy night with stunning and sassy Daisy Fowler. Seeing her again sets his blood on fire, but he's about to embark on the most dangerous undercover op of his life. Love has no place in his world, but when Daisy is threatened, he'll destroy anyone in his path to protect her.